Adam Gurowski

Diary from November 18, 1862 to October 18, 1863

Adam Gurowski

Diary from November 18, 1862 to October 18, 1863

ISBN/EAN: 9783337184520

Printed in Europe, USA, Canada, Australia, Japan

Cover: Foto ©Raphael Reischuk / pixelio.de

More available books at **www.hansebooks.com**

DIARY,

FROM

NOVEMBER 18, 1862, TO OCTOBER 18, 1863

BY

ADAM GUROWSKI.

VOLUME SECOND.

NEW-YORK:

Carleton, Publisher, 413 Broadway.

MDCCCLXIV.

OF all the peoples known in history, the American people most readily forgets YESTERDAY ;

I publish this DIARY in order to recall YESTERDAY to the memory of my countrymen.

GUROWSKI.

WASHINGTON, October, 1863.

CONTENTS.

NOVEMBER, 1862.

PAGE

Secretary Chase—French Mediation—The Decembriseur—Diplomatic
Bendings.. 11

DECEMBER, 1862.

President's Message — Political Position — Fredericksburgh — Fog —
Accident—Crisis in the Cabinet—Secretary Chase—Burnside—
Halleck—The Butchers—The Lickspittle Republican Press—
War Committee Patriots—Youth—People—Ring out........... 22

JANUARY, 1863.

Proclamation—Parade—Halleck — Diplomats — Herodians — Inspired
Men—War Powers — Rosecrans — Butler — Seward — Doctores

PAGE

Constitutionis — Hogarth — Rhetors — European Enemies —
Second Sight — Senator Wright, the Patriot — Populus Ro-
manus — Future Historian — English People — Gen. Mitchel —
Hooker in Command — Staffs — Arming Africo - Americans —
Thurlow Weed, &c.. 61

FEBRUARY, 1863.

The Problems before the People — The Circassian — Department of
State and International Laws — Foresight — Patriot Stanton
and the Rats — Honest Conventions — Sanitary Commission —
Harper's Ferry — John Brown — The Yellow Book — The
Republican Party — Epitaph — Prize Courts — Suum cuique —
Academy of Sciences — Democratic Rank and File, etc....... 119

MARCH, 1863.

Press — Ethics — President's Powers — Seward's Manifestoes — Cavalry —
Letters of Marque — Halleck — Sigel — Fighting — McDowell —
Schalk — Hooker — Etat Major-General — Gold — Cloaca Maxima
— Alliance — Burnside — Halleckiana — Had we but Generals, how
often Lee could have been destroyed, etc.. 159

APRIL, 1863.

Lord Lyons — Blue Book — Diplomats — Butler — Franklin — Bancroft —
Homunculi — Fetishism — Committee on the Conduct of the
War — Non-intercourse — Peterhoff — Sultan's Firman — Seward —
Halleck — Race — Capua — Feint — Letter-writing — England — Rus-
sia — American Revolution — Renovation — Women — Monroe
Doctrine, etc... 182

MAY, 1863.

PAGE

Advance—Crossing—Chancellorsville—Hooker—Staff—Lee—Jackson—Stunned—Suggestions—Meade—Swinton—La Fayette—Happy Grant—Rosecrans—Halleck—Foote—Elections—Re-elections—Tracks—Seward—413, etc...................................... 215

JUNE, 1863.

Banks—"The Enemy Crippled"—Count Zippelin—Hooker—Stanton—"Give Him a Chance"—Mr. Lincoln's Looks—Rappahannock—Slaughter—North Invaded—"To be Stirred up"—Blasphemous Curtin — Banquetting — Groping — Retaliation — Foote—Hooker — Seward — Panama — Chase — Relieved—Meade—Nobody's Fault—Staffs, etc.. 238

JULY, 1863.

Eneas—Anchises—General Warren—Aldie—General Pleasanton—Superior Mettle — Gettysburgh — Cholera Morbus—Vicksburgh—Army of Heroes—Apotheosis—"Not Name the Generals"—Indian Warfare—Politicians—Spittoons—Riots—Council of War—Lords and Lordlings—Williamsport—Shame—Wadsworth—"To meet the Empress Eugenie," etc........................... 257

AUGUST, 1863.

Stanton—Twenty Thousand — Canadians — Peterhoff—Coffey—Initiation—Electioneering—Reports—Grant—McClellan—Belligerent Rights — Menagerie — Watson — Jury — Democrats — Bristles — "Where is Stanton?" — "Fight the Monster"—Chasiana—Luminaries—Ballistic—Political Economy, etc.................... 286

SEPTEMBER, 1862.

PAGE.

Jeff Davis—Incubuerunt—O, Youth !—Lucubrations—Genuine Europe—It is Forgotten—Fremont—Prof. Draper—New Yorkers—Senator Sumner's Gauntlet—Prince Gortschakoff—Governor Andrew—New Englanders—Re-elections—Loyalty—Cruizers—Matamoras—Hurrah for Lincoln—Rosecrans—Strategy—Sabine Pass, etc............................... 310

OCTOBER, 1862.

Aghast—Firing—Supported—Russian Fleet—Opposition—Amor scelerated — Cautious — Mastiffs — *Grande Guerre* — Manœuvring — Tambour battant—Warning, etc............................... 338

DIARY.

NOVEMBER, 1862.

**Secretary Chase—French Mediation—the Decembriseur—Diplomatic
Bendings.**

November 18.—In the street a soldier offered
to sell me the pay already several months over-
due to him. As I could not help him, as
gladly I would have done, being poor, he sold
it to a curb-stone broker, a street note-shaver.
I need not say that the poor soldier sustained
a loss of twenty-five per cent. by the operation! He wanted to send the money home to his
poor wife and children; yet one fourth of it was
thus given into the hands of a stay-at-home specu-
lator. Alas, for me! I could not save the poor
fellow from the remorseless shaver, but I could and
did join him in a very energetic cursing of Chase,
that at once pompous and passive patriot.

This induced me to enter upon a further and

more particular investigation, and I found that hundreds of similar cases were of almost daily occurrence; and that this cheating of the soldiers out of their nobly and patriotically earned pay, may quite fairly be denounced as rather the rule than as the exception. The army is unpaid! Unspeakable infamy! Before,—long before, the intellectually poor occupant of the White House, long before *any* civil employé, big or little, the Army ought to be paid. Common humanity, common sense, and sound policy affirm this; and common decency, to say nothing about chivalric feelings, adds that when paymasters are sent to the army at all, their first payments should be made to the rank and file; the generals and their subordinate officers to be paid, not before, but afterwards. Oh! for the Congress, for the Congress to meet once again! My hope is in the Congress, to resist, and sternly put an end to, such heaven-defying and man-torturing injustice as now braves the curses of outraged men, and the anger of God. How this pompous Chase disappoints every one, even those who at first were inclined to be even weakly credulous and hopeful of his official career. And why is Stanton silent? He ought to roar. As for Lincoln—he, ah! * * * * The curses of all the books of all the prophets, be upon the culprits who have thus compelled our gallant and patriotic soldiery to mingle their tears with their own blood and the blood of the enemy!

Nov. 18.—Again Seward assures Lord Lyons that the national troubles will soon be over, and that the general affairs of the country "stand where he wanted them." Seward's crew circulate in the most positive terms, that the country will be pacified by the State Department! England, moved by the State papers and official notes—England, officially and non-officially, will stop the iron-clads, built and launched in English ports and harbors for the use of the rebels, and for the annoyance and injury of the United States. England, these Americans say, England, no doubt, has said some hard words, and has been guilty of some detestably treacherous actions; but all will probably be settled by the benign influence of Mr. Seward's despatches, which, as everyone knows, are perfectly irresistible. How the wily Palmerston must chuckle in Downing Street.

The difference between Seward and a real statesman, is this: that a statesman is always, and very wisely, chary about committing himself in writing, and only does it when compelled by absolutely irresistible circumstances, or by temptations brilliant enough to overrule all other considerations; for, such a statesman never for one moment forgets or disregards the old adage which saith that "*Verba volant, scripta manent.*" But Seward, on the contrary, literally revels in a flood of ink, and fancies that the more he writes, the greater statesman he becomes.

At the beginning of this month, I wrote to the French minister, M. Mercier, a friendly and respectful note, warning him against meddling with politicians and busybodies. I told him that, before he could even suspect it, such men would bring his name before the public in a way neither pleasant nor profitable to him. M. Mercier took it in good part, and cordially thanked me for my advice.

Nov. 19.—Burnside means well, and has a good heart; but something more is required to make a capable captain, more especially in such times as those in which we are living. It is said that his staff is well organized; God be praised for that, if it really is so. In that case, Burnside will be the first among the loudly-lauded and self-conceited West-Point men, forcibly to impress both the military and the civilian mind in America, with a wholesome consciousness of the paramount importance to an army of a thoroughly competent and trustworthy staff.

The division of the army into three grand corps is good; it is at once wise and well-timed, following the example set by Napoleon, when he invaded Russia in 1812. If his subordinate generals will but do well, I have entire confidence in Hooker. He is the man for the time and for the place. As a fighting man, Sumner is fully and unquestionably reliable; but I have my doubts about Franklin. He is cold, calculating, and ambitious, and he has the especially bad quality of being addicted to the alternate blowing of hot and cold. Burnside did a good thing in confiding to General Siegel a separate command.

The *New York Times* begins to mend its bad ways; but how long will it continue in the better path?

Nov. 20.—England stirs up and backs up rebellion and disunion here; but, in Europe, for the sake of the unity of barbarism, Islamism, and Turkey, England throttles, and manacles, and lays prostrate beneath the feet of the Osmanli, the Greeks, the Sclavi, the heroic Montenegrins. England is the very incarnation of a treachery and a perfidy previously unexampled in the history of the world. The *Punica fides*, so fiercely denounced and so bitterly satirized by the historians and poets of old Rome, was truthful if compared to the *Fides Anglica* of our own day.

Nov. 22.—Our army seems to be massed so as to

be able to wedge itself in between Jackson in the valley and Lee at Gordonsville. By a bold manœuvre, each of them could be separately attacked, and, I firmly believe, destroyed. But, unfortunately, boldness and manœuvre, that highest gift, that supreme inspiration of the consummate captain, have no abiding place in the bemuddled brains of the West-Pointers, who are a dead weight and drag-chain upon the victimised and humiliated Army of the Potomac.

Nov. 25.—The Army is stuck fast in the mud, and the march towards Fredericksburgh is not at all unlikely to end in smoke. There seems to be an utter absence of executive energy. Why not mask our movements before Gordonsville from the observation of Lee ? Or, if preferable, what is to hinder the interposition of *un rideau vivant*, a *living curtain*, in the form of a false attack, a feint in considerable force, behind which the whole army might be securely thrown across the Rappahannock, by which at least two days' march would be gained on Lee, and our troops would be on the direct line for Fredericksburg, if Fredericksburg is really to be the base for future operations. In this way, the army would have marched against Fredericksburg on both sides of the river. Or, supposing those plans to be rejected, why not throw a whole army corps at once, say 40,000 to 50,000 strong, across the Rappahannock. On either plan, I repeat it, at least two days' march would have been stolen upon Lee; three or four days of forced marches would have been healthy for our army, and a bloodless victory would have been obtained by the taking of the seemingly undefended Fredericksburg. A dense cloud enveloped this whole enterprise, and it is not even improbable, that the campaign may become a dead failure even before it has accomplished the half of its projected and loudly vaunted course. But bold conceptions, and energetic movements to match them, are just about as possible to Halleck or Burnside as railroad speed to the tedious tortoise.

Nov. 25.—Oh! So Louis Napoleon could not keep quiet. He offers his mediation, which, in plain English, means his moral support to the South. Oh! that enemy to the whole human race. That *Decembriseur.** Our military slowness, if nothing else is the matter, our administrative and governmental helplessness, and Seward's

---

* The men who, in the great French revolution, and under the leadership of Danton and of the municipality of Paris, massacred the political prisoners in September, 1792, are recorded in history under the name of *Septembriseurs.* Louis Napoleon may no less justly be called the *Decembriseur,* from that frightful massacre on the 2nd of December, from which he dates his despotism.

lying and all-confusing foreign policy have encouraged foreign impertinence and foreign meddling. I have all along anticipated them as an at least very possible result of the above mentioned causes. [See vol. I of the Diary.] Nevertheless, I scarcely expected such results to appear so soon. Perhaps this same impertinent French action may prove a second French *faux pas*, to follow in the wake of the first and very egregious *faux pas* in Mexico. The best that we can say for the *Decembriseur* is, that he is getting old. England refuses to join in his at once wild and atrocious schemes, and makes a very Tomfool of the bloody Fox of the Tuileries. My, Russia—ah! I am very confident of that—will refuse to join in the dirty and treacherous conspiracy for the preservation of slavery. Well for mediation. But Mr. *Decembriseur*, what think you and your diplomatic lackeys; what judgment and what determination do you and they form as to the terms and the termination, too, of your diabolical scheme? Descend, sir, from your shilly-shally generalities and verbal fallacies. Is it to be a commercial union, this hobby of your minister here? What is it; let us in all plainness of speech know what it is that you really and positively intend. Propound to us the plain meaning and scope of your imperial proposition.

Nov. 27.—Lee, with his army, marches or marched on the south side of the river, in a parallel to the line of Burnside on the north side of the river, and Jackson quietly, but quickly follows. They are at Fredericksburg, and our army looms up, calm, but stern; still, but defiant and menacing. I heartily wish that Burnside may be successful, and that I may prove to have been a false prophet. But the great *Fatum*, FATE, seems to declare against Burnside, and Fate generally takes sides with bold conceptions and their energetic execution.

Nov. 28.—The French despatch-scheme reads very like a Washington concoction, and does not at all bear the marks of Parisian origin. I find in it whole phrases which, for months past, I have repeatedly heard from the French minister here. Perhaps Mr. Mercier, in his turn, may have caught many of Mr. Seward's much-cherished generalities, unintelligible, very probably, even to himself, and quite certainly so to every one but himself. Perhaps, I say, Mr. Mercier may have caught up some of them, and making them up at hap-hazard into a *macedoine*, a hash, a hotch-potch, has served up the second-hand and heterogeneous mess to his master in Paris. The Despatch expresses the fear of a servile war; this may very well have been copied from Mr. Seward's despatch to Mr. Adams, (May, 1862,) wherein Seward attempted to frighten England by a prophecy of a servile war in this country.

Nov. 30. — Mr. Seward semi-officially and conveniently accepts the French impudence. Computing the time and space, the scheme corresponds with McClellan's inactivity after Antietam, and with the raising of the banner of the Copperheads. I spoke of this before, (see Diary for November and December, 1861, in Vol. I.) and repeatedly warned Stanton.

Nov. 30.—Mercier, the French diplomat, rapidly gravitates towards the Copperheads—Democrats. Is he acting thus *in obedience to orders?* After all, some of the diplomats here, and especially those of what call themselves the "three great powers," almost openly sympathize and side with secessionists, and patronize Copperheads, traitors, and spies. The exceptions to this rule are but few; strictly speaking, indeed, I should except only one young man. Some diplomats justify this conduct on the plea that the Republican Congressmen are "great bores," who will not play at cards, or dine and drink copiously; accomplishments in which the Secesh was so pre-eminent as to win his way to the inner depths of the diplomatic heart. The people, I am sure, will heartily applaud those of its representatives for thus incurring the contempt of dissipated diplomats.

Some persons maintain that Stanton breaks down, perhaps that he suffers, physically as well as mentally, from his necessitated contact with his official colleagues and his and their persistent, inevitablo and inexorable hangers-on and supplicants. I do not perceive the alleged failure of his health or powers, and I do not believe it; but assuredly, it were no marvel if such really were the case. It must be an adamantine constitution and temper that could long bear with impunity the daily contact with a Lincoln, a Seward, a Halleck, and others less noted, indeed, but not the less contagious.

President's Message—Political position—Fredericksburgh—Fog—Accident — Crisis in the Cabinet — Secretary Chase — Burnside — Halleck — the Butchers—The Lickspittle Republican Press—War Committee patriots —Youth—People—Ring out.

GRAMMARIANS may criticize the syntax of the President's message, and the style. It reads uneasy, forced, tortuous, and it declares that it is *impossible* to subdue the rebels by force of arms. Of course it is impossible with Lincoln for President, and first McClellan and then Halleck to counterfeit the parts of the first Napoleon, and the at once energetic and scientific Carnot. Were the great heart of THE PEOPLE left to itself, it would be very *possible* and even quite easily *possible*.

The message is written with an eye turned towards the Democrats; they are to be satisfied with the prospect of a convention.   Seward puts lies into Lincoln's pen, in relation to foreign nations. But all is well, in the judgment of our *Great Statesmen*.   Even the poor logic is, according to them, quite admirable.

Contrariwise, Stanton's report corresponds to the height and the gravity of events, and is worthy alike of the writer, and of the people to whom it is addressed.

Dec. 6.—Nearly four weeks the campaign has been opened ; the enemy adds fortifications to fortifications before the very eyes of our army, yet nothing has been done towards preventing the rebels from working upon the formidable strongholds.

Does Halleck-Burnside intend to wait until the rebels shall be thoroughly prepared to repel any attack that may be made upon them?   Either there is foul play going on, or there is stupendous stupidity pervading the entire management.   But no one sees it, or rather few, if any, wish to see it. Stanton, I am quite sure, has nothing to do with the special plans of this enterprise.   All is planned and ruled by Lincoln, Halleck and Burnside.

Dec. 7.—The political situation to-day, may be summarily stated as follows: the Republicans are confused by recent electoral defeats, and by the administrative and governmental helplessness, as exhibited every day by their leaders; the Democrats, flushed with success, display an unusual activity in evil doing, and are risking everything to preserve Slavery and the South from destruction. I speak of the Simon-pure Democrats, *alias* Copperheads, such as the Woods, the Seymours, the Vallandighams, the Coxes, the Biddles, &c. The Sewards and the Weeds are ready for a compromise. The masses of the people, staggered by all this bewildering turmoil and impure factiousness, are nevertheless, stubbornly determined to persevere and to succeed in saving their country.

Dec. 7.—The European wiseacres, the would-be statesmen, whether in or out of power, especially in England, and that opprobrium of our century, the English and the Franco-Bonapartist press, have decided to do all that their clever brains can scheme towards preventing this noble American people from working out its mighty and beneficent destinies, and from elaborating and making more glorious than ever its own already very glorious history. As well might the brainless and heartless conspirators against human progress and human liberty endeavor to arrest the rotation of a planet by the stroke of a pickaxe.

Ah! Mr. *Decembriseur*, with your base crew of lickspittles, your pigmy, though treacherous efforts,

even contending with those of the English enemies
of light, and of right, your common hatred of Freedom and Freemen will end in being the destruction
of yourself.

Dec. 7.—Burnside complains of the manner in
which he is victimised, and explains his inactivity
by the fact that the War Department neglected to
furnish him with the necessary pontoons. How, in
fact, was Burnside to move a great army without
pontoons? But it was the duty of Halleck, and his
lazy or incompetent, or traitorous staff, to have seen
to the sending on of the pontoons. However, supposing Burnside and *his* staff to have as much wit
as an average twelve-year-old school boy, they
could have found in the army not merely hundreds,
but even thousands of proficient workmen in a vari-
ety of mechanical trades, who would have constructed on the spot, and at the shortest notice, any
number of bridges, pontoons, &c. Oh, how little
are those wiseacre generals, the conceited and swag-
gering West Pointers; oh, how very little, if at all
are they aware of the inexhaustible ingenuity and
resources, the marvelous skill and power of such
intelligent masses as those of which they are the
unintelligent, the unsympathising and the thoroughly unblessed leaders !

On a Sunday, exactly four weeks back from the

day which I wrote these lines, McClellan was dismissed, and was succeeded by Burnside. But, after the established McClellan fashion, the great, great army was marched 30 to 50 miles, and then halts for weeks up to its knees in mud, and occupies itself in throwing up earthworks. And this is called making War! and the Hallecks are great men in the sight of Abraham Lincoln, and of all who profess and call themselves Lincolnites, and the rest stand around wondering and agape :

Conticuere omnes intentique era (asinina) tenebant.

Stanton's magnificent report states that there are about 700,000 men under arms; yet this tremendous force is paralysed by the inactivity of most of the generals; those in the West, however, forming a bright and truly honorable exception. But, to be candid, how can activity and dash be expected from generals who have at their head, a shallow brained pedant like Halleck? Napoleon had about 500,000 men, when, in between four and five months, he marched from the Rhine to Moscow. Yet he had the aid of no rail-road, on land, no steam, that practical annihilator of distance, no electric telegraph, with which to be in all but instantaneous communication with his distant

generals, and had not similar material resources.

Dec. 10.—Mr. Seward's long correspondence with
Mr. Adams shows to Europe that Mr. Seward imitated the rebels, and tried to frighten England with
the bugbear of King Cotton; and also that he has
no solid and abiding convictions whatever.   Now,
he preaches emancipation, yet, at the beginning of
his *great* diplomatic activity, he openly sided with
slavery; aye, he is still willing to save it for the
sake of the Union, and, above all, and before all, for
his own chances for the next Presidency.

Dec. 10.—Burnside has finally crossed the Rappahannock.   Of course I do not know the respective positions.   But I am sure that if the rebels
have not a perfectly enormous advantage of position, and if the leading of the generals be worthy
of the courage of their men, the victory must be
ours.   Oh! were all our generals Hookers, and not
Burnsides!

General 'McDowell's Court of Inquiry produces
some strange revelations.   The inquiry will not end
in making a thorough general of McDowell.   He
may have been somewhat unfortunate, no doubt;
but his want of good fortune was at least equalled
by his want of good generalship.   I, and many
others besides, were quite mistaken in our early es-

timate of McDowell. He should not so easily have swallowed the second Bull Run. He should at least have been wounded, if only ever so slightly; his best friends must wish that. But to be defeated, and come out without even a scratch! What a digestion the man must have for the hardest kinds of humiliation! But neither the President nor that curse of the country, McClellan, has great reason to plume himself much upon his share in the revelations that are made in the course of this Inquiry. McDowell himself seems to have been intended, by nature for a scheming and adroit politician. * * * *

Dec. 10.—The Congress feels the ground, hesitates, and apparently lacks the necessary energy to come to a determination. Lincoln, even such as he is, contrives to humbug most of the Congressmen. Well! The first of January is close at hand, and Seward, the Congressional cook, will concoct unpalatable and costly dishes for Congressional digestion. Seward is the incarnation of confusion, and of political faithlessness.

I have only now discovered certain of the reasons why the Battle of Antietam, so bravely fought by our army, had no *ensemble* and such marvelously poor results. Burnside, with his corps, got into line many hours too late. The rebels were thus enabled to concentrate on the wing opposed to

Hooker and Sumner, the right wing and centre of the rebels being for the time unthreatened. And that is generalship! The blame of a blunder so glaring, and in its effect so mischievous, attaches equally to Burnside and to McClellan. The victory, such as it was, was due to the subordinate generals, and to the heroic bravery of the rank and file of the army.

When Burnside was invested with the command of the Army of the Potomac, he for nearly twenty-four hours retained McClellan in camp, with the intention of returning the command of the army to him if the rebels had attacked, as it was expected they would, during Sunday and Monday.

Dec. 13.—Night. Fight at Fredericksburgh. No news. O God!

Dec. 14.—As the consequence of Halleck-Burnside's slowness, our troops storm positions which are said to be impregnable by nature, and still farther strengthened by artificial works.

The President is even worse than I had imagined him to be. He has no earnestness, but is altogether in the hands of Seward and Halleck. He cannot, even in this supreme crisis, be earnest and serious for half an hour. Such was the severe but terribly true verdict passed upon him by Fessenden of Maine.

Dec. 15.—Slaughter and infamy! Slaughter of our troops who fought like Titans, though handled in a style to reflect nothing but infamy upon their commanders. When the rebel works had become impregnable, then, but not until then, our troops were hurled against them! The flower of the army has thus been butchered by the surpassing stupidity of its commanders. The details of that slaughter, and of the imbecility displayed by our officers in high command, — those details, when published, will be horrible. The Lincoln-Seward-Halleck-influence gave Burnside the command because he was to take care of the army. And how Burnside has fulfilled their expectations! It seems that the best way to take care of an army is to make it victorious.

My brave and patriotic Wadsworth has gone in the field, also his two sons; one of them, (Tick,) was at Fredericksburgh, and his bravery was remarkable, even among all the heroism of that most glorious and most accursed day. How many such patriots as Wadsworth, can we boast of? Yet the miserable Halleck had the impudence to say—" Wadsworth may go wherever he pleases, even if he pleases to go to Hell!"

Hell itself, would be too good a place for Halleck; imbeciles are not admitted there!

Dec. 17.—The details are coming in.   The disaster of our army is terrible—indescribable; the heroic people bleeds, bleeds!   And all this calamity and all this suffering and humiliation, are brought on by the stupidity of Burnside and Halleck, or both of them.   The curse of the people ought to rest for centuries upon the very names of the authors of such frightful disaster.   They are fiends, yea, worse, even, than the very fiends themselves.

Why, even the very rabble in Constantinople would storm the seraglio after such a massacre. But here—oh, here, it just reminds Mr. Lincoln of a little anecdote.

Dec. 17.—I meet with but few such as Wade, Grimes, Chandler and other radicals in both Houses of Congress, who seem to feel all the heart burning and bitterness of soul at this awful Fredericksburgh disaster.   The real criminals, those who ought, in the agonies of a great shame, call upon the rocks and the mountains to fall upon them not, blush not, sorrow not.

In many of the general public, I have no doubt that the feeling of shame and sympathy, are blunted by these repeated military calamities, and by Mr. Lincoln's undaunted i..........

      *   *   *   *   *   and men,
Have wept enough, for what ?   To weep,
To weep again.

Dec. 17.—About ten days ago, Mr. Seward again sent forth to Europe and to her Cabinets, one of his stale, and by no means Delphic oracles, predicting the success of Burnside's campaign, and immediately follows a bloody and disgraceful calamity ! Such is always the result of Seward's prophecies ! A diplomat calls Seward the evil eye of the Cabinet, and of the country. I suggested to some of the senators that a resolution be passed prohibiting Mr. Seward from playing either the prophet or the fool.

Burnside took care of the army, no doubt, but it was of the rebel army. Our soldiers have been brought by him to the block, to an easy slaughter, he himself being some few miles in the rear, and having between him the river, and the intervening miles of land. All this, however, was according to the regulations, and on the most approved Halleck-McClellan fashion of fighting great battles.

Dec. 18.—The disaster was inaugurated by the shelling of Fredericksburgh. One hundred and forty-seven, (147 !) guns playing upon a few houses. It was the play of a maddened child, exhibiting in equal proportions, reckless ferocity and egregious stupidity ; and it is difficult to find one dyslogistic term which will adequately describe and condemn it.

From what I can already gather of the details of the attack, it may be peremptorily concluded that Burnside, Sumner, and above all, Franklin, are utterly incompetent of a skillful and effective handling of great masses of troops.   They attacked by brigades, positions so formidable, that if they could possibly be carried by any exertion of human skill and strength, they could only be carried by large masses impetuously hurled against them. Franklin seems especially to have acted ill in not at once throwing in 10,000 men to be followed rapidly and again and again by 10,000 more.   In that wise and only in that wise, he might possibly have broken and turned the enemy, and thrown him on his own centre.   It is said that Franklin had 60,000.   If so, he could easily have risked some 20,000 in the first onslaught.   Sixty thousand! Great God!   Why, it is an army in itself, in the hands of a general at all deserving of that name. If those great West Pointers had only even the slightest idea of military history!   More battles have been fought and won with 60,000 men, and with fewer still, than with larger numbers, and at Fredericksburgh Franklin's force formed only a wing against an enemy whose whole army could number but little more than 60,000. I want the reports with the full and positive details.

The clear-sighted and warlike TRIBUNE discovered in Burnside high, brilliant, and soldier-like qualities —admirably borne out and illustrated no doubt, by the Fredericksburgh butchery! To the hospital of imbeciles with all such imbeciles!

The *Times* was manly in its appreciation, and flunkeyed to no one under hand, that is, confidentially and for newspaper publication.

Mr. Seward reveals to the world at large, that, besides his volume of 700 pages, containing the last diplomatic correspondence, he has still an equal number of masterpieces as yet not published. What a dreadful dysentery of despatch-writing the poor man and his still more afflicted readers must labor under.

The Lincoln-Seward policy, has rebuilt the awful Democratic party, which was brooken up, prostrated in the dust. Lincoln—Seward—Weed, partially emasculated the Republican party, and may even emasculate the thus far thoroughly virile and devoted patriotism of the people.

A helpless imbecile in the hands of a cunning and selfish and ruthless charlatan, is the sight that daily meets our eyes in Washington.

General Bayard, one of the slaughtered at Fredericksburgh, was a true Bayard of the army, and one of the very few West Pointers free from conceit, that corrosive and terribly prevalent malady of the West Point clique.

Dec. 18.—Senators waking up to their duties, and to the consciousness of their power. These patriots have said to Seward, *Averte Sathanas*, and overboard he goes, after having done as much evil as only *he* could do.

The most contradictory rumors are in circulation about Stanton. I cannot find out the truth. I do not believe all that is said, but it is necessary to put the rumors on record. It is said then, that Stanton stands up for the butchers and asses in the army and in his department. I believe that in all this, there is not a single word of truth; but if it were true, then I should say, Stanton is ruined by bad company, and down with him and with them!

Quoniam sic Fata tulerunt. But worthy Senators and Representatives, believe still in Stanton, and so do I; only the Seward - Blair - McClellan clique tears Stanton's reputation to pieces. Stanton seems to be, in some measure, infatuated with Halleck, who, perhaps, humbugs Stanton with military technicalities, which Halleck so well knows how to pass current for military science.

Dec. 20.—The American generals, at least those

in the Army of the Potomac, for the sake of shirk-
ing responsibility, maintain that when once in line
of battle, they must rigidly abide by the orders
given to them.   No doubt, such is the military law
and rule, but it is susceptible of exceptions.
The generals of the Potomac shun the exceptions,
and thus deprive their action of all spontaneity.
Perhaps, indeed, spontaneity of action is not among
their military gifts.   Thus we have from them,
none of those *coups d'eclat*, those sudden, brilliant,
and impetuously improvised dashes, which so often
decide the fate of the day, and turn imminent defeat and partial panic into glorious and crowning
victory.   We find none such, if we except some actions of Hooker and Kearney, on a small scale, and
at the beginning of the campaign in the Chickahominy, or the Peninsula.   The most celebrated *coups
d'eclat* in general military history, have mostly
been, so to speak, the children of inspiration, seiz-
ing Time by the forelock,—thus using opportunity which sometimes exists but for a few minutes,
and thus a doubtful struggle terminates in a brilliant success.   At such critical moments, the commander of a wing, or a corps, nay, even a division,
ought to have the courage, the lofty self-abnegation,
and firm confidence in his star or good luck, and still
more in the enduring pluck of his men, and boldly

strike for the accomplishment of that which the
"Orders" have not mentioned or foreseen. Such
a general acts on his own inspiration, and at the
same time reports to the Commander-in-Chief, what
he has determined upon. If instead of acting thus
promptly, he sends and waits for further orders, the
auspicious opportunity may pass away; the decisive
moments in a battle are very rapid, and a single
hour lost, loses the day, or reduces the results of a
victory.

I respectfully submit these undeniable but much
disregarded truths to the Hallecks, McClellans, Mc-
Dowells, and other great West Pointers.

Dec. 20.—The political cesspool is deeper, broader,
filthier and more feculent than ever. Seward is
triumphant, and the patriots have very much elon-
gated countenances.

Dec. 21.—Senator Wilson has learned from Halleck, Burnside, and from some other and similarly
great captains, that the affair of Fredericksburgh,
and the re-crossing of the river, brilliantly compares with the countermarchings of Wagram, and
with that celebrated crossing of the Danube. As
there is not, in reality, a single point of similitude,
the comparison is well selected, aud does great
honor to the judgment of the military wiseacres.
At all events, never was the memory of a Napoleon,

a Massena, or a Davoust, more ignominiously desecrated than by this comparison.

Dec. 22.—So, then, Sathanas Seward remains,
and Mr. Lincoln scorns the advice of the wisest and
most patriotic Senators. To be snubbed by Lincoln,
and Seward, is the greatest of all possible humilia-
tions. Border-state politicians, Harrises, Brownings
and other etceteras of grain, are the confidential advisers. Political manhood is utterly, and to all
seeming, irretrievably lost.

Stanton still holds with Seward. *Embrassons
nous, et que cela finisse.*

How brilliantly do even the very basest times of
any government whatever, Parliamentary, royal or
despotic, compare with what I now daily see here
in the capital of the great republic!

Since the earliest existence of political parties,
rarely, if ever, has a party been in such a difficult,
and, at times, even disgraceful position, as that of
the patriots of both houses of Congress. Against
the combined attacks of all stripes of traitors, such
as ultra Conservatives, Constitutionalists, Copperheads and pure and impure Democrats, the patriots
must defend an administration which they them
selves condemn, and with the personnel of which,
(Stanton and Wells excepted,) they have no sympathy and no identity of ideas. They must defend

an administration which opposes even measures
which they, the patriots, demand,—an administration which, in the recent elections, either
betrayed or disgraced the whole party, and which
brought into suspicion, if not into actual contempt,
the name, nay, even the principles of the Republicans. And thus the patriots have the dead weight
to support, and are wholly unsupported. The
narrow-minded and shallow Republican press, has
no comprehension of the difficulty of the position
in which the patriots are placed ; and that press,
being in various ways connected with the administration, rarely, if ever, supports the patriots,
and even mostly neutralises their best and noblest
efforts. Thus, in the move against Seward, and
for a reform in the Cabinet, the enlightened and
patriotic Republican press of New York, was
either persistently mute or hostile to the movement. Every day I am the more firmly convinced
that Seward is the great stumbling block alike
to Mr. Lincoln and the country at large.

Dec. 22.—Utterly incapable as is McClellan, and
absolutely unfitted by nature to be a great captain
as is Burnside, yet I think it quite clear that
neither of them would have blundered quite so
terribly if he had been provided with a really

competent, zealous and faithful staff, as the generals of continental Europe invariably are. But it seems that here, neither the generals nor the government even desire to understand the true nature, duty, and value of the staff of an army, or what the chief of such a staff ought to know and ought to do. What, in fact, can we at all reasonably expect from a Halleck! After all, however, and shallow as are his brains, this mock Carnot must have read books on military science; and yet he has not learned either the use or the composition of a staff for an army! Had he done so, he would have organized a staff for himself, and one for each of the commanders in the field. It is true that in this country there is no school of staffs, and West Pointers are generally ignorant on that point. Nevertheless, with a little good will and care, it would be easy enough to find intelligent officers of all grades fit for staff duties as arranged for staff officers in Europe. But then, the necessary good will and good judgment are wanting in the head of this military organization. And this Halleck, this Halleck is a mere mockery, a mere sciolist, a shallow pretender to military science. He may have the capacity to translate a book, but nothing of all that he translates effects any hold upon his brain, or he would, long before now,

have done something towards .organising the army.
A general inspector is the first necessity.   Then
establish the necessary proportions of each arm of the
service, *i. e.*, of infantry, cavalry and artillery
for each division.   Then organise the cavalry as a
body.   When you do this, or even a considerable
part of all this, oh, sham-Carnot, Halleck! then
your chance to be considered a military authority
will be established.   Oh, science, oh, insulted
science!   How desecrated is thy name in the
high places here, and especially on the right and
left of the White House.   And oh! you really
great and intelligent American PEOPLE, how ignominiously you are cheated of your blood, your
time, your money, and most of all, of your so
recently magnificent national reputation !

What your military wiseacres show you as an organized army, would actually thrill, as with the
death-shudder, any European military organizer.

Dec. 23.—I learn that the day following the
butchery at Fredericksburgh, Burnside wished to
renew the attack.   What madness!   The generals
protested, and Burnside, greatly exasperated, declared that at the head of his former corps, the
9th, he would himself storm the miniature Torres
Vedras.   If all this is true, then Burnside is weaker
' headed than I had judged him to be; but I will

not do him the injustice to say that he really intended to play a mere farce. What, in the name of common sense, could he do with a single corps, when the whole army was repulsed?

I am warned by a friend, that the Army of the Potomac is so infected with McClellanism, that is to say, by presumption, intriguing, envy and misconception of what is true generalship,—that the army must undergo the process of strong purification, fumigation, pruning and weeding, (and especially among the higher branches,) before it can ever again be made truly useful and reliable.

Dec. 22.—Burnside's report. I am sure that the great luminaries of the press, and the declaimers, the intriguants and the imbeciles, will be thrown into fits of ecstatic admiration of what they will call the manly and straightforward conduct of Burnside in assuming the responsibility and confessing his own fault. But what else could he do? And if he acted thus in obedience to the orders of Halleck, then instead of manliness, his conduct is almost treasonable towards the people, for in withholding the truth as to the orders given by Halleck, he gives that incarnation of calamity the power to repeat the butchery and ensure the ill success of our armies.

The report is altogether unsoldierly; it is fussy

and inflated ; a full blown specimen of the pomp-
ously inane.   How can Burnside venture to say
that after the repulse, during three days he expected the enemy to leave his stronghold and attack
him—Burnside?   The rebels never did anything to
justify such a supposition.   They are neither idiots
nor madmen, and only from a McClellan, or some
bright pupils of the McClellan school, could such
imbecility, such gratuitously ruinous playing into
the hands of an enemy be expected.   A commander ought to be on the watch for any mistake
that his antagonist may commit, but he is not justified in setting that antagonist down as an ass.
For two days the army was unnecessarily kept under the guns of the enemy, that is the truth, and I
will make the truth known, no matter who may
try to conceal it.   Here, for the present, I stop in
sheer and uncontrolable disgust.   By and by, however, I will return to the consideration of this report.

Oh! American people! In so very many respects,
truly great people!   Far, very far beyond my
poor powers of expression are the great love and
veneration with which ever and always I look upon you.   But allow me, pray allow me to use the
frank familiarity of a true friend, so far as just
plainly to tell you, that even I, your sincere friend,

should love you none the less, and certainly should hold you in all the greater reverence, were you not quite so ultra-favorable in judgment of your civil and military rulers and pastors and masters and nincompoops generally !

Further back in this diary, I termed Mr. Secretary Chase a *passive patriot. Peccavi.* And here let me write down my recantation ! Chase exerted himself for the retaining of Seward in the cabinet, and it was by Chase alone that the efforts of the patriots to expel Seward, were baffled. And yet, from the first day of the official assemblage of this cabinet down to the day of the meeting of the present session of Congress, Chase was more vigorously vicious than any other living man in daily, hourly, *all the time*, denunciation of Seward,—of course, behind Seward's back !   Several insoluble problems, no doubt, there are; but there is not one thing, physical or not physical, which so completely defies any comprehension and baffles my most persistent inquiry, as just this.

How, unless Chase has drank of the waters of Lethe, how can he possibly look, now, in the face of, for instance, Fessenden of Maine, to whom he has said so many bitter things against the now belauded "Secretary Seward !"   Bah ! Chase most certainly must have a forty-or-fifty-diplomatist power of commanding—literally and not slangishly be it spoken!—his *cheek*, if, without burning blushes he can look in the face of Fessenden, Sumner or any honest man and say,—" I admire and I support Secretary Seward!" God! If all who, during the last two years, have come into contact with Chase, would but come forward and speak out! In that case, thousands would stand forth, a " cloud of witnesses," to confirm this statement. Chase! Faugh! I hereby brand him, and leave him to the bitter judgment of all men who can conscientiously claim to be even *half honest.*

In merest and barest justice to Seward, greatly as I disapprove of his general course, I must here note the fact that he is by no means addicted to evil speaking about any one. Not that this reticence proceeds from scrupulous feeling or a proud stern spirit. Seward, however, never speaks evil of any one unless to destroy, and to one who sympathises in that same amiable wish. To undermine a rival or to destroy an enemy, Seward will expend any amount of slander; but, in the absence of personal interest, Seward, though officially civilian, is, by nature, far too good and too old a soldier to waste ammunition upon worthless game.

Dec. 23.—Why could not Mr. Lincoln choose for

his Secretary of State some man who has a holy
and wholesome horror of pen, ink, and paper?
Some man gifted with a sound brain, who never
is quick at writing a dispatch, and would demand
double salary as the price of writing one? Oh!
Mr. Lincoln, had you but done this, not only would
all America, but all Europe also be truly thankful
for great immunity from the curse of morbid
attempts at diplomacy and statesmanship.

Dec. 23.—Mr. Lincoln's proclamation to the
butchered army! For heaven's sake let us know,
pray, *pray* let us know who was Lincoln's amanuensis? I hope it was not Stanton. The army is
defiled. "An accident," says this precious proclamation, "has prevented victory." *What* accident? Let the country know the precise nature
of that same accident, and the manner, time, and
place of its occurrence! Burnside talks about a
fog! Oh! yes, a deep, dense terribly foul fog—in
the *cerebellum!* Is that the *accident* of which the
precious proclamation so impudently speaks?
Lincoln makes the wonderful discovery that the
crossing and the recrossing of the river are
quite peerless, absolutely unparallelled military
achievements.

Happy it was for the army, and happy for the
country that at Fredericksburgh, our heroic sol-

diers gave far other and nobler proofs of more than human courage and fortitude than the mere crossing and recrossing of a river.

The *Tribune* is either in its dotage, or still worse. Burnside's unsoldierly blundering is compared to the great victorious splendors of Asperm, Esslingen, Wagram, and the tyrant-crushing three days. of immortal Waterloo! The *Tribune* lauds the crossing and the recrossing of the river, as an act of superhuman bravery; and Lincoln sympathises with the heavily wounded, and twaddles extensively about *comparative* losses. Comparative to what? Oh! spirits of Napoleon and his braves; oh! spirit of true history, veil your blushing brows! And the *Tribune* dares to make this impudent attempt at befogging the American people, and at the same time dares to tell that people that it is " intelligent."

But let us not forget those comparative losses! Comparative to what? To those of the enemy? What knows he about them?

Dec. 24.—Crisis in the Seward cabinet. The " little Villain " of the *Times*, repeated what he did after the first " Bull Run." But he did not now confess to his dining with Seward, as formerly he did with the great " anaconda Scott!" The New

York Republican press is attracted to Seward by natural affinity of election. Seward, however, holds the honey pot, and the flies are all eager to dip into it.

I wish, yet dread to hear the exact particulars of Stanton's behavior during the crisis in the cabinet. It is so very, *very* painful to be rudely awakened to distrust of those whom once we have too implicitly, too fondly believed. Lincoln has now become accustomed to Seward, as the hunchback is to his protuberance. What man who has an ugly excrescence on his face does not dread the surgeon's knife, although he knows that momentary pain will be followed by permanent relief?

At the public dinner of " The New England Society," John Van Buren nominated McClellan for next President, and proposed the health of Secretary Seward. *Oh ! quam pulchra societas !*

I am charged with being " dissatisfied with every thing, and abusing every body." The charge is unjust. I speak most lovingly and in most sincere admiration of the millions, of the great, toiling, brave, honest People, and of the hundreds of thousands of the gallant people-militant—the army ! But I *do* censure some thirty or forty individuals who dispense favors and appoint to fat offices, and, quite naturally, every dirty-souled lickspittle is indignant against me therefor! The blame of such people is far preferable to their praise!

I am rejoiced, I am almost proud that Hooker insisted .upon crossing the Rappahannock, and marching to Fredericksburgh, and that he opposed the subsequent attack.

But of what benefit to me is this fatal, this Cassandra gift of foreseeing? Alas! Better, happier would it be for me could I not have foreseen and vainly, all vainly foretold, the terrible butchery of a brave people during two long and fatal years!

Dec. 24.—It is impossible to keep cool while reading Burnside's report. Once more this report justifies and corroborates Prince Napoleon's judgment on American generals, *i. e.*, that their plan of campaigns will always be deficient in practice, like the theoretical war-exercises of schoolboys. From this sweeping and terribly true charge, however, we must except the Grants and the—alas! how few!—Rosecranses.

The report says, "but for the fog," etc. All lost battles in the world had for cause some *buts* —except the genuine *but*—in the brains of the commander.

"How near we came to accomplishing," etc.—is

only a repetition of what, *ad nauseam*, is recorded by history as lamentations of defeated generals.

"The battle would have been far more decisive." Of course it would have been so, if—won.

"As it was, we were very near success," etc. So the man who takes the chance in the lottery. He has No. 4, and No. 3 wins the prize.

The apostrophe to the heroism of the soldiers is sickly and pale. The heroism of the soldiers! It is as brilliant, as pure, and as certain as the sun.

The attack was planned, (see paragraph 2 of the report,) on the circumstance or supposition that the enemy extended too much his line, and thus scattered his forces. But in paragraph 4, Burnside stated that the fog, (O, fog!) etc., gave the enemy twenty-four hours' time to concentrate his forces in his strong positions—when the calculation based on the enemy's *division of forces* failed, and the attack lost all the chances considered propitious.

The whole plan had for its basis probabilities and impossibilities—schoolroom' speculations—instead of being, as it ought to have been, as every plan of a battle should be, based on the chances of the *terrain*, by the position of the enemy, and other conditions, almost wholly depending upon which the armies operate. It is natural that martial Hooker objected to it.

Oh! could I have blood, blood, blood, instead of ink!

Constructing the bridge over the Rappahannock, our engineers were killed in scores by the sharp-shooters of the enemy. Malediction on those imbecile staffs! The *A B C* of warfare, and of sound common sense teach, that such works are to be made either under cover of a powerful artillery fire, or, what is still better, if possible, a general sends over the river in some way, with infantry to clear its banks, and to dislodge the enemy. In such cases one engineer saved, and time won, justify the loss of almost twenty soldiers to one workman. Some one finally suggested an expedition and they did at the end what ought to have been done at the start. O West Point! thy science is marvellous! The staff treated the construction of a bridge over the Rappahannock as if it were building some railroad bridge, in times of peace!

I am told that Stanton took sides with Seward. I deny it; Stanton remained rather passive. But were it true that Stanton, too, is *Seward-ized,*—then, Oh Mud, how powerful thou art!

In Boston, the B.s and Curtises, and all of that kidney, make a great fuss and invoke the name of Webster.   If so, they are only *excrementa Websteriana.*

Dec. 24.—Patriots in both Houses of Congress! your efforts to put the conduct of the national affairs in honorable hands, and on honorable tracks, to prevent the very life blood of the people from being sacrilegiously wasted, to prevent the people's wealth from being recklessly squandered ; your efforts to introduce order and spirit in certain parts of a spiritless Administration, to fill the higher and inferior offices with men whose hearts and minds are in the cause, and to expel therefrom, if not absolute disloyalty, at least, the most criminal indifference to the people's cause and welfare; your efforts to make us speak to Europe like men of sense, and not in the senseless oracles which justly evoke the scorn and the sneers of all European statesmen ; all these your efforts as patriots rebounded against a nameless stubbornness.

Nevertheless you fulfilled a noble, sacred and patriotic duty. Whatever be to-day the outcry of the Flatfoots, lickspittles, intriguers, imbeciles ; whatever be the subserviency or want of civic courage in the public press—when all these stinking, suffocating, deleterious vapors shall be destroyed by the ever-living light of truth, then the grateful people will bless your names, which, pure and luminous, will shine high above the stupidity, conceit, heartlessness, turpitude, selfish ambition, indirect and direct treason darkening now the national horizon.

Dec. 25. — *Christmas.* The Angel of Death hovers over thousands and thousands of hearths. Thousands and thousands of families in tears and shrouds. Communities, villages, huts and log-houses, nursing their crippled, invalid, patriotic heroes! A year ago, all was quiet on the *Potomac*—now all is quiet on the *Rappahannock.*

What a progress we have made in a year! and at the small, insignificant cost of about sixty to eighty thousand killed or crippled, and of one thousand millions of dollars! But it matters not! The quietude of the official butchers and money squanderers is, and must remain undisturbed in their mansions, whatever be the moral leprosy dwelling therein !

A young man from New England, (whom I saw for the first time,) told me that my Diary stirred up the youth. Oh, if so, then I feel happy. Youth ! youth ! you are all the promise and the realization ! But why do you suffer yourselves to be crushed down by the upper-crust of senile nincompoops ? Oh youth, arise, and sun-like penetrate through and through the magnitude of the work to be accomplished, and save the cause of humanity!

Dec. 25.—As it was and is in all Revolutions and upheavals, so here. A part of the people constitute the winners, in various ways, (through shoddy names, jobs, positions, etc.) while the immense majority bleeds and sacrifices. Here many people left poorly salaried desks, railroads, shops, &c. to become great men but poor statesmen, cursed Generals, and mischief-makers in every possible way and manner. The people's true children abandoned homes, families, honest pursuits of an industrious and laborious life—in one word, their ALL, to bleed, to be butchered, to die in the country's cause. The former are the winners, the sacrificers, and the butchers; the second are the victims.

The evidence before the War Committee shows, to a most disgusting satiety, that General Halleck is exclusively a red-tapist, and a small pettifogger, who is unworthy to be even a non-commissioned officer; General Burnside an honest, well intentioned soldier, thoroughly brave, but as thoroughly destitute of generalship; General Sumner an unquestionably brave but headlong trooper; and Hooker alone in possession of all the capacity and resources of a captain. General Woodbury's evidence is that of a man under difficulties, on whom his superiors in rank have thrown the responsibility of their own crime.

Halleck alone is responsible for the non-arrival of the pontoons. Burnside could not look for them; it was the duty of Halleck to order some of the semi-geniuses of his staff to the special duty of seeing to their delivery at Fredericksburgh, to give them necessary power to use roads, steamers, water, animals and men for transportation, and make it a capital responsibility if Sumner finds not the pontoons on the spot, and at the precise day and hour when he wanted them. Then, Gen. Meigs, who coolly asserts that he " gave orders." O yes! but he never dreamed it was his duty to look for their execution. The fate of the campaign depended upon the pontoons, and Halleck-Meigs " gave orders," and there was an end of it. In any other country, such culprits would have been at the least dismissed—cashiered, if not shot; here, their influence is on the increase. Halleck and Meigs are still great before Mr. Lincoln, and before the mass of nincompoops.

Rhetors and sham-erudites are ecstatic about Burnside's conduct. Well! Burnside is good-natured—that is all. They forget the example of Canrobert and Pellisier, in the Crimea. Canrobert, after having commanded the army, gave up the command, and served under Pellisier. Oh declaimers! Oh imbeciles! ransack not the world—let Rome alone, and its Punic wars, its Varrus, etc.—Disturb not history, which, for you, is a book with seventy-seven seals. You understand not events under your long noses, and before your opaque eyes.

When in animal bodies the brains are diseased, the whole body's functions are more or less paralyzed. The official brains of the nation are in a morbid condition. *That* explains all.

Dec. 27.—I wish I could succeed in bringing about the organization of a good Staff for the army. *Etat Major General de l'Armée* Stanton seems to understand it, but the Hallecks and other West Pointers have neither the first idea of it, nor the will to see it done.

Dec. 28.—The so-called great papers of the Republican party in New York, as well as some would-be statesmen here, discuss the probability of some new manifestation by Louis Napoleon, or by other European powers, of interference in our internal affairs. The probability of such a demonstration by European meddlers can only have one of the following causes:—Our terrible disaster at Fredericksburg, or, what even is worse than that slaughter, the absolute incapacity of our leaders to

cope with such great and terrible events as
this last one.   The bravery, the heroism of our soldiers will be applauded, admired, and pitied in Europe, but the utter intellectual marasmus, as shown
by our administration, will and must embolden the
European marplots to attempt to stop what they
consider a further unnecessary massacre. General
Burnside's report, and the evidence before the War
Committee are before the country and before Europe. Therefore Europe and our country are to
judge.

During his last visit in summer to New York, etc.
the French Minister came in contact with low
French adventurers, (Courriers des Etats Unis) with
copperheads and with democrats, and now he is
taken with sickly diplomatic sentimentalism to conciliate, to mediate, to unite, to meddle, and to get
a feather in his diplomatic cap. I am sorry for him,
for in other respects he has considerable sound
judgment. *Mais il est toqué sur cette question çi.*
He is ignorant of the temper of the masses, and considers the assertions of adventurers, of traitors, and
of meddlers, as being the expression of the sentiments of the people. But sensible diplomats are
rari aves.

Hooker, because he alone is a *captain*, cannot be
in command. Infamous intriguers, traitors, and

imbeciles, prevent Hooker from being intrusted with the destinies of our army. Whole regiments claim to serve under him, and above all such regiments as fought under others in the peninsula, and always have been worsted, and who wish once to be led to success and victory, as were always Hooker's soldiers. The Franklins, and other marplotters in the Potomac Army, menace to resign if Hooker is put in command. The sooner the better for the army to get rid of such trash. But the imbeciles and the intriguers in power think not so; and all may remain as it was, and a new slaughter of our heroes may loom in the future.

Dec. 29.—General Butler's proclamation to his soldiers in New Orleans is the best and noblest document written since this war. It is good, because it records noble and patriotic deeds. During those eighteen months General Butler has shown capacity, activity, energy, fertility of resources and readiness to meet any emergency, unequalled by any one in the administration or in command. And for this, Butler is superseded, because Seward promised it to the *Decembriseur* in the Tuilleries, and because he is a *man*, and *conservative patriots, alias* traitors, could not get at him.

Dec. 30.—Angel of wrath, smite, smite! Oh, genius of humanity, take into thy mercy this noble people !   Oh, eternal reason, send the feeblest breath of divine emanation and arrest this all-devouring torrent of imbecility, selfishness and conceit that is reigning paramount here.   Only the PEOPLE's devotion and patriotism, only the *unnamed* save the country !

Dec. 30.—Those foreign caterwaulings against Butler.   England, in 1848–9, whipped women in Ireland, and how many thousands have been murdered by the *Decembriseur ?*   And the Russian minister joining in this music.   A shame for him and for his government !

Dec. 30.—Poor Greeley looks for intervention, mediation, arbitration ; and selects Switzerland for the fitting arbitrator !   How little—nay—nothing at all, he knows about Switzerland and the Swiss ! Stop ! stop ! respectable old man !

Dec. 31.—Stanton is not at all responsible for the slaughter at Fredericksburgh, or for the infamy of the belated pontoons.   Halleck has the exclusive control of all military movements, etc., in the field. But Stanton ought not be benumbed by a Halleck or a Meigs.

The people at large cannot realize the really awful position of patriotic members of Congress, and above all, of such senators as Wade, Grimes, Fessenden, Wilson, Morrill, Chandler and others, or the almost similar position of Stanton, in his contact with the double-dealings or the obstinacy of Lincoln.

Dec. 31.—To-morrow few, if any, shall miss the occasion to shake hands with the official butchers, with men dripping with the gore of their brethren. Oh, Cains! oh, fratricides !

Dec. 31.—*Midnight.*—Disappear! oh year of disgraces, year of slaughters and of sacrifices.

Tschto den griadoustchi nam gotowit ? (Puschkine.)

Ring out the false, ring in the true,
Ring out the grief that saps the mind,
    *   *   *
    *   *   *

Ring in REDRESS *for all mankind !*

Proclamation—Parade—Halleck—Diplomats—Herodians—Inspired Men—
War Powers—Rosecrans—Butler—Seward—Doctores Constitutiouis—Ho-
garth—Rhetors—European Enemies—Second Sight—Senator Wright the
Patriot—Populus Romanus—Future Historian—English People—Gen.
Mitchell—Hooker in Command—Staffs—Arming Africo-Americans—Thur-
low Weed, &c.   .

Jan. 1.—The morning papers.   No proclamation!
Has Lincoln played false to humanity?

The proclamation will appear.   All right so far!
Hallelujah!   How the friends of darkness, how the
demons must wince and tremble.

There!   Red-tape commander-in-chief, field marshal (who never saw a field of battle!) parades at
the head of victorious generals, of intelligent staffs,
of active pontoon providers, and of really and highly qualified quartermasters general.   To the White
House!   They will congratulate Mr. Lincoln. Upon
what?   Upon Fredericksburgh and other massa-
cres; but especially they will congratulate Mr. Lin-

coln upon the fact of his being surrounded by such a bright galaxy of know-nothings and do-nothings!

Death-knell to slavery and to the slaveocracy. The foulest relic of the past will at length be destroyed. The new era has a glorious dawn; it rises in the glories of sacrifices made by a generous and inspired people. Yes! The new era rises above darkness, selfishness, and imbecility. The shades of the slaughtered are now at length propitiated; their slaughter is at least in part atoned for; and outraged humanity is, at least in part, avenged! Let rebels and conservatives remain hardened in crime; a just and condign vengeance shall overtake them.

> *Nunc pede libero*
> *Pulsandu tellus.*

Jan. 2.—Shallow and brainless diplomats sneer at the proclamation. So did the Herodians sneer at the star of Bethlehem; and where now are the Herodians? Oh! shallow and heartless diplomats, your days are numbered, too!

Jan. 2.—A man inspired by conviction and glowing with a fervent faith, thoroughly knows what he is about. Strong in his faith, and by his faith, he clearly sees his way, and steadily walks in it, while others grope hither and thither amidst shadows and darkness and bewildering doubts! Such a man boldly takes the initiative, marches onward, and is as a beacon-light to a nation, to a people; often, sometimes, even for all humanity. A man who has a profound faith in his convictions has coruscations, fierce flashes of that second-sight for the signs of the times. The mere trimming and selfish politician is ever ready to swim with the stream which he had neither strength nor skill to breast; he never ventures to take the initiative. In issuing the proclamation, Mr. Lincoln gives legal sanction, form, and record to what the storm of events and the loud cry of the best of the people have long demanded and now inexorably dictate.

History will pitilessly tell the truth, the whole truth, and nothing but the truth; and small credit will history give to Lincoln beyond that of being the legal recorder of a righteous deed, and not even that credit will be given to the countersigner, Seward.

Mr. Seward countersigned both proclamations of freedom. Europe is filled with his despatches, written at first plainly for, then lukewarmly tolerating, and, at length, flatly against, slavery. European statesmen have thus the exact measure of Mr. Seward's political character. They know that to the very last he defended slavery, and then countersigned the decree of its destruction! In Europe, self-respecting statesmen resign rather than countersign a measure which they disapprove or have strongly opposed.

Jan. 3.—Emancipation under war powers. A mistake by a contradiction. Spoke of it before. And nevertheless : under war powers alone, emancipation is palatable to a great many, nay, almost to millions of small, narrow intellects, dried up by the formulas, and who in the Constitution see only the latter, and not the expanding, all-embracing principle and spirit. O, Rabbis! O, Talmudists !

Lincoln is very unhappy in his phraseology. He invites the sympathies of humanity on a measure decided by him to favor the war. It is a contradiction ; humanity and war are antipodic.

The papers in the confidence of Seward, such as the *Intelligencer* (without intelligence,) the border-state friends of Lincoln, and all that is muddy and rotten, even the supposed to be well-informed diplomats unanimously assert that Mr. Lincoln has no confidence in his proclamation. As for Seward—this Lincoln's evil genius—no doubt exists concerning his contempt for the proclamation. Ask the diplomats. But these highest pilots in this administration are bound—as by a terrible oath—to violate all the laws of psychology, of human nature, of sense, of logic and of honor, to make the people bleed and suffer in its honor.

Well, pompous Chase; how do you feel for having sided with Seward?

Gen. Butler's farewell proclamation to New Orleans rings the purest and most patriotic harmony. Compare Butler's with Lincoln's writings. All the hearts in the country resounded with Butler; and because he acted as he did, Lincoln-Seward-Blair-Halleck's policy shelved Butler.

Jan. 3.—By the united efforts of Lincoln-Seward-Blair, of the *Herald*, and of that cesspool of infamies, the *World*, of McClellan, and of his tail, by the stupifying influence of Halleck, the Potomac army, notwithstanding its matchless heroism, and equipped as well as any army in Europe; up to this day the Potomac army serves to—establish—the military superiority of the rebels, to morally strengthen, nay, even to nurse the rebellion. Lincoln-Halleck dare not entrust the army into the hands of a true soldier,—Stanton is outvoted. The next commander inherits all the faults generated by Lincoln, McClellan, Halleck, Burnside, and it would otherwise tax a Napoleon's brains to reorganize the army but for the patriotic spirit of the rank and file and most of the officers.

Jan. 3.—What a pity that petty, quibbling constitutionalism alone is understood by Lincoln and by his followers. To emancipate in virtue of a war power is scarcely to perform half the work, and is a full logical incongruity. Like all kind of war power, that of the president has for its geographical limits the pickets of his army—has no executive authority beyond, besides being obligatory only as long as bayonets back it. Such a power cannot change social and municipal conditions, laws or relations (see Vol. I.)

The civil power of the president penetrates beyond the pickets, and in virtue of that civil power, and of the sacred duty to save the fatherland, the President of the United States, and not the Commander-in-Chief, can say to the slaves: "Arise, you are free, you have no servitude, no duties towards a rebel and traitor to the Union. I, the president, dissolve your bonds in the name of the American people."

Jan. 4.—How the tempest of events changes or modifies principles. The South rebelled in the name of State rights, and now Jeff Davis absorbs all States and all parliamentary rights for the sake of *salus populi* or rather of *salus* of slavocracy. Jeff Davis nominates officers in the regiments whatever be the opposition of the respective Governors. In the North, the Governors, all of them, (Seymour?)

true patroits, insist upon power and the right to organize new regiments, and resist the centralization by the United States Government. Perhaps— as the satraps and martinets assert—thereby the organisation of the army is thrown on a false track. Whether so or not, one thing is certain, but for the States and Governors, Lincoln, Scott, Seward, McClellan, Halleck, or the Union, would be nowhere.

Jan. 4.—They fight battles in the West. Generals, to be victorious, must be in spiritual and in electric communion with the heroic soldiers. So it was at Murfreesborough. Rosecrans, at the head of his cavalry or body guard, dashes in the thickest, and turns the dame fortune, who smiles on heroes, but never smiled on McClellan nor on his tail. Rosecrans sticks not to regulations, and keeps not a few miles in the rear. Franklin, at Fredericksburgh mounted not even his horse but stood in front of his tent. Similar to Rosecrans here was Kearney, the bravest of the brave, more of a captain than any of the West-Point high-nosed nurslings; so is Heintzelman, Hooker, Reno, Sigel and many, many others, whom McClellanism, Halleckism, Lincolnism kept or keeps down.

I positively learned that in the last days of the summer of 1862, a list without heading circulated in the Potomac army, and all who signed it bound themselves to obey only McClellan. The McClellan clique originated this conspiracy, which extended throughout all the grades.

: What confusion prevails about the rights of existence of slavery. How they discuss it. How they pettifog. Why not establish the rights of existence of syphilis, of *plica* in the human body. O, casuists. O, *Intelligencers.* O, *Worlds !*

Well, to me, slavery seems to legally (cursed legality) exist in virtue of the special State rights, and not in virtue of the Constitution. But for the State rights, the Africo-American is a man and citizen of the United States—and this under the Constitution which is paramount to State rights. The rebellion annihilates the State rights, and all special constitutions guaranteed by the Union, and at the same time annihilates the relation of the Africo-American to the specific States or constitutions. It restores to him the rights of man guaranteed to him as man by the Union and the Constitution of the United States. The Africo-American recovers his rights, lost and annihilated by specific State rights and municipal, local laws. The president had to issue his proclamation as guardian and executor of the Constitution, and then Africo-Americans recovered their citizenship on firmer and broader grounds than under, or by the war power. Calhoun, the father of the rebellion—as Milton's Satan —and all the rebels now curse or cursed the preamble of the Constitution as Satan cursed the light. I suppose Calhoun's and the rebels reasons are similar to me. *Inde iræ.*

The commanders in the West bear evidence of the devotion, the heroism and the endurance of the Africo-Americans, sacrificing their lives without hope; martyrs by the rebels as well as by Hallecks and the like.

I met a farmer from Maine. He was rather old and poor. Had two sons—lost them both—they were all his hope. He spoke simply of it, but to break one's heart. *He grudged not,* (his own words,) his hopes and blood for the cause, and considered it good luck to have recovered the body of one of his boys, and brought it back home to the "old woman," (wife, mother.) I shook hands with him. I ought to have kissed him. Unknown, unnamed hero-patriot! and similar are hundreds of thousands, and such is the true people. And so sacrilegiously dealt with by insane helplessness.

Jan. 5.—The *Doctors Constitutionis* break their formula brains concerning the constitutionality of the proclamation, and foretell endless complications. If so, if complications arise, the reasons thereof are moral, logical and practical. 1st.—The emancipation was neither conceived nor executed in love ; but it was for Lincoln as Vulcan for Jupiter. The proclamation is generated neither by Lincoln's brains, heart or soul, and what is born in such a way is always monstrous.   2d.—Legally and logically, the proclamation has the smallest and the most narrow basis that could have been selected.   When one has the free choice between two bases, it is more logical to select the broader one.   The written Constitution had neither slavery nor emancipation in view, but it is in the preamble, and the emancipation ought to be deduced from the preamble.   Many other reasons can be enumerated pregnant with complications and above all when Lincoln-Seward are the *accoucheurs*.   My hope and confidence is in the logic of events always stronger than man's helplessness and imbecility.

Jan. 5.—European rulers, wiseacres, meddlers, humbugs, traitors, demons, diplomats, assert that they must interfere here because European interests suffer by the war.   Indeed !   You have the whole old continent and Australia to boot, and about nine hundreds millions of population ; can you not organise yourself so as not to depend from us ?   And if by your misrules, etc., our interests were to suffer, you would find very strange any complaint made on our part.   Keep aloof with your good wishes, and with your advices, and with your interference. You may burn your noses, and even lose your little scalps. You robbers, murderers, hypocrites, surrounded by your liveried lackeys, you presumptuous, arrogant curses of the human race, stand off, and let these people whose worst criminal is a saint when compared to a Decembriseur—let this people work out its destinies, be it for good or for evil.

Jan. 5.—Early in December, 1860, therefore soon after Mr. Lincoln's election, a shrewd and clear-sighted politician, Gen. Walsh, from New York, visited Springfield, and made his bow to the rising sun. On his return from the Illinois Medira, I asked the general what was his opinion concerning the new President. "Well, sir," was the general's answer, "in parting, I advised Mr. Lincoln to get a very eminent man for his private secretary."— *Sapienti sat.*

, *Jan.* 6.—Oh for a voice of thousand storms to render justice to the patriots in Congress, to make the masses of the people know and appreciate them, and to show up the littleness and the ignorance of the pillars of the Republican press. Never and in no country has the so-called good press shown itself so below the great emergencies of the day as are the old hacks semperliving in the press.

Jan. 7.—The great military qualities shown by Gen. Rosecrans, thrilled with joy all the best men in the Potomac Army. The war horse Hooker is the loudest to admire Rosecrans. Happy the Western heroes to be beyond the immediate influence of Washington—of the White House—and above all, of such as Halleck!

Rosecrans has revealed all the higher qualities of a captain; coolness, resolution, stubbornness and inspiration. His army began to break,—he ordered the attack on the whole line, and thus transformed defeat into victory. Not of McClellan's school, is Rosecrans.

Jan. 7.—Senator Summer who, during the ministerial crisis, ought to have exposed to the country the mischievous direction given by Mr. Seward to our foreign relations, and who ought to have done it nobly, boldly, authoritatively, patriotically, and from his Senatorial chair, Senator Sumner preferred to keep stoically quiet, notwithstanding that his personal friends and the country expected it from him. Yet next to Chase, Senator Sumner, more than any body, attacks Seward in private conversation! I read in the papers that Senator Sumner's influence on Mr. Linclon is considerable (nevertheless Seward remained as the greatest curse to the country,) and that he, Sumner, is a *power behind the throne.*   Has Sumner insinuated this himself to some newspaper reporter in *extremis* for news? *Power behind the throne,* what a tableau : Sumner and Lincoln! O, Hogarth, O, Callot! Oh, for your crayon! and now—of course—the country is safe, having such *Power behind the throne.*

Mr. Lincoln's good intentions I hear talked about right and left. Oh, for one sensible, good, energetic action, and all his intentions may go where the French proverb puts them.

Jan. 7.—The city crowded with Major Generals and Brigadier-Generals not in activity. When Mr. Lincoln is cornered, then he makes a Brigadier or a Major General, according to circumstances and in obedience to political or to backstairs influence. From the beginning of the war, no sound notions directed the nominations, either under Cameron, Scott, or McClellan, or now; at the beginning of the war they had Generals without troops, then troops without Generals, and now they have Generals who have not commanded, or cannot command, troops. If, during the war in Poland in 1831, Warsaw, the Capital, had been overrun in such a way by do-nothing Generals, the chambermaids in the city would have taken the affair into their fair hands, and armed with certain night effluvia made short work with the military drones.

Jan. 8.—A poor negro woman with her child was refused entrance into the cars. It snowed and stormed, and she was allowed to shiver on the platform. A so-called abolitionist Congress and President gave the charter to the constructors of the city railroad and the members of Congress have free tickets, and the Africo-American is treated as a dog. Human honesty and justice!

Jan. 8.—Horse contracts the word. Never in my life saw I the horse so maltreated and the cavalry so poorly, badly, brainlessly organised drilled and used. Some few exceptions change not the truth of my assertions, and McClellan is considered a great organiser. They ruin more horses here in this war than did Napoleon I. in Russia, (I speak not of the cold which killed thousands at once.)

How ignorant and conceited! Halleck solicits Rarey, the horse-tamer, for instructions. O, Halleck, you are unique! Officers who have served in armies with large, good, well-organised and well-drilled cavalry—such officers will teach you more than Rarey. But such officers are from Europe, and it would be a shame for a West-Point incarnation of ignorance and conceit to learn anything from an officer of European experience. Bayard, however, thought not so. Justice to his name.

The rebels are not so conceited as the simon pure

West-Pointers. Above all the rebels wish success, and have no objections to learn ; they imported good European cavalry officers, and have now under Stuart (his chief of staff is a Prussian officer) a cavalry which has made a mark in this war.

Jan. 8.—O rhetors ! O, rhetors ! malediction upon you and upon the politicians ! You have no heart, no sensibilities. Not one, not one has yet uttered a single word for the fallen, for the suffering, the dying and nameless heroes of our armies. It seems, O rhetors and politicians ! that the people ought to bleed that you may prosper. Corpses are needed for your stepping stones ! The fallen are not mentioned now in Congress, as you never mentioned them in your poor stump speeches. O, you whitened sepulchres !

O rhetors and politicians ! O, powers on, before, and " behind the throne !" In your selfish, heartless conceit, you imagine that the Emancipation is and will be your work, and will be credited to you. Oh yes, but by old women.

The people's blood, the fallen heroes, tore the divine work of emancipation, from the hands of jelously watching demons. To the shadows of the fallen the glory, and not to your round, polished or unpolished phrases. Not the pen with which the proclamation was written is a trophy and a relic, but the blood steaming to heaven, the corpses of the fallen, corpses mouldering scattered on all the fields of the Union.

Jan. 8.—As a rapid spring tide, so higher and higher, and with all parties—even with the decided Copperheads—rises the haughty contempt toward the crowned, the official, the aristocratic, and the flatfooted (livery stable) part of Europe. Good and just! Marshy, rotten rulers and aristocrats who scarcely can keep your various shaky and undermined seats, you and your lackeys, you take on airs of advisors, of guardians, of initiators of civilization! Forsooth! I except Russia. In Russia the sovereign, his ministers and nine-tenths of the aristocracy are in *uni sono* with the whole nation; and all are against slavery, against the rebels, against traitors. The Russian government and the Russian nation often are misrepresented by their official or diplomatic agents.

Any well organized American village in the free States contains more genuine, moral and intellectual civilization than prevails among European higher circles, those gilded pasteboards. This is all that you, you conceited advisors, represent in that splendid, all-embracing edifice of civilization! At the best you are ornaments, or—with Wilhelm von Humboldt—you are culture, but not the higher, man-inspiring civilization.   A John S. Mill, a Godwin Smith, and those many outside of the *would-be-something* strata in England, in France, almost the whole Germany, those are the representatives of the genuine civilized Europe.

The freemen of the North, on whom you European exquisites look superciliously down with your albino eyes, the freemen of the North, bleeding in this deadly struggle, are the confessors for the general civilization, and stand on the level with any martyrs, with any progressive people on record on history.

Jan. 9.—Quo, quo scelesti ruitis.........

It is maddening to witness for so many months the reckless waste of men, of time, of money, and of material means, and all this squandered by governmental and administrative helplessness and conceit.   In the military part, notwithstanding Stanton's devotion and efforts, that Halleck, *excrementum Scotti*, as by appointment, carries out everything contrary to common sense, to well established and experienced (Halleck and experience, ah! .... military practice, and Mr. Lincoln is as perfectly) charmed by it, as is the innocent bird by the snake.

And thus the sacrifices and the blood of the people run out as does the mighty Rhine — they run out in sand.   O, Lincoln-Seward's domestic policy. O, Lincoln-Halleck's war power! You make one shudder as with a death pang.

January 9.—The worshippers of slavery, that is, the Democrats, of the Scymour's, Wood's, and the *World's* church, call the war waged for the defence of human rights, for civilization and for maintaining the genuine rational self-government, they call it an unholy war. In some respects the Copperheads are right. The holy war loses its holiness in the hands of Lincoln, Seward, Halleck, and their disciples and followers, because those leaders violate all the laws of logic and of reason, this holy of holies. At times I would prefer peace than see devoted men so recklessly murdered by such....

A critique of the first volume of the "Diary" asserts that all my statements are made after the events occurred, *ex post*. To a very respectable General I showed a part of the original manuscript which squared with the printed book. Often I am ashamed to find that the bit of study and experience acquired by me goes so far when compared with many around me, and in action. I foresee, because I have no earthly personal views, no cares, nothing in the world to think off or to aim at, no charms, no ties—only my heart, my ideas, my convictions, and civilization is my worship. Nothing prevents me, day and night, from concentrating whatever powers and reading I can have in one single focus. This cause, this people, this war, its conduct, are the events amidst which I breathe. Uninterruptedly I turn and return all that is in my mind—that is all. And I am proud to have my heart in harmony with my head.

Almost every event has its undercurrent, and of ten the little undercurrents pre-eminently shape the events themselves. The truth of this axiom is illustrated principally in the recall of the resolute, indefatigable, far and clear-sighted patriot and statesman, General Butler. To jump to a conclusion without much ado, the recall of Butler from New Orleans is due principally, if not even exclusively, to the united efforts—or conspiracy—of Mr. Seward and Mr. Reverdy Johnson. Thirteen months ago Mr. Seward expected, as he still expects for the future, an uprising of a Union Party in the hottest hot-bed of Secessia. That such are the Secretary of State's expectations, I emphatically assert, and as proof, it may be stated that only yester day, January 9th, Mr. Seward most authoritatively tried to impress upon foreign diplomats the speedy reunion and *restoration* of the Union as it was, notwithstanding the Proclamation, *still considered by the Secretary of State* as being *a waste of paper*. How far the foreign diplomats believe the like oracular decisions, is another question; certain it is that they shrug their shoulders.

But to return to Butler and New Orleans. The patriotic activity by which General Butler won, conquered and maintained the rebel city for the Union, was emphatically considered by Mr. Seward, as crushing out every spark of any latent Union feeling among the rebels. Thurlow Weed, then abroad, urged Mr. Seward to find out the said Union feeling, to blow it into almighty fire and to rely ex-clusively upon it. Here Reverdy Johnson was and is, the principal Union crony of the Secretary of State, and Seaton of the *Intelligencer*; but above all, since the murder of Massachusetts men at Balti-more in 1861, Reverdy Johnson was the devoted advocate of all rich traitors, as the Winans and others, who were called by him " misled Union men." When Gen. Butler dealt deserved justice to rich traitors in New Orleans, the Washington Union-ists surrounding Mr. Chase and Mr. Seward—some of them from New Orleans—urged an investigation. The Secretary of State eagerly seized the occasion to dispatch to the Crescent City Mr. Reverdy John-son with the principal secret mission to gather toge-ther the elements of the scattered Union feeling in Louisiana and in the South, and to make them blaze—in honor of the Secretary of State. It was a rich harvest in every way for Reverdy Johnson ; he harvested it, and on his return fully convinced the Secretary of State, that the Union could not be saved if Gen. Butler remained in his command in the Department of the Gulf.

This surreptitious undermining of General Butler by the Secretary of State, is one more evidence of how truly patriotic was the effort of the Republican Senators and Congressmen to liberate the President and the country from the all-choking and all-poisoning influence of Mr. Seward, and how cursed must remain forever the conduct of Mr. Chase, who, after having during two years cried against Seward, accusing him almost of treason, when the hour struck, preferred to embarrass the patriots and the President rather that to let Mr. Seward retire and deprive the people of his *patriotic* services.   It was moreover expected that, thus warned by the patriots, the President would seize the first occasion to infuse energy into his Cabinet. But there is a Mr. Usher, a docile nonentity, made Secretary of the Interior ; of course the Secretary of State will be strengthened thereby

January 10.—Senator Wright of Indiana, in an ardent and lofty—of course, not rhetorical, speech, hit the nail on the head, when, rendering due homage to Rosecrans, he called him " the first general

who fights for the people and not for the White
House." The greatest praise for the man, and the
most saddening picture of our internal sores.

January 10.—As the pure *populus Romanus*
had an inborn aversion to Kings and diadems, and
could not patiently bear their neighborhood, so the
genuine American Democrat, one by principles
and not by a party name or by a party organization, such a Democrat feels it to be death for his institutions to have slavocracy in his country or in its
neighborhood.

Jan. 10.—O how is to be pitied the future historian
of this bloody tragedy ! Through what a loathsome
cesspool of documentary evidence, preserved in the
various State Archives, the unhappy historian will
have to wade, and wade deep to his chin. Original
works of Lincoln, Seward, etc.

It is easy to play a game at chess with a far superior player, then at least one learns something ;
but impossible to sit at a chess board with a child
who throws all into confusion. The national chess-
board is very confused in the White House. Cunning is good for, and only succeeds in dealing with,
mean and petty facts.

Jun. 10.—Halleck's congratulatory order to Rosecrans and to the Western heroes. How cold and
pedantic. How differently, how enthusiastically

and fiery rang Stanton's words on the capture of forts Henry and Donelson and to Lander's (now dead) troops. Why is Stanton silent? Is it the Constitution, the Statute, is it the incarnate four years formula which seals Stanton's heart and brains? or is Stanton eaten up by the rats in the Cabinet?

January 10.—The messages of the loyal Governors, not copperheads, (as is Seymour of N. Y.) above all, the message of Andrew of Massachuetts, throw a ray of hope and promise over this dark, cold, un patriotic confusion so eminent here in Washington. This confusion, this groping, double-dealing and helplessness can be only cured by a wonder, or else all will be lost. The wonder is daily perpetrated by the all enduring, all-sacrificing people.

Those criminals who ought to have been shot, or, at the mildest, cashiered for the slaughter at Fredericksburgh, the engineers, mock-Jominis, the sham soldiers : all these Washington engineers of that recent butchery, assert now, that, after all, the possession of Fredericksburgh was immaterial ; that Lee would have then selected a better position. All this is thrown to the public to palliate the crime of the Washington military conclave, and to weaken and invalidate Hooker's evidence before the War Committee. It must be admitted that if Hooker— having fifty thousand in hand, and one hundred

thousand in his rear, had seized the Fredericksburgh
heights, he would not have allowed Lee to so easily
select a position and to fortify it. Nay, I suppose,
that not only Hooker, but even a Halleck, a Cullum
or a Meigs would have prevented Lee from settling
in any comfortable position. However, I might be
mistaken. Corinth, Corinth, for Halleck, Those
great night-caps here have so original and so new
military conceptions, their general comprehension
of warfare so widely differs from science, experience,
and from common sense, that, holding Fredericksburgh they might have invited Lee to select whatever
ever he wanted as a strong position.

I learn that Halleck is at work to translate some
French military book. What an inimitable narrow-
minded pedant. If Halleck had brains, he could
not have an hour leisure for translation. But in
such way he humbugs Mr. Lincoln, who looks on
Halleck as the quintescence of military knowledge and genins. A man who can translate a
French book must be a genius. Is it not so, Lincoln?
And thus Halleck translates a book instead of taking
care that the pontoons be sent in time ; and Halleck
prepared sheets for the press, and our soldiers to be
massacred,

Burnside prepares a movement ; Franklin, to undermine Burnside, to appear great, or to get hold

of the army, denounces Burnside secretly to the President: the President forbids the movement. What a confusion! Mr. Lincoln, either accept Burnside's resignation, which he has repeatedly of-fered, or kick down the denouncers. Accident made me discover almost next day, the names of the two generals sent by Franklin on this denunci-atory errand — John Cochran and Newton. I instantly told all to Stanton, who was almost igno-rant of Franklin's surreptitiousness. I also told it to several Senators.

The Army of the Potomac is altogether demoral-ized—above all, in the higher grades. It could not be otherwise if they were angels. McClellanism was and is propitious to general disorder, and how Mr. Lincoln improves is exemplified above. Inde-pendent men, independent Senators and Represent-atives who approach Mr. Lincoln, find him peevish, irritable, intractable to all patriots. *All these are criteria of a lofty mind and character.* Weed, Seward, Harris, Blair, and such ones alone, are agreeable in the White House.

So much is spoken of the war powers of the Pre-sident; I study, and study, and cannot find them as absolute as the Lincolnites construe them. All that I read in the Constitution are the real *war powers* in the Congress, and the President is only the executor of those powers. The President must have permission for every thing, almost at every step— and has no right to issue decrees. He has no war powers over those of Congress, and can act very little on his own hook. It seems to me that Congress, misled, confused by casuists, expounders, and by small intellects worshipping routine, that Congress rather abdicated their powers, and that the bunglers around Lincoln, in his name greedily seized the above powers.

Poor Lincoln! As the devil dreads holy water, so Mr. Lincoln dreads to be surrounded with stern, earnest, ardent, patriotic advisers. Such men would not listen to stories!

January 11.—The thus-called metropolitan press is in the hands of old politicians, old hacks—and no new forces or intellects pierce through. It is a phenomenon. In any whatever country in Europe, at every convulsion the press bristles with new, fresh intellects. Here, the old nightcaps have the monopoly. Farther: those respectable fossils reside at a distance from the focus of affairs, are not directly in contact with events and men, and are in no communion with them. The Grand Lamas of the press depend for information upon the correspondents, who catch news and ideas at random, and nourish with them their employers and the public.

January 11.—Senator Sumner has made a motion to give homesteads to the liberated Africo-Americans. That is a better and a nobler action than all his declamations put together.

January 12.—Sentinels in double line surrounding the White House. Odious, ridiculous, unnecessary, and an aspect unwonted in this country—giving the aspect to the White House of an abode of a tyrant, when it is only that of a shifting politician. It is Halleck, who, with the like futilities and absurdities, amuses Lincoln and gets the better of him.

Mr. Lincoln is very depressed at the condition of the Army of the Potomac, and decides—nothing for its reorganization. But for Halleck, Stanton would reorganize and give a new and healthy life to the army. I mean the upper grades, and not the rank and file, who are patriotic and healthy.

After Corinth, Halleck-Buell disorganized the Western, now Halleck is at work to do the same with the Potomac Army. I know that in the presence of a diplomat, Halleck complained that he is paid only five thousand dollars, and earned by far more in California. He had better return to California and to his pettifogging.

Since the beginning of this Administration, Mr. Seward wrote, I am sure, more dispatches than

France, England, Prussia, Russia, Austria, Spain, and Italy put together during the Crimean war, and up to this day. Great is ink, and paper is patient !

January 13.—It is more than probable that Mr. Mercier stirred up, or at least heartily supported the mediation scheme. The Frenchmen in New York maintain that Mr. Mercier derives his knowledge of America and his political inspirations from that foul sheet, the *Courrier des Etats Unis*. There is some truth in this assertion, as the reasons enumerated to justify mediation can be found in various numbers of that sheet. I am sorry that Mr. Mercier has fallen so low; as for his master, he is a fit associate for the *Courrier*.

January 13.—Ralph Waldo Emerson, inspired and not silenced by the storm. He alone stands up from among the Athenian school. He alone is undaunted. So would be Longfellow, but for the terrible domestic calamity whose crushing blow no man's heart could resist. I never was a great admirer of Emerson, but now I bow, and burn to him my humble incense.

January 15.—The patriotic, and at times inspired orator—not rhetor—Kelly, from Pennsylvania, told me that all is at sixes and sevens in the Administration, and in the army. I believe it. How could it be otherwise, with Lincoln, Seward and Halleck at the head?

Mr. Seward did his utmost to defeat the re-election of Judge Potter from Wisconsin, one among the best and noblest patriots in the country. For this object Mr. Seward used the influence of the pro-Catholic Bonzes. Then Mr. Seward wrote a letter denying all this—a letter which not in the least convinced the brave Judge, as I have it from himself.

If all the lies could only be ferreted out with which Seward bamboozles Lincoln, even the God of Lies himself would shudder.

January 15.—The noble and lofty voice of the genuine English people, the voice of the working classes, begins to be heard. The people re-echo the key-note struck by a J. S. Mills, by a Bright, a Cobden, and others of like pure mind and noble heart. The voice of the genuine English people resounds altogether differently from the shrill *falsetto* with which turf hunters, rent-roll devourers, lords, lordlings, and all the like shams and whelps try to intimidate the patriotic North, and comfort the traitors, the rebels.

January 16.—But for the truly enlightened and patriotic efforts of the Senators Wade, Lane, (of Kansas) and Trumbull, the debate of yesterday,

Thursday, on the appropriation for the West Point Military Academy would have gone to the country, absolutely misleading and stultifying the noble and enlightened people. It was most sorrowful, nay, wholly disgusting to witness how Senators who, until then, had stood firmly against small influences and narrow prejudices, blended together in an unholy alliance to sustain the accursed clique of West Point engineers. Much allowance is to be made for the allied Senators' ignorance of the matter, and for the natural wish to appear wise. The country, the people, ought to treasure the names of the ten patriotic Senators whose voices protested against futher sustaining that cursed nursery of arrogance, of pro-slavery, or of something worse.

Whatever might have been the efforts of the Senatoral patrons and the allies of the engineers, the following facts remained for ever unalterable : 1st. That the spirit of close educational corporation which have exclusive monopoly and patronage, is perfectly similar to the spirit which prevailed and still prevails in monasteries, and permeates the pupils durring their whole after life; 2d. That the prevailing spirit in West Point was and is rather monarchical and altogether Pro-Slavery; 3d, that of course some noble exceptions are to be found and made,—but they are exceptions; 4th, that such educational monasteries nurse conceit and arrogance ; and this the mass of West Pointers have prominently shown during this war in their relations with the noble and devoted volunteers, and that this arrogant spirit of clique and of caste works mischievously in the army ; 5th, that exceptions, noble and patriotic, as a Reno, a Lyons, a Bayard, a Stevens, and other such heroes and patriots, do not disprove the general rule ; 6th, that Lyons, Grant, Rosecrans, Hooker, Heintzelman, etc., have shown glorious qualities not on account of what they learnt in West Point, but by what they did not learn there ; 7th, that these heroes rose above the dry and narrow school wisdom, and are what they are, not because educated in West Point, but notwithstanding their education there. And here I interrupt the further enumeration to give an extract from a private letter directed to me by one of the most eminent pupils from West Point, and the ablest *true*, not *mock*, engineer in our army :

"In regard to your views of West Point's influence I am at a loss to make any answer," (the writer is a great defender of West Point,) "but would suggest that it may be after all not West Point, but the want of *a supreme hand* to our military affairs to *combine* and *use* the materials West Point furnishes, that is in fault. * * * *West Point cannot make a general*—no military school can—but it can· and does furnish good soldiers. All the distinguished Confederate generals are West Pointers. and yet we know the men, and know that neither Lee, nor Johnson nor Jackson, nor Beauregard, nor the Hills are men of any very extraordinary ability," etc., etc., etc.

To this I answer: the rebels are with their heart and soul in their cause, and thus their capacities are expanded, they are inspired on the field of battle. (Similar answer I gave to General McDowell about six months ago.) So was our Lyon, so are Rosecrans, Hooker, Grant, and a few others; and for such generals, Senators Trumbull, Wade and Lane ardently called in the above debate.

I continue the enumeration: 8th. The military direction of the war is exclusively in the hands of a West Point clique, and of West Point engineers,—not *very much* with their hearts in the people's cause; 9th, that that clique of West Point engineers from McClellan down to Halleck prevents any truly higher military capacity getting a free untramelled scope, (General Halleck with all his might opposes giving the command of the army to Hooker,) and this Halleck, an engineer from West Point, who never saw a cartridge burnt or a file of soldiers fighting, to-day decides the military fate of our country on the authority of a book said to be on military science, but if such a book had been written by any officer in the armies of France, Prussia or Russia, the ignorant author would have had the friendly advice from his superiors to resign and select some pursuit in life more congenial to his intellectual capacities; further, this Halleck complains in following words: "that they (the Administration) made him leave a profitable business in San Francisco, and pay him only 5,000 dollars to fight THEIR (not his) battles." So much for a Halleck. 10th, That the West Point clique of engineers, the McClellans, the Hallecks, the Franklins, etc., have brought the country to the verge of the grave, as stated by Senator Lane.

Such were the facts established by the patriotic and not would-be-wise Senators; and there is an illustration recorded in history as proof that the above not engineering Senators were right in their assertions. Frederick II. was in no military school; the captains second to Napoleon in the French wars were Hoche, Moreau, and Massena, all of them from private life.

—The clique of engineers has the Potomac Army altogether in its grasp, and has reduced and perverted the spirit of the noble children of the people. Oh, the sooner this army shall be torn from the hands of the clique the nearer and surer will be the salvation of the country.

The clique accuses the volunteers; but the clique, the engineers in power have disorganized, morally and materially, and disgraced the Army of the Potomac. They did this from the day of the encampments around Washington, in the fall of 1861, down to the day of Fredericksburgh. Fredericksburgh was altogether prepared by engineers; at Fredericksburgh the engineer Franklin did not even mount his horse when his soldiers were mis-led and miscommanded—by himself.

—Stragglers are generated by generals. Besides, to explain straggling, I quote from a *genuine* book on genuine military science, published in Berlin in 1862, by Captain Boehu, the most eminent professor at the military school in Potsdam: "The greatest losses, during a war, inflicted on an army are by maladies and by straggling. Such losses are five times greater than those of killed and wounded; and an *intelligent administration* takes preparatory measures to meet the losses and to compensate them. Such measures of foresight consist in organizing depots for batallions, which depots ought to equal one sixth of the number of the active army." O, Halleck, where are the depots?

—"In any ordinary campaign, excepting a winter campaign, the losses amount (as established by experience) to one half in infantry one fourth in cavalry, and to one third in artillery." (Do you know any thing about it, O, Halleck?)

Let the people be warned, and they may understand the location of the cause generating further disasters. If the Army the Potomac shall win glory, it will win it notwithstanding the West Point clique of engineers. The disasters have root in the

White House, where the advice of such a Halleck prevails.

—I know very well that the formation of the volunteers in respective States and by the Governors of such States raises a great difficulty in organizing and preparing reserves. But talent and genius reveal themselves by overpowering difficulties considered to be insurmountable. And Halleck is a man both of genius and talent.

Taking into account the patriotism, the devotion of the governors of the respective states, [not *à la* Copperhead Seymour], it would have been possible, nay, even easy to organize some kind of reserves. O, Halleck, O, fogies!

January 17.—Mr. Lincoln loads on his shoulders all kinds of responsibilities, more so than even Jackson would have dared to take. Admirable if generated by the boldness of self-consciousness, of faith, and of convictions. True men measure the danger—and the means in their grasp to meet the emergency; others play unconsciously with events, as do children with explosive and death-dealing matters.

January 17.—General and astronomer Mitchel's death may be credited to Halleck. Halleck and Buell's envy—if not worse—paralysed Mitchel and Turtschin's activity in the West. Mitchel and Turtschin were too quick, that is, too patriotic. In early summer, 1862, they were sure to take

Chattanooga, a genuine strategic point, one of those principal knots and nurseries in the life of the secesh. How imprudent! Chattanooga is still in the hands of the rebels, and if we ever take it, it will cost streams of blood and millions of money. Down with Mitchel and Turtschin. Mitchel's *excrementa* were more valuable than are Halleck's heavy, but not expanding, brains. Mitchel revealed at once all the qualities of an eminent, if not of a great general. Quickness of mind, fertility of resources. An astronomer, a mathematician, Mitchel's mind was familiar with broad combinations. Such a mind penetrated space, calculated means and chances, balanced forces and probabilities. Not to compare, however, is it to be borne in mind that Napoleon was a mathematician in the fullest sense, and not an engineer, not a translator.

January 18.—Mr. Lincoln's letter to McClellan when the hero of the Copperheads was in search of mud in the Peninsula. The letter rings as sound common sense ; it shows, however, that common sense debarred of strong will remains unproductive of good. Mr. Lincoln commonly shows strong will, in the wrong place.

————— cin Theil von jener Krafft,
Die stehts das Guthe will, und stehts das Boese schaff.

January 18.—The emancipation proclamation is out. Very well. But until yet not the slightest signs of any measures to execute the proclamation, at once, and in its broadest sense. Now days, even hours, are equal to years in common times. Had Lincoln his heart in the proclamation, on January 2d he would began to work out its expansion, realization, execution. I wish Lincoln may lift himself, or be lifted by angels to the grandeur of the work. But it is impossible. Surrounded as he is, and led in the strings by Seward, Blair, Halleck, and by border-state politicians, the best that can be expected are belated half measures.

Stanton comprehends broadly and thoroughly the question of emancipation and of arming the Africo-Americans. As I intend to realize my plans of last year and organise Africo-American regiments, I had conversations with Stanton, and find him more thorough about the matter than is any body whom I met. He agreed with me, that the cursed land of Secessia ought to be surrounded by camps to enlist and organise the enslaved, as a scorpion surrounded with burning coals. Such organizations introduced rapidly and simultaneously on all points, would shake Secessia to its foundations, and put an end to guerillas, *alias* murderers and robbers. We will again think and talk it over. But as is wont with Lincoln, he will hesitate, hesitate, until much of precious time will be lost.

January 18.—A surgeon in one of the hospitals in Alexandria writes in a private note:

"Our wounded bear their sufferings nobly; I have hardly heard a word of complaint from one of them. A soldier from the 'stern and rock bound coast' of Maine—a victim of the slaughter at Fredericksburgh—lay in this hospital, his life ebbing away from a fatal wound. He had a father, brothers and sisters, a wife, and one little boy of two or three years old, on whom his, heart seemed set. Half an hour before he ceased to breathe, I stood by his side, holding his hand. He was in the full exercise of his intellectual faculties, and knew he had but a brief time to live. He was asked if he had any message to leave for his dear ones whom he loved so well. "*Tell them,*" said he, "*how I died—they know how I lived!*"

January 19.—Senator Wright, of Indiana, stirred the hearts of the Senate and of the people. It was not the oration of a rhetor—it was the confession of an ardent, pure patriot. I never heard or witnessed anything so inspiring and so kindling to soul and heart.

January 20.—General Butler palsied and shelved, Halleck all powerful and with full steam running the country and the army to destruction—such is the truest photograph of the situation. But as an adamantine rock among storms, so Mr. Lincoln remains unmoved. Unmoved by the yawning, bleeding wounds of the devoted, noble people—unmoved by the prayers and supplication of patriots—of his — once — best friends. Mr. Lincoln answers, with dignity not Roman, and with obstinacy unparalleled even by Jackson, that he will stand or fall with his present advisers, and that he takes the responsibility for all the cursed misdeeds of Seward, Halleck, Chase, and others. So children are ready to set a match to a powder magazine unconscious of the terrible results—unconscious of the awful responsibility for its destructive action.

A death pang runs through one's body to see how rapidly the dial marks the disappearing hours, and how unrelentingly approaches March 4th, and the death-knell of this present patriotic, devoted Congress. For this terrible storm and clash of events, the people, perhaps, feel not the immensity of the loss. Paralyzed as Congress has been and now is, by the infernal machinations of Seward, Chase, and others, and by Mr. Lincoln's stubborn helplessness, the patriots in both Houses nevertheless, succeeded in redeeming the pledge which the name of America gives to the expansive progress of humanity. The patriots of both Houses, as the exponents of the noble and loftiest aspirations of the American people, whipped in—and this literally, not figuratively—whipped Mr. Lincoln into the glory of having issued the Emancipation Proclamation. The laws promulgated by this dying Congress initiated the Emancipation—generated the Proclamation of the 22d September, and of January 1st.

History will not allow one to wear borrowed plumage.

—Congress ought not to have so easily abdicated its well established rights of more absolute and direct control of the deeds of the Administration and of its clerks, *alias* Secretaries of Departments. It is to be eternally regretted that Congress has shown such unnecessary leniency ; but in justice it must be said that the patriotic and high-minded members of Congress wished to avoid the degrading necessity of showing the nation the prurient administrative sores. Advised, directed, tutored and pushed by Seward, Blair and Chase, Mr. Lincoln is—innocently—as grasping for power, as are any of those despots not over respectfully recorded by history.

With all this, the presence of Congress keeps in awe the reckless and unscrupulous Administration, as, according to the pious belief of medieval times, holy water awed the devil. But Congress once out of the way, without having succeeded in rescuing Mr. Lincoln from the hands of those mean, ignorant, egotistic bunglers, all the time squinting towards the succession to the White House, and unable to surround the President with men and patriots, then all the plagues of Egypt may easily overrun this fated country. Such conjurors of evil as the Sewards, Hallecks, and others, will have no dread of any holy water before them, and they will be sure that the great party of the " Copperheads" in the future

Congress will applaud them for all the mischief done, and lift them sky high, if they succeed in treading down in the gutter, or in any way palsying emancipation, tarnishing the people's noble creed, and endangering the country's holiest cause.

General Fitz-John Porter's trial before court-martial ended in his dismissal, but ought punishment to fall on him alone, when the butchers of Fredericksburgh and when the pontoon men are in high command? when a Franklin is still sustained, when a Seward and a Halleck remain firm in their high places as the gates of hell?

January 20.—Wrote a respectful letter to the President on Halleck's military science, his book, and capacity. Told respectfully to Mr. Lincoln that not even the Sultan would dare to palm such a Halleck on his army and on his people.

Mr. Lincoln in his greatness says that "he will stand and fall with his Cabinet." O, Mr. Lincoln! O, Mr. Lincoln! purple-born sovereigns can no more speak so!

Mr. Lincoln! with the gang of politicians, your advisers and friends, *you all desire immensely, and will feebly.* You desire the reconstruction of the Union, and you almost shun the ways and means to do it. And thus this noble people is dragged to a slaughter house.

> Parumne campis atque Neptuno super
> Fusum est—[Yankee] sanguinis ?

January 21.—Deep, irreconcilable as is my hatred of slavocrats and rebels, neverthelesss I am
forced to admire the high intellectual qualities of
their chiefs, when compared with that of ours. Of
Lincoln *versus* Jeff Davis I spoke in the first volume. But now Lee, Jackson, Hill, Ewall, *versus*
Halleck, McClellan, McDowell, Franklin, etc.

Januáry 22.—Wendell Phillips's *Amen* oration
to the Proclamation is noble and torrent-like orato-
ry. Greeley is the better Greeley of former
times. I heartily wish to admire and speak well
of Greeley, as of every body else. Is it my fault
that they give me no occasion ?

January 23.—General Fitz-John Porter, Mc-
Clellan's pet, told me to-day, that after the battle
at Hanover Court House, he supplicated Mc-
Clellan to attack Richmond at once—which in Porter's opinion could have been taken without much
ado,—and not to change his base to James River;
and even Fitz-John could not prevail on this demi-
god of imbeciles, traitors and intriguers.

January 24.—Here is one of the thousand flagrant
lies with which Seward entangles Lincoln, as with
a net of steel. Lincoln assured General Ashley
that the public is unjust toward Seward in accusing
him of having worked for the defeat of Wadsworth. That they have been the best friends for
long years; that, when Military Governor of
Washington, Wadsworth was a daily visitor in

Seward's house; and that, during the canvass, Wadsworth consulted with Seward concerning his (Wadsworth's) actions.

Mr. Seward knows that every one of those assertions which he or Thurlow Weed pushed down the throat of Mr. Lincoln is a flagrant lie. Every one knows that for many, many years the high-toned Wadsworth had in utter detestation Mr. Seward's character as a lawyer or as a public man, and that he never spoke to him, and never was his political or private friend.

I am sorry to bring such details before the public, but how otherwise convict a liar? As for Thurlow Weed's secret and open machinations against the election of Wadsworth, only an idiot or a s.... doubts them. Ask the New York politicians, provided they have manhood to tell the truth.

January 24th.—Caveant Senators and Representatives! cannot be too often hurled into the ears of the people and of the Congressmen. The time runs lightning like—the 4th of March approaches with comet-like velocity. If the tempest is not roaring, its signs are visible, and most of the helmsmen are blind or unsteady. Oh! could every move of the pendulums of the clocks of the Senate Chamber and the Representatives' Hall, thunder-like repeat that *caveant,* transmitted by the purest and best days of Rome! The Republicans and many of the war

Democrats are faithful and true to the people and to its sacred cause; but the names of the "filibustering" traitors in both houses ought to be nailed to the gallows!

European winds bring Louis Napoleon's opening speech, and the confession, that although once rebuked, he, the dissolute, the profligate, with his corrosive breath still intends to pollute the virginity of our country; for such is the indelible stain to any nation, to any people which accepts or submits to any, even the most friendly, foreign mediation or arbitration. Never, never any great nation or any self-respecting government, accepted or submitted to any similar foreign interference. Of the peoples, nations and governments, which allowed such interference, some collapsed into degradation for a long time, only slowly recovering, like Spain; others, like Poland, disappeared. Those who advocate such mediation unveil their weakness, their thorough ignorance of the world's history and of the historic and political bearings of the words, *mediation*, and *arbitration;* and to crown all, these advocates bring to market their imbecility.

The Africo-Americans ought to receive military organization and be armed. But it ought to be done instantly and without loss of time; it ought to be done earnestly, boldly, broadly ; it ought to be done at once on all points and on the largest scale; it ought to be done here in Washington, under the eyes of the chief of the people; here in the heart of the country; here, so to speak, in the face of slave-breeding Virginia, this most intense focus of treason; it ought to be done here, that the loyal freemen of Virginia's soil be enabled to fight and crush the F. F. V's, the progeny of hell; it ought to be done here on every inch of soil covered with shattered shackles; and not partially on the out-skirts, in the Carolinas and Louisiana. Stanton, alone, and Welles among the helmsmen, are so in-spired; but alas, for the rest of the crew.

On the flags of the Africo-Americans under my command, I shall inscribe: *Hic niger est! hunc tu (rebel) caveto!* I shall inculcate upon my men that they had better not make prisoners in the battle, and not allow themselves to be taken alive.

January 25th.—So Gen. McClellan's services to the rebellion are acknowledged by the gift of a splendid mansion situated in New York, in the so-cial sewer of American society. The donors, are the shavers from Wall Street, individuals who coin money from the blood and from the misfortunes of the people, and who by high rents mercilessly crush the poor; who sacrifice nothing for the sacred cause; who, if they put their names as voluntary contributors of a trifle for the war, thousand and thousand times recover that trifle which they osten-tatiously throw to gull the good-natured public opinion; not to speak of those so numerous among the McClellanites, who openly or secretly are in mental communion with treason and rebellion. Naturally, all this gang honors its hero.

McClellan's pedestal is already built of the corpses of hundreds of thousands butchered by his generalship, poisoned in the Chickahominy, and decimated by diseases. His trophies are the wooden guns from Centreville and Manassas.

January 25th.—What from the beginning of this war, I witness as administrative acts and dispositions, and further the debates in Congress on the various bills for military organizations and for the organization of the various branches of the military medical, surgical, and quartermaster's service; all this fully convinces me that the military and administrative routine, as transmitted by Gen. Scott, or by his school, and as continued by his pets and remnants, is almost the paramount cause of all mischief and evils. In the medical, surgical, and in the quartermasters' offices, ought have been appointed young civilians and business men as chiefs, having under them some old routinists for the sake of technicalities of the service. Such men would have done by far better than those old intellectual drones. A merchant accustomed to carry on an extensive and complicated business would have been by far a better quartermaster-general—*Intendant des armées*—than the wholly inexperienced Gen. Meigs. This last would serve as an aid to the merchant. At the beginning of the war, I suggested to Senator Wilson to import such quartermasters from France or Russia, men experienced and accustomed to provide for armies of 100,000 men each. By paying well, such men could have been easily found, and the military medical and surgical bureau, as organized by Scott, was about sixty years behind real science. These senile representatives of non-science snubbed off Professor Van Buren of the New York academy, to whom they compare as the light of a common match to that of calcium. If men like Dr. Van Buren, Dr. Barker, and others of real science from New York, Boston, Philadelphia, etc., had been listened to, thousands and thousands of limbs and lives would have been saved and preserved.

January 25th.—Mr. Lincoln relishes the idea that if the cause of the North is victorious, no one can claim much credit for it. I put this on record for some future assumptions. Mr. Lincoln is the best judge of the merits of his clerks and lieutenants. But Mr. Lincoln forgets that the success will be due exclusively to the people—and, *per contra*, he alone will be arrayed for the failure. His friends and advisers, as the Sewards, the Weeds, the Blairs, the Hallecks, will very cleverly wash their gored hands from any complicity with him—Lincoln.

The army to be formed from Africo-Americans is to be entrusted to converted conservatives. It is feared that sincere abolitionists if entrusted with the command, may use the forces for some awful, untold aims. It is feared that abolitionists once possessed of arms and troops, may use them indiscriminately, and emancipate right and left, by friend and foe, paying no attention to the shrieks of border-States, of old women, of politicians, of cowards, of Sewardites; nay, it is feared that genuine abolitionists may carry too far their notions of absolute equality of races, and without hesitation treat the white rebels with even more severity than they threaten to treat loyal armed Africo-Americans. And why not? ....

The history of England, the history of any free country has not on record a position thus anomalous, even humiliating, as is that of the patriots in Congress, thanks to Mr. Lincoln's helpless stubbornness. The patriots forcibly must consider Mr. Lincoln, even Sewardised, Blairised, Halleckised as he is, as being the only legal power for the salvation of the country. The patriots must support him, and instead of exposing the wretched faults, mistakes, often ill-will of his administration, must defend the administration against the attacks of the Copperheads, who try to destroy or disorganize the administration on account of that atom of good that it accidentally carries out on its own hook. And thus the patriots must suffer and bear patiently abuses heaped on them by the treasonable or by the stupid press, by intriguers and traitors; and patriots cannot make even the slightest attempt to vindicate their names.

January 26th.—The visits to the White House and the "*I had a talk with the President,*" are among the prominent causes of the distracted condition of affairs. With comparatively few exceptions, almost everybody expands a few inches in his own estimation, when he says to his listeners, nay, to his friends : "I had a talk with the President." Of course it is no harm in private individuals to have such *a talk*, but I have frequently observed and experienced that public men had better refrain from having any talk with him. Very often he is not a jot improved by their talk, and they come out from the interview worsted in some sort or other.

Sumner, the Roman, the Cicero, was to-day urged by several abolitionists from Boston to expose the mischief of both the foreign and the domestic policy of Seward. The Senator replied that he is more certain to succeed against that public nuisance and public enemy by not attacking him openly. I vainly ransack my recollection of my classic reading for the name of any Roman who ever made such a reply.

January 26th : Two o'clock P. M.—Hooker is in command! And patriotic hearts thrill with joy! Mud, bad season, mortality, loss of time, demoralization, such is the inheritance left by McClellan, Halleck and Burnside—such are the results prepared by the infamous West Point and other muddy intriguers in Washington, and in the army,—such is the inheritance transmitted to Hooker, by the cursed Administration procrastinations. In all military history there is seldom, if ever, a record of a commander receiving an army under such ominous circumstances. If Hooker succeeds, then his genius will astonish even his warmest friends.

When Hooker was wounded, and in the hospital, he repeatedly complained to me of the deficiency of the staffs. I reminded him of it, and he promised to do his best to organize a staff without a flaw.

I immediately wrote to Stanton, sending him several pages translated from the German works of Boehn (before spoken of) to give to the Secretary a general idea of what are the qualities, the science, the knowledge and the duties of a good chief of staff. I explained that the staff and the chief of the staff of an army are to it what the brains and the nervous system are to the human body.

9 o'clock, P. M.—I am told that Hooker wished to have for his chief of staff General Stone, (whitewashed) who is considered to be one of the most brilliant capacities of the army. If so, it was a good choice, and the opposition made by Stanton is for me—at the best—unintelligible.

Hooker selected Butterfield. What a fall from Stone to Butterfield. Between the two extend hundreds, nay, thousands, of various gradations. Gen. Butterfield is brave, can well organize a regiment or a brigade, but he has not and can not have the first atom of knowledge required in a chief of staff of such a large army. Staff duties require special studies, they are the highest military science; and where, in the name of all, could Butterfield have acquired it? I am certain Butterfield is not even aware that staff duties are a special science. All this is a very bad omen, very bad, very bad. Literally they laugh at me; now they hurrah for Hooker. May they not cry very soon on account of Hooker's staff. When I warn, Senators and Representatives tell me that I am very difficult to be satisfied. We will see.

January 27.—It is said that Franklin, Sumner, and even Heintzelman declared. they would not serve under Hooker. Let them go. Bow them out, the hole in the army will be invisible. I am sorry that Heintzelman plays such pranks, as he is a very good general and a very good man. Well, a new galaxy of generals and commanders is the inevitable gestation of every war. Seldom if ever the same men end a war who began it. New men will prove better than the present sickly reputations consecrated by Scott, West Point and Washington.

January 27.—Governor Andrew—the man always to the point, or as the French would say *toujours à la hauteur de la question*—insists on forming African or black regiments in Boston from free blacks. Such formations interfere not with my project, as I principally, nay exclusively, look to contrabands, to actual slaves. Governor Andrew wishes to give the start, to stir up the Government and other Governors and to drag them in his footsteps. He is the representative man of the new and better generation which ought to have the affairs of the country in hand, and not these old worn-out hacks who are at it now. If such new men were at the helm in both civil and military affairs, Secesh would have been already crushed and Emancipation accomplished. To such a new generation belongs Coffey, one of the Assistant Attorney Generals, Austin Stevens, Jr., Charles Dana, Woodman, etc., etc. The country bristles with such men, and only prejudices, stupidity, and routine prevents them from becoming really active and from saving the country.

January 27.—The patriotic majorities of both Houses of Congress pass laws after laws concerning the finances, arming the Africo-Americans, increasing the powers of the President, etc., each of which taken alone, would not only save the cause but raise it triumphant over the ruins of crime and of slavery, if used by patriotic, firm, devoted, unegotistic hands and brains. But alas! alas! very little of such, except in one or two individuals, is located

in the various edifices in and around the presidential quarters.

The military organization of Africo-Americans is a
powerful social and military engine by which slavery, secession, rebellion, and all other dark and
criminal Northern and Southern excrescences can
be crushed and pulverized to atoms, and this in a
trice. But as is the case with all other powerful
and explosive gases, elements, forces, etc. this mighty
element put in the hands of the Administration
must be handled resolutely, and with unquivering
hands and intellect; otherwise the explosion may
turn out useless for the country and for humanity.

At present the indications are very small that
the administration has a decided, clear comprehension how to use this accession of loyal forces on a
large scale; how to bring them boldly into action
in Virginia, as the heart of the rebellion. Nothing
yet indicates that the administration intends to arm
and equip Africo-Americans here under the eyes of
the government. Nothing indicates that it intends
to do this avowedly and openly, and thereby terrify
and strike the proud slave-breeders, the F. F. V's.
of Virginia, in the heart of treason, and do it by
their own once chattels, now their betters.

January 28.—The Congress almost expires; and
will or can the incarnated constitutional formula
save the country? It is a chilling thought to doubt,
yet how can we have confidence! All in the

people! the people alone and its true men will not and cannot fail, and they alone are up to the mission.

The dying Congress can no more reconquer its abdicated power. This noble and patriotic majority —many of them, are not re-elected, thanks to Lincoln-Seward—provide the incarnate formula with all imaginable legal, constitutional powers, more than twice sufficient to save the country. Could only the brains and hands entrusted with laws, be able to execute them! Oh for a legal, constitutional, statute Cromwell, ready to behead treason, rebellion, slavocracy and slavo-sympathy, as the great Oliver beheaded and crushed the poisonous weeds of his time. If the democratic-copperhead vermin had the possibility, they would make a McClellan-Seymour dictatorship, and extinguish for a century at least, light, right, justice, and freedom. Not yet! Oh, Copperheads! not yet.

January 29.—They dance to madness in New York, they dance here and give dancing parties! O what a heartlessness, recklessness, flippancy, and crime, of those mothers, wives and young crinolines, when one half of the population is already in mourning, when they have fathers, brothers, husbands in the army. I hope that Boston and New England as well as the towns and villages of the country all over, spit on this example given by New York and Washington. My friend N———, progressive,

enlightened and therefore a true Russian, is amazed
and displeased with such an intolerable flippancy.
During the Crimean war, no one danced in Russia
from the Imperial palace down to the remotest
village; the people's indignation would have prevented any body—even the Czar, from such a sacrilegious display of recklessness when the country's
integrity and honor were at stake, when the
nation's blood was pouring in torrents.

Unspeakably worse, is the cold indifference
with which many generals, many men in power, the
rhetors and the politicians, speak of what is more
than a sacrifice in a sacred cause, is an unholy and
demoniac waste of human life.   But some one
—some avenging angel, will call them all to a terrible account.

January 30.—I would have ex-Governor Boutwell, of Massachusetts, Secretary of State.   The
conduct of European affairs requires pure patriotism—that is, conscientiousness of being an American by principle, in the noblest philosophical
sense, sound common sense, discretion, simplicity,
sobriety of mind, firmness, clearsightedness.   Boutwell would be a Secretary of State similar to
Marcy.

January 30.—Wrote a letter to Stanton with
the following suggestions for the organization of a
large and efficacious force, nay, army, from the
Africo-Americans.

Some of the points submitted to this genuine patriot have been already variously mentioned above ; here are some others.

1. It may be possible—even probable—on account of inveterate prejudices and stupidity, that an Africo-American regiment may be left unsupported during a battle.

2. It would be therefore more available to organize such a force at once on a large scale, so as to be able to have strong brigades, and even divisions. At the head of six to eight thousand men, resistance is possible for several hours if the enemy outnumbers not in too great proportions—four or five to one, and if the terrain is not altogether against the smaller force.

3. The Africo-Americans ought to be formed, drilled and armed principally with the view to constitute light infantry—and, if possible, light cavalry—but above all, for a *set fight.*

4. Their dress must be adapted to such a light service—as ought to be the dress of our whole infantry, facilitating to the utmost the quick and easy movements of the body and of the feet ; both impossible or at least difficult in the present equipment of the American infantry. On account of the modern improvements in fire-arms, the fights begin at longer distances, and it is important that the soldier be trained to march as quickly as possible, so as to force the enemy from their positions at the

point of the bayonet. In this country of clay, bad roads, forests and underbrush, even more than care must be bestowed upon the feet and legs of the infantry. I suggested an imitation of the equipment of the French infantry.

5. In the case of the arsenals not having the requisite number of fire-arms, I would have the third line armed with scythes. As a Pole, I am familiar with that really terrible weapon.

6. To adapt the drill to the object in view—to free it as far as possible from needless technicalities, and to reduce it to the most urgently needed and the most readily comprehended particulars.

7. In view of the above-mentioned reasons, I would have the Tactics now in use very carefully revised, or have an entirely new book of Tactics and Regulations.

8. Suggested that General Casey should be entrusted with the matters treated of in suggestions 6 and 7.

January 31.—The Copperheads in Congress are shedding crocodile tears over the doom that awaits those Africo-Americans who may unfortunately be taken prisoners by the rebels. Now, in the first place enlisted Africo-Americans are under the protection of the United States Government, and that Government will not be guilty of the infamy of seeing its captured soldiers murdered in cold blood— and in the next place the Africo-American will prove anything rather than an easily-made captive to Southern murderers. The Africo-Americans will sell their lives so dearly as to disgust the rebels with the task of attempting to capture them.

January 31.—Few people can understand the intensity of the disgust with which I find myself often obliged to mention Thurlow Weed—that darkest incarnation of all that is evil in black mail, lobbyism, and all hideous corruptions. It is not my fault that such a man is allowed to exert a malign influence on the country's fate, and I am obliged to give the dark as well as the bright parts of the great social picture. How deeply I regret my inability to collect and record, in part at least, if not as a whole, all the deeds of heroism and devotion, of generous and brave self-abnegation, which have been done by thousands, even by millions of those who are both falsely and foolishly called the lower classes.

FEBRUARY, 1863.

The Problems before the People—the Circassian—Department of State and International Laws—Foresight—Patriot Stanton and the Rats—Honest Conventions—Sanitary Commission—Harper's Ferry—John Brown—the Yellow Book—the Republican Party—Epitaph—Prize Courts—Suum cuique—Academy of Sciences—Democratic Rank and File, etc. etc. etc.

February 1.—THE task which this great American people has on its hands is one utterly unexampled in the history of the world. While in the midst of a great civil war, and struggling as it were in very death-throes, to emancipate and organize four millions of men, most of whom, up to this very day, have by deliberate legislation been kept in ignorance and savagery. Thoroughly to comprehend the immensity of such a task, we must also reflect that the men to whom that task is intrusted are anything rather than intellectual giants. Yet the true solution of the problem will be given by the principle of self-government and by the self-governing People. And it is therein that consists the genuine American originality which Europe finds it so impossible to understand. And it is just as little understood by most of the diplomatists here, and what

is still worse, it is not even studied by them. It is
wretched work to be obliged to witness the low, the
actually ignoble parts which many men play in
the great farce of political life. I could easily mention a full score of would-be-eminent men, who are
unsurpassed by the meanest of the vulgar herd in
flippancy and an utter want of self-respect.

The diary published in London by Bull Run Russell deserves to be read by every American. Russell deals blows to slavery which will tell in England. However annoying may be to many the dis-
closures made by this indiscreet confidant of their
vanity, Russell's revelations establish firmly the
broad historical—not gossipping—fact, that before
and after Sumter, the most absolute want of earnestness, of statesmanlike foresight, and the most
childish but fathomless vanity inspired all the actions of the American Secretary of State. I am one
of the few who, having often met Russell here, never fawned to him, nay who not even took any notice
of him; but I am grateful to him for his falsely-
called indiscreetness—for his having done the utmost to bring out truth—in his own way. It is the
best that I have seen, or heard, or read of him.
Flatterers, Secretaries, Senators, and Generals
crowded to Russell and to his table, and he exposes
them. Among others, General McDowell was Russell's guest, very likely to show his gratitude to the

slanderer of the volunteers, whom McDowell did not understand how to lead to victory.

Seward showed to Russell his dispatches to Lord John Russell. Mr. Sumner, at Bull Run Russell's table, asked Russell's aid to keep peace with England. Good! Unspeakably good!

Not only the Emancipation problem must be solved, so to speak, amidst the storm of battle—but other and very mighty problems, social, constitutional, jurisprudential, and financial, must be similarly and promptly dealt with. And these great questions must be debated to the accompaniment of the music of musketry and cannon. In some respects the situation of America at present may be said to resemble that of France in the days of her great Revolution. But affairs here and now are still more complicated than they were in France from 1789 to 1793.

Formerly I took a more active part than I now take in revolutionary and reformatory struggles, and was seldom daunted by their difficult problems, or by their most violent tempests. But now I have a chilling sense of weariness and disgust as I note the strange things that are done under my very eyes.

The burden of taxes laid upon a people who have an inborn hatred of taxation, a debt created in a few months surpassing that which England and France contracted in half a century; and that debt contracted as if by magic, and in the very crisis of a civil war such as any foreign war would be mere baby's play to.

The people at large see the precipice, and hear the roaring of the breakers ahead, but despair not! Sublime phenomena for the future historian to dwell upon ! All this is genuine American originality. In its sublime presence, down, down upon your knees in the dust, all you European wiseacres !

The capture of the *Circassian*, an English blockade runner, gave birth to some very delicate international complications. The decision of the Prize Court shows up the absolute destitution of statesmanship in the Department of State, generally coruscated with ignorance of international principles, rules of judicial international decisions, and of belligerent rights and observances. Every day shows what a masterly stroke it was of the Secretary of State to have proclaimed the blockade in April, 1861, and to have been the first to recognize the rebels in the character of independent belligerents. The more blockade runners will be captured by our cruisers, the more the complications will grow. A false first step generates false conditions *ad infinitum*. The question of the *Circassian* is only the beginning, and not even the worst. The worst will come by and by. But Seward is great before Allah ! The truth is, that Mr. Seward and the Department are as innocent of any familiarity with international laws, as can be. The people, the intelligent people would be horror-stricken could they suddenly be made acquainted with all the shameful ignorance which is corrosively fermenting in the State Department.

To every intelligent and well regulated Government in Europe, the Department of Foreign Affairs —which in America is called the State Department —has attached to it a board of advisers for the solution of all international questions.

In England, for instance, all such questions are referred to the Crown Lawyers, i. e. the Attorney and Solicitor General, and, in specially important cases, to the Lord High Chancellor, and one or two of the Judges.   And in order to obtain the advice he obviously stands so much in need of, Mr. Seward ought to have consulted two or three American juriconsults of eminence.   Mr. Seward ought to have foreseen that the war would necessarily give rise to international, commercial, and maritime complications.   Such men as Charles Eames, Upton, etc. would have been excellent advisers on all international and statutory questions.   Presumptuous that I am—to venture upon the mere supposition that Seward the Great can possibly need advice!   Not he, of course—not he.   Mr. Seward is the Alpha and Omega—knows everything, and can do every thing himself.   Happily, the people at large is the genuine statesman, and can correct the mistakes— and worse—of its blundering, bungling servants.

American pilots and statesmen ! Forget not that foresight is the germ of action. Foresight reveals to the mind the opportunenesss of the needed meas- ure by which a solution is to be given, a question decided, and the hoped-for results obtained.

American people ! How much foresight have your—dearly-paid—servants shown ? You, the peo- ple alone, you have been far-seeing and prophetic; but not they.

February 2.—All the efforts of the worshippers of treason, of darkness, of barbarism, of cruelty, and of infamy—all their manœuvres and menaces could not prevail. The majority of the Congress has decided that the powerful element of Africo- Americans is to be used on behalf of justice, of freedom, and of human rights. The bill passed both the Houses.   It is to be observed that the " big" diplomats swallowed *col gusto* all the pro- slavery speeches, and snubbed off the patriotic ones. The noblest eulogy of the patriots !

The patriots may throb with joy ! The President intends great changes in his policy, and has tele- graphed for——Thurlow Weed, that prince of dregs, to get from him light about the condition of the country.

The conservative " Copperheads" of Boston and of other places in New England press as a baby to their bosom, and lift to worship McClellan, the conservative, and all this out of deepest hatred towards all that is noble, humane, and lofty in the genuine American people. Well they may ! If by his generalship McClellan butchered hundreds of thousands in the field, he was always very conservative of his precious little self.

Biting snow storm all over Virginia ! Our soldiers ! our soldiers in the camp ! It is heart-rending to think of them. Conservative McClellan so conservatively campaigned until last November as to preserve—the rebel armies, and make a terrible winter campaign an inevitable necessity. O, Copperheads and Boston conservatives ! When you bend your knees before McClellan, you dip them in the best and purest blood of the people !

February 3.—The Secretary of War appointed General Casey to shorten the general tactics for the use of Africo-American regiments to use them as light infantry.

The devotion of American women to the sick and wounded soldiers, makes them be envied by the angels in Heaven (provided there are any). This devotion of these genuine gentlewomen atones for the ignoble flippancy of dancing-crinolines.

Down, down goes slavery notwithstanding the *gates of hell*, and their guard, the McClellans, the Sewards, amorously embracing the Copperheads and all that is dark and criminal. Humanity is avenged and Eternal Justice is satisfied.

February 4.—Sumner is re-elected to the Senate. His re-election vindicates a sound principle, because his opponents were all the Copperheads and slavery-saviours in Massachusetts. Sumner's influence in the Senate is rather limited. Politically he is on all points most honest; but his conduct towards Seward is not calculated to impress one with any very high esteem for his manhood.

It is not force, or decision, or power, that is cruel in revolutionary times — but, weakness. All societies have had their epochs of progress and of retrogression. Sylla was a conservative, and so too was Phocion. The Pharisees were reactionists and conservatives. Europe has millions of them, of various hues, shapes, tendencies and convictions. But the reactionists and conservatives in the past of Europe all have been and are of a purer metal than the conservatives here, and their impure organs, as the National Intelligencer, the World, the Boston Courier, and the rest of that fetish creed.

February 4.—The French Yellow Book, or State Correspondence, justifies my forebodings of November last. Mr. Mercier's diplomatic sentimentalism, and his associations, germinated the *Decembriseur's* scheme for mediation and humiliation.

Further is to be found in the Yellow Book the evidence how, from the start of this dark rebellion, Mr. Seward, the master spirit of the Administration, dealt death blows to all energetic, unyielding prosecution of the war for crushing the rebellion, and that he was double-dealing in all his public actions. The published state papers of the French government disclose the fact that nine months ago Mr. Seward sent the French minister to Richmond with a mission to invite the Jeff. Davises, Hunters, Wigfalls, Benjamins and others to come back to their seats in the Senate, and in the name of the cruelly outraged North, Mr. Seward proffered to the traitors a hearty welcome. So says the French diplomat in his official dispatch to the French Secretary of Foreign Affairs. Such underhanded dealings should not be allowed, and most assuredly would be stringently punished, if perpetrated under similar circumstances by the minister of any European government dealing with treason in arms. But here, Mr. Seward's impudence—if not worse —displays its flying colors. The Republican press will swallow all this, and Senator Sumner as Chairman of the Committee will—keep quiet.

That confidential mission entrusted to the French diplomat by Mr. Seward, was more than sufficient to evoke the subsequent attempt at mediation, because it revealed to the piercing eye of European statesmanship, how the Administration, and above all how its master spirit had little confidence in the cause; it revealed the want of earnestness in official quarters. I hate and denounce all attempts, even by the most friendly foreign power, to meddle with the internal affairs of our country. But I have some little knowledge of European statecraft, of European diplomacy, of European rulers, and of European diplomats; and I assert, emphatically, that they are emboldened to offer their meddlesome services because they have very little if any respect for our official leaders; and because the want of energy and of good faith to the principles of the North as displayed by Seward, he nevertherless remaining at the helm, has firmly settled the conviction in European minds, that the rebels cannot be crushed by such traffickers and used up politicians as have in their hands the destinies of the Union.

February 5.—The new Copperhead Senators—in their appearance resembling bushwhackers; the pillars of Copperheadism in the House, take umbrage at the sight and the name of New England, and abuse the New England spirit with all their coppery might. Well they may. So did Satan hate and abuse light.

Patriot Stanton is earnestly at work concerning the organization of Africo-Americans on a mighty scale; busy against him, likewise, are the intriguers, the traitors, the cavillers, the Sewardites and the McClellanites, all being of the same kidney. Seward sighs for McClellan. But Stanton will override the muddy storm. He has at his side men as pure, energetic and devoted as Watson, a patriot wtthout a flaw.

Stanton surrounds himself and selects young men —as far as he can, he crowds out the remains of Scott, so tenderly protected by Lincoln. Could he only have swept out the rest of the old fogies! Undoubtedly these young men in the War Department would give new life to it.

February 6.—The people at large are at a loss to find the cause of the recent disasters. The general axiom is, " we are not a military nation." Neither is the South. But here they forget that every great or small effect has its—not only—cause, but several causes. Many such causes have been repeatedly pointed out. Old routine in military organization stands foremost. Few, if any, understand wherein consists the proper organization of an army, and most have notions reaching back sixty years. The medical and surgical bureaus are obsolete. Governor Andrew of Massachusetts, who is always on the right side, and with him many young men, insisted upon organizing the above services as they are organized in the Continental armies of Europe. But even in the Senate prevailed the respect for dusty, rusty, domestic tradition. The few changes forced by the outcry of the people cure not the evil. Skeletons and not men are at work, and if they are not skeletons they are leeches of the government and of the people's blood.

Thus likewise, when the organizations of the staffs was discussed, no one had the first notion of the nature and duties of a staff; and the military authorities were as ignorant as the civilians. Of course a McClellan, then a Halleck, Meigs, Hitchcock, etc., could not disperse the fog. Many Congressmen were thunderstruck by the display of words which, as they were purely technical terms, the Congressmen in question could not understand. Others sought for guidance in the Staff of Wellington, and thus oddly but unmistakeably proved themselves completely in the dark as to the difference between the personal staff of the commander of an army, and the Staff of that Army itself. And all this in a country of the most rapid movement and progress, and amongst a people which unhesitatingly adopts and adapts to its own needs and welfare almost every novelty from almost every part of the world. The great fault committed by the People is its too great respect for false authorities and false prophets.

The so-called honest Conservatives have exercised and still continue to exercise a most fatal influence on public affairs, and especially on what is called the domestic policy. These same " honest Conservatives" are more dangerous than the out-spoken Copperheads ; more dangerous, perhaps, than all the friends of slavery and foes of the Union combined. These "honest Conservatives" have contrived to surround themselves with a halo of honesty and respectability. But they as cordially hate and dread every vivid light and vigorous progress as the traitors themselves do. Those Conservatives opposed every vigorous measure. They spoke tenderly of the "misguided brethren" in the South, and took their own servile and blundering, though quite possibly sincere fancies, for actual and tangible facts. The honest Conservatives will support whatever is slow, double-dealing, and, therefore, conservative. The honest Conservatives took McClellan to their honest hearts, and not one of them has any clear notion of military affairs, and still less can any of them fathom the awful depth of McClellan's military criminality. I repeat what I said in the first volume of my Diary : McClellan and his tail fell, not on account of their Democratism, or their pro-slavery creed, but because McClellan repeatedly displayed all the worst qualities of a thoroughly unsoldierly commander. No one would have uttered a word of censure if McClellan with his hundred and eighty thousand men had surrounded the thirty to forty thousand rebels in Centreville and Manassas in the winter of 1861–2, and taken some nobler trophies than camp manure and maple guns! The honest Conservatives attack and hate Stanton, yet not one of them has

any notion whatever of Stanton's action towards
McClellan. Stanton would have been the first to
raise McClellan sky-high if McClellan had preferred
to fight instead of reposing in his bed in Washington, and then in various muds. Such is your knowledge of this and of all other public affairs, O respectable soul and spiritless body of honest Conservatives! Historians of this country! collect the
names of the *honest* Conservatives, but expose them
not to the abomination of coming generations.

February 7.—The Sanitary Commission, with all
its branches and subdivisions, is among the noblest
manifestations of what can be done by a free people, and how private enterprise of intelligent, patriotic and unselfish men can confer benefit. Nor
must the praise of that great work be limited to
men. Warm-hearted gentlewomen also have done
their share in it.   The Sanitary Commission is one
of the best out-croppings of self-government, and
does honor to the people, and softens and amelior-
ates the warlike roughness of the times.

The Sanitary Commission marks a new era in the
history of genuine and not bogus and merely verbal philanthropy, and its spontaneity and expansion
were only possible in free, and therefore humane
and enlightened America.

February 8.—Mr. Seward is busily at work en-
deavoring to crush the radicals, and to make the
Emancipation Proclamation a mere sheet of waste

paper.   All that is mean and nasty, all that is reeking and foul with all kinds of corruptions, takes Seward for its standard-bearer.   The so-called radical press aids Seward with all its might.

February 9.—Gen. Casey adopts some of my ideas and suggestions, which I discussed with him. Gen. Casey is honestly at work, and the new tactics will be in print.

Stanton would wish to establish a thorough military camp on a large scale, for organizing Africo-Americans.   But the higher powers are against it. Virginia, the most populous slave state, the nursery of slaves, must, scorpion - like, be surrounded with glowing contraband camps.   What a splendid position for such a camp is Harper's Ferry under the shadow of immortal John Brown!

A few days ago, Mr. Lincoln was full of joy because the defences of Washington are in excellent condition.   Thus the country will learn with joy that the——spade is still at work, that the military curse hurled by Scott and McClellan is still influencing the operation of the war, that Halleck is the worthy continuator of his predecessors, that Mr. Lincoln's fears and uneasiness about the fate of the city of Washington are slowly, slowly assuaged, that the President's fancy is nursed, that the construction of the extensive fortifications around the capital is still continued, that new forts are continually erected, that the fear of an attack on Washington is still paramount, and that to-day—sixty to seventy thousand troops are kept idle in these old and new forts—when Rosecraus has no succor, when Texas is lost, and when the whole rebel region trembles under the tread of savage hordes.

Through one of its clerks, the State Department intends to sue me for libel, contained, as they say, in the first volume of my *Diary*. Well, great masters, if you swallow me, you may not digest me. Let us try.*

February 10.—....mens agitat molem....oh, could I only believe that such is the case with Mr. Lincoln, how devoted I could become, and loyal to him, according to the new theory of the lickspittles and politicians !

February 10.—Resolute Senator Grimes did what was the duty of Sumner to have done long ago. Grimes presented resolutions relative to the mission of Mercier to Richmond, a mission allowed, almost authorized by Mr. Seward. Mercier cannot be blamed, and his veracity is supported by the fact that Lord Lyons was at once informed of the whole transaction, and Lord Lyons is to be believed. Seward will play the innocent, and take his refuge in the god of—lies.

---

* I must here record that Mr. Carlisle, the eminent lawyer in Washington, although in every respect opposed to my political and social views, behaved, in this affair, as a thorough man of honor. I am sorry that on a similar former occasion, not in Washington, my political friends showed themselves not Carlisles.

February 12.—In his answer to the Senate, Mr. Seward gives to Mercier the lie direct. It will be rich if Mercier stands square.

February 12.—Congress draws to its close. Lincoln accumulates powers, responsibilities, and hereafter perhaps curses, sufficient to break the turtle on which stands the elephant that sustains the Sanscrit world.

February 13.—The almost imperceptible ripple on the diplomatic pool of Washington has disappeared. Simple people might have believed that there was an issue of veracity between Mr. Seward and the French Minister. But since a long, a very long time, Seward and veracity have run in different orbits, and diplomats, Talleyrand-like, ought to be the incarnation of equanimity even if any one— diplomatically—treads on their toes. Besides, the answer given to the Senate before it reached its destination *might have been arranged* at any such confidential chat as was that one where the little innocent, nobody-hurting (no, not even the people's honour) trip to Richmond was concocted. The French Minister's name *appears not* in the document sent to the Senate; so the lie direct is after all only a constructive lie; nobody is hurt. A general shaking of hands and all is well. But strange things may come out yet, and others may not be so blazened out.

The soap bubble of mediation exploded under the

nose of the French schemers. The soap used by them was of the finest and most aromatic quality, but the democratic nerves of the American people resisted the Franco-diplomatic cunningly mixed aroma. The applause gained by Mr. Seward's very indifferent document, wherein the great initiator of the Latin race on this free continent was rebuked, the satisfaction shown by the public, ought to open the eyes of the sentimental French trio. They ought to understand, by this time, that Seward's argumentative dispatch, incomplete and below mark as it is, won applause, although it expresses only the hundredth of the patriotic ire bursting from the people's bosom. Otherwise the people would have at once found out all skillfully, cunningly, chameleon-like Seward dodges, which ignore before Europe the sublime character of the struggle forced by treason upon the loyal free States; and in which how he avoids to hurt the slavocracy.

The Imperial mediator and bottle-holder to slavocracy belies not his bloody origin and his bloody appetites. The events in Egypt, the negro kidnapping in Alexandria, have torn the mask from his astute policy. If, for his filibustering raid into Mexico, Louis Napoleon wanted colored soldiers accustomed to the climate, he could raise them among the free colored population of the French possessions in Martinique, Guadaloupe, etc. But to use the freemen from the Antilles would have set a bad example to the Africo-Americans in the revolted States ; Louis Napoleon wished not to hurt or offend his slaveocratic pets and traitors; by kidnapping slaves in Egypt the French ruler showed how highly he values the stealing qualities of the Southern chivalry—and he paid a tribute to the principle of slavery.

But while treating with all possible horror and disrespect the French officiousness, the American people ought not to forget the innermost interconnection of events. If the French diplomacy, if the French Cabinet became sentimental at the sight of our deadly struggle with the demon of treason, it was because they witnessed our helplessness, and witnessed the uninterrupted chain of faults and of bad policy; it was because they and the whole world saw the want of earnestness in our official leaders; and from all this these *Messieurs* concluded that the patriots of the North never will be able to crush the traitors in the South. So speak the French diplomatic documents, so speaks Mercier, Drouyn de l'Huys and Louis Napoleon; and has not the Seward-Weed influence, paramount in the policy of the Government, brought about all these bad results, palsied the war, and thus almost justified the officiousness of the *Messieurs?*

February 13.—Many forebode the downfall, the dissolution, and the disappearance of the Republican party. That may be, and if so then one of the cardinal laws of human progress, development and ascension, will be fullfilled. *The initiator either perishes by the initiated, or the initiator perishes, disappears because his special mission, his task is done.*

The progress of humanity is marked by the sacrifice and death of its initiators. Such was the end of the founders of religions, of societies ; such of political bodies. Osiris, Lycurgus, Romulus, Christ, the martyrs, the apostles, are a few from numberless illustrations that might be cited. The Long Parliament, the French Convention, disappeared after having fullfilled the work of destruction pointed out to them by the genius of progress and of our race. As an organized political party the Republican may disappear with the war, for slavery is finally destroyed. This is the noble initiation and solution fulfilled by the Republican party. To destroy slavery and the political defenders and props of slavery, was the mission that was fatally thrown or entrusted by inexorable destiny to the Republican party. With the destruction of slavery, disappears from the political life of America the *Northern man with Southern principles;* those very dregs of dregs of all times and of all political bodies and societies. Slavery is destroyed both virtually and *de facto,* new issues are looming, new solutions will be given, and new men will bear the new word.

All in creation, and in every party, has its light

and its shadow, its pure principle, its pure men and
its dregs. Every party has its faults and its short-
comings. The dregs fall, and the work of the
party is done. Some of the chiefs and leaders of
the Republican party became faithless, (Seward,)
went over to darkness, but thereby the onward
march to the sacred aim was not arrested. The
irresistible current of events and of human affairs
carried onwards the Republican party. Perhaps
unconsciously, but nevertheless emphatically, the
Republican party in its *ensemble* was a providential
agency; it became the incarnation of the loftiest
aspirations of the best among the American people.
Against its wish and will, contrary to expectations, the Republican party was challenged to action ;
the sword of law, of justice and of right, was forcibly
thrust into the party's hand, and slavocracy, the
challenger, is already bleeding its life-blood, and its
death-knell resounds from pole to pole. To speak
the language of politicians ; abolition, emancipation
by the sword, was forced upon the Republican party.

And the Republican party carried out the principle of the preamble of the bill of rights ; a principle
eternal as right, but nevertheless hitherto only
partially realized. The Republican party has
borne the brunt, and accomplished the appointed
evolutions of progress ; and the Republican party
has deserved well of the American people, of history and of humanity. And the children and grand-

children of those who to-day cavil, defile and stone
the party, they hereafter will bless the Republican
party, who, with noble consciousness can say to the
spirit of light and of duty : *Nunc dimitte in pacem
servum tuum Domine.*

One of the best evidences of purity and of the
elevation of the Republican party in its noblest representative men is that the obtusest among the
great diplomats shunned the Republicans as little
monsters shun the daylight. I mention this as a
collateral illustration without intending to raise a
diplomat or the poor diplomacy of the world to an
undeserved significance, for I bear in mind the be-
hest, *ne misceantur sacra prophanis.*

The nobleness of the accomplished mission, the
glorious Sunset wherein will disappear the Republican party, frees, not from reproaches nor from
maledictions, those Republicans who, by their selfishness and faithlessness, obstructed its progress,
and polluted the party. Their names remain nailed
to the pillory.

I may here observe that I never belonged and
never claimed to belong to the Republican party.
For nearly half a century my creed has been—Onward ! onward ! struggle, fight, sacrifice for light,
for progress, for human rights ; for that cause fight
and struggle under every banner, under every
name, and in rank and file with every body.

February 13.—Seward seizes by the hair the

.occasion proffered to him by the *Decembriseur's*
offer of mediation, and tries to reconquer the confidence of the public.   This shows to Drouyn de
l'Huys and to his master, that they are misinformed
concerning the condition of America, (also M. Mercier misinformed them; how could he do otherwise?)   The despatch to Dayton, February 7, will
lead astray public opinion.   The majority will forget and lose sight of the intercatenation of events
and actions perpetrated by Mr. Seward.   O Chase!
O Sumner!   Seward rises with his patient pen and
paper in the inky glory of a patriot, and you——
cave in.

Speaking of Mr. Seward's answer to France, a
diplomat observed to me: "The European Cabinets
are so accustomed to Mr. Seward's duplicity and
want of veracity, that now that Seward refuses to
accept mediation, in Europe they will conclude that
Seward's acceptation of mediation is at hand."

February 14.—The struggle is for the rights of
man, for the Christian idea, purified of all dogma
and worship.   Those who see it not, are similar to
a fish from the Kentucky Cave.

February 14.—Could Mr. Lincoln only be inspired, be warmed by the sacred fire of enthusiasm,
then his natural and selected affinities would be
other minds than those of a Seward, a Weed, a Halleck, etc.; then what is night could become light;
and where he painfully gropes along his path, Mr.

Lincoln would march with a firm, almost with a godlike step, at the head of such a peerless people as those of whom he is the Chief Magistrate.

But as it is now, I may turn the mind in any direction whatever, all the causes of mishaps and disasters converge on Mr. Lincoln. According to his partisans, Mr. Lincoln's intentions are the best, and he is always trying to conciliate—and to shift. It is useless to discuss Mr. Lincoln's peculiar ways. In most cases, Mr. Lincoln uses old, rotten tools for a new and heavy work. I have it from the most truthful and positive authority, that Mr. Lincoln is fully acquainted with the opinions of the so called *dissatisfied*, of those with Southern propensities, proclivities and affinities, of whom many are in the superior civil and military service. Contrary to the advice of patriots in the Cabinet and out of it, Mr. Lincoln insists upon keeping such at their post— doubtless always expecting that they will *turn round*. Such a heavy difficulty and task as is the present, must be worked out, with absolute devotion and sincerity ; and can this logically be expected from men whose hearts and minds are not in their actions ? Mr. Lincoln forgets that thousands of lives and millions of money are sacrificed to the experiment as to whether the insincere officials will *turn round*.

The cause will not fail, light will not be extinguish, even if the leaders break down or betray,

even if the Copperheads frighten some of the
pilots, or if some of the faithless pilots shake hands
with the Copperheads, as was the case in the elections of November last in New York and else-
where. The people will save light, dissipate darkness, save the cause, save the leaders, the pilots and
the politicians.

February 15.—Some days ago in compliance with
summons, that pedler of all corruptions, Thurlow
Weed, came to Washington, and with Mr. Seward,
his *fidus Achates*, was for days or nights closeted
with Mr. Lincoln, pouring into the president's soul as
much poison and darkness as was possible. That
such was the case can, besides, easily be concluded
from what that incarnation of all perversions predi-
cated to all who came within his nauseous preach-
ings here. According to Mr. T. Weed's revelations, " *The proclamation is an absurdity, and the
Union will soon—as it ought—be ruled by the
rebels.*" So it was told me. Perhaps it is already
done through Thurlow Weed's mediation and in-
strumentality.

Continually inspired by Weed, Mr. Seward is
therefore untiring in his over-patriotic efforts to
preserve the former Union and Slavery—to save the
matricide slave-holders.

In what clutches is Mr. Lincoln! Even I pity
him. Even I am forced to give him credit for
being what he is—considering his intimacies and

his surroundings. Few men entrusted with power over nations have resisted such fatal influences,— not even Cromwell and Napoleon. History has not yet settled how it was with Cæsar, and so far as I know, Frederick the Great of Prussia is of the very few who have been unimpressionable. Pericles coruscates over ruins and the night of the ancient world; Pericles's intimacy was with the best and the manliest Athenians.

But has Mr. Lincoln an unlimited confidence in the few men with large brains and with big hearts, brains and hearts burning with the sacred and purest patriotic fire? Or are not rather all his favorites—not even whitened—sepulchres of manhood, of mind and of sacred intellect ?

February 16.—It is asserted, and some day or other it will be verified, that the Committee on the Conduct of the War have investigated how far certain generals from the army on the Rappahannock used their influence with the President to paralyze a movement against the enemy ordered by Burnside. That facts discovered may be published or not, for the Administration shuns publicity. *The Committee discovered that Mr. Seward was implicated in that conspiracy of generals against Burnside.* Any qualification of such conduct is impossible, and the vocabulary of crimes has no name for it; let it, therefore, be *Sewardism.* The editors of the New

York *Tribune* did their utmost to prevent *Seward-ism* being exposed.

February 16.—Often, so to speak, the hand refuses to record what the head hears and sees, what the reason must judge. To witness how one of the greatest events in the development of mankind, how the deadly struggle between right and crime, between good and evil, how the blood and sweat of *such a people* are dealt with by—counterfeits !

February 17.—Poor Banks ! He is ruined by having been last year pressed to Seward's bosom, and having been thus initiated into the Seward-Weed Union and slavery-restoring policy. Banks and Louis Napoleon in Mexico and in his mediation scheme ; both Banks and Napoleon were ruined by yielding to bad advice—Banks to that of Seward, and Louis Napoleon to that of his diplomats. I hope that Banks will shake off the night-mare that is throttling him now ; that he will no more write senseless proclamations, will give up the attempt to save slave-holders, and will march staight to the great task of crushing the rebellion and rebels. He will blot slavery, that Cain's mark on the brow of the Union ; blot it and throw it into the marshes of the parishes of Louisiana. I rely upon Banks's sound common sense. He will come out from among the evil ones.

February 18.—Under no other transcendent leadership than that of its patriotism and convictions, the majority of this expiring Congress boldly and squarely faced the emergencies and all the necessities daily, hourly evoked by the Rebellion, and unhesitatingly met them. If the majority was at times confused, the confusion was generated by many acts of the administration, and not by any shrinking before the mighty and crushing task, or by the attempt to evade the responsibility. The impartial historian will find in the Statutes an undisputable confirmation of my assertions. The majority met all the prejudices against taxation, indebtedness, paper currency, draft, and other similar cases.

And all the time the majority of Congress was stormed by traitors, by intriguers, by falsifiers and prisoners of public opinion; the minority in Congress taking the lead therein. Many who ought to have supported the majority either fainted or played false. The so-called good press, neither resolute nor clear-sighted, nor far-seeing, more than once confused, and as a whole seldom thoroughly supported the majority.

If the good press had the indomitable courage in behalf of good and truth, that the *Herald* has in behalf of untruth and of mischief, how differently would the affairs look and stand!

February 19.—Jackson first formed, attracted and led on the people's opinion. Has not Mr. Lincoln thrown confusion around?

February 19.—The Supreme Court of the United States has before it the prize cases resulting from captures made by our navy. The counsel for the English

and rebel blockade-runners and pilferers find the best
point of legal defence in the unstatesmanlike and un-
legal wording of the proclamation of the blockade, as
concocted and issued by Mr. Seward, and in the repeated declarations contained in the voluminous
diplomatic correspondence of our Secretary of State,—
declarations asserting that *no war whatever is going
on in the Federal Republic.* No war, therefore no
lawful prizes on the ocean. So ignorance, and humbug
mark every step of this foremost among the pilots of a
noble, high-minded, but too confiding people.

The facts, the rules, and the principles in these prize
cases are almost unprecedented and new; new in the
international laws, and new in the history of governments of nations. Seldom, if ever, were so complicated the powers of government, its rights, and the
duties of neutrals, the rights and the duties of
the captors, and the condition of the captured.
This rebellion is, so to speak, *sui generis*, almost
unprecedented on land and sea. The difficulties and
complications thus arising, became more complicated by the either reckless or unscientific (or both)
turn given by the State Department in conceding to
the rebels the condition of belligerents. Thus the
great statutory power of the sovereign, (that is, of the
Union through its president) for the suppression of the
rebellion was palsied at the start. The insurrection of
the Netherlands alone has some very small similarity
with our civil war; however, that insurrection took

place at a time when very few, if any, principles of international laws were generally laid down and generally recognized.   Here the municipal laws, the right of the sovereign and his duty to save itself and the people, the rights and the laws of war, wrongly applied to such virtual outlaws as the rebels, the maritime code of prize laws and rules, play into and intertwine each other.   When Mr. Seward penned his doleful proclamation of the blockade, etc., he never had before his mind what a mess he generated ; what complications might arise therefrom.   I am sure he never know that such proclamation was *a priori* pregnant with complications, and that at least its wording ought to have been very careful.   Mr. Seward was not at all cognizant of the fact that the wording of a proclamation of a blockade, for the time being, lays down a rule for the judges in the prize courts.   For him it was rather a declamation than a proclamation ; he who believed the rebellion would end in July, 1861, and that no occasion would arise to apply the rules of the blockade.

Thus Mr. Seward, with his thorough knowledge of international law rendered difficult the position of the captors; he equally increased the difficulty for the judge to administer justice.   By this proclamation and the commentaries put on it, Mr. Seward curtailed the rights of the government of which he is a part, conceded undue conditions to the rebels, and facilitated to the neutrals the means of violating his blockade.

So much is clear and palpable to-day, and I am sure
more complications and imbecilities are in store.   If
Mr. Seward had had good advisors for these nice and
difficult questions, he would not have blundered in
this way.   Thus Charles Eames, who in the pleadings
before the Superior United States Court has shown a
consummate mastery in prize questions—Eames could
teach Mr. Seward a great deal about the constitutional powers of the president to suppress the rebellion,
and about the meaning and the bearing of international maritime laws, rights, duties and rules.

February 20.—A Mr. Funk, a member of the Illinois Senate, a farmer, and a man of sixty-five years, on
February 13, made a speech in that body which
sounds better than all the rhetories and oratories.   It
was the sound and genuine utterance of a man from
the people, and I hope some future historian will
record the speech and the name of the old, indomitable
patriot.

February 20.—Stimulated by a pure Athenian
breeze, the Congress passed a law organizing an
Academy of Sciences.   What a gigantic folly; the
only one committed by this Congress.   The pressure
was very great, and exercised by the bottomless vanity of certain scientific, self-styled magnates, and by
the Athenians.   Up to this day, the American scientific development and progress consisted in its freedom
and independence.   No legal corporation impeded
and trammeled the limitless scope of the intellectual

and scientific development.   That was the soul and secret of our rapid and luminous onward march.   Now fifty patented, incorporated respectabilities will put the curb on, will hamper the expansion.   Academies turn to fossils.   My hope is that the true American spirit will soar above the vanity and pettiness of corporated wisdom, and that this scientific Academy bubble will end in inanity and in ridicule.   I am sorry that Congress was taken in, and committed such a blunder.   It was caught napping.

Mr. Chase's bank bill, prospective of money, and as many say, prospective of presidency, passed the house. What fools are they already begin to direct their steps and their ardent wishes toward the White House.

February 22.—The, at any price, supporters of the Administration, point with satisfaction to the various successes, and to the space of land already redeemed from rebellion.   I protest against such explanation given to events, and call to it the attentionof every future historian.   Never had the *suum cuique* required a more stringent, philosophical application.   With the various inexhaustible means at its disposal, with the unextinguishable enthusiasm of the people, far different and more conclusive results, *could* and ought to have been obtained.   The ship makes headway if even, by the negligence of the officers and of the crew; she drags a cable or an anchor.   The ship is the people dragging its administrators.

A western Democrat, but patriot, said to me that

Lincoln compares to Jeff Davis, as a wheel-barrow does to a steam engine!

The Democrats claim to be the genuine fighting element, and to be possessed of the civic courage, and of governmental capacity. How, then, can the Democrats rave for McClellan, the most unfighting soldier ever known?

The future historian must be warned not to look to the newspapers for information concerning facts and concerning the spirit of the people. The *Tribune's* senile clamor for peace, for arbitration, for meditation, its Jewitt, Mercier, Napoleon, and Switzerland combinations, fell dead and in ridicule before the sound judgment of ninety-nine hundreths of the people.

February 24.—In Europe I had experience of political prisons and of their horror. But I would prefer to rot, to be eaten up by rats, rather than be defended by such arch-copperheads as are the Coxes, the Biddles, the Powells, etc., etc.

In the discussion concerning the issue of the letters of marque, Sumner was dwelling in sentimentalities and generalities, altogether losing sight of the means of defense of the country, and the genuine national resources. With all respect for high and sentimental principles and patriotism, with due reverence of the opinion, the applause or the condemnatory verdict to be issued by philanthropists, by doctors, and other Tommities, my heart and my brains prefer the resolute, patriotic, manly Grimes, Wades, etc., the various *skippers* and masters, all of whom look not over the ocean for applause, but above all have in view to save or to defend the country, whatever be the rules or expectations of the self-constituted Doctors of International laws.

February 25.—The Union-Slavery saviours, led on by the *Herald*, by Seward, by Weed, etc., all are busily at work.

Let us break their bands asunder, and cast away their cords from us.

I hear that great disorder prevails in the Quartermaster's Department. It is no wonder. In all armies, countries, government and wars, the Quartermaster's Department is always disorderly. Why shall it not be so here, when want of energy is the word? At times Napoleon hung or shot such infamous thieves, as by their thefts skinned and destroyed the soldiers and the army; at times in Russia, such curses are sent to Siberia. But as yet, I have not heard that any body was hurt here, with the exception of the treasury of the country, and of the soldiers. The chain-gang of those quartermaster's thieves, contractors, jobbers and lobbyists must be strong, very long, and composed of all kind of influential and not-influential vampyres. Somebody told me, perhaps in joke, that all of them constitute a kind of free-masonry, and have signs of recognition. After all, that may be true. Impudence, brazen brow, and blank conscience may be among such signs of recognition.

February 26.—O, could I only win confidence in Mr. Lincoln, it would be one of the most cheerful days and events in my life. Perhaps, elephant-like, Mr. Lincoln slowly, cautiously but surely feels his way across a bridge leading over a precipice. Perhaps so ; only his slowness is marked with blood and disasters. But the most discouraging and distressing is his *cortège*, his official and unofficial friends. Mars Stanton, Neptune Welles, are good and reliable, but have no decided preponderance. Astrea-Themis-Bates is mostly right when disinfected from border-State's policy, and from fear of direct, unconditional emancipation. But neither in Olympus nor in Tartarus, neither in heaven nor in hell, can I find names of prototypes for the official and unofficial body-guard which, commanded by Seward, surrounds and watches Mr. Lincoln, so that no ray of light, no breath of spirit and energy may reach him.

February 26.—This civil war with its *cortège* of losses and disasters, which after all fall most bloodily and crushingly on the laborious, and rather comparatively, poorer part of the whole people ; perhaps all this will form the education of the rank and file of the political Democratic party. The like Democratic masses are intellectually by far inferior to the Republican masses. Experience will perhaps teach those unwashed Democrats how degrading was their submission to slavocracy, which reduced them to the condition of political helots. This rank and file may find out how they were blindfolded by slave breeders and their northern abettors. A part of the Democratic masses were, and still are kept in as brutal political ignorance and depravity as are the poor whites in the South, under whatever name one may record them. Now, or never, is the time for the *unwashed* to find out that during their alliance with the Southern traitors, all genuine manhood, all that ennobles, elevates the man and warms his heart, was poisoned or violently torn from them—that brutality is not liberty, and finally, that the Northern leaders have been or are more abject than abjectness itself. If the rank and file finds out all this, the blood and disasters are, in part at least, atoned for.

February 27.—O! could I from every word, from every page of this Diary, for eternities, make coruscate the nobleness, the simple faith with which the people sacrifices all to the cause. To be biblical, the sacrifice of the people is as pure as was that made by Abel; that made by the people's captains, leaders, pilots is Cain-like.

February 27.—All the Copperheads fused together have done less mischief, have less distorted and less thrown out of the track the holy cause, they have exercised a less fatal and sacrilegious influence, they are responsible for less blood and lives, than is Mr. Seward, with all his arguments and spread-eagleism. Even McClellan and McClellanism recede before Seward and Sewardism, the latter having

generated the former.   In times of political con-
vulsions,   perverse   minds   and   intellects   at the
helm, more fatally influence the fate of a nation than
do lost battles.   Lost battles often harden the temper of a people ; a perverse mind vitiates it.

February 27.—Gold rises, and no panic, a phenomenon upsetting the old theories of political economy.
This rise will not affect the public credit, will not
even ruin the poor.   I am sure it will be so, and political economy, as every thing else in this country,
will receive new and more true solutions for its old,
absolute problems.   The genuine credit, the prosperity of this country, is wholly independent of this or
that financial or governmental would-be capacity ; is
independent of European exchanges, and of the appreciation by the Rothschilds, the Barings, and whatever
be the names of the European appraisers.   The American credit is based on the consciousness of the people,
and on the faith in its own vitality, in its inexhaustible
intellectual and material resources.   The people
credits to itself, it asks not the foreigners to open for
it any credit.   The foreign capitalists will come and
beg.   The nation is not composed here as it is composed all over Europe, of a large body of oppressed,
who are cheated, taxed by the upper-strata and by
a Government.   Thus credit and discredit in America
have other causes and foundations, their fluctuations differ from all that decides such adventualities in Europe.

I am sure that subsequent events will justify these my assertions.

February 28.—Inveterate West Pointers got hold of the dizzy brains of some Senators and of other Congressmen, and Congress wasted its precious time in regulating the military position of engineers. This action of Congress is a *pendant* to the Academy of Sciences. The leaders in this discussion proved to *nausea*, 1st. Their utter ignorance of the whole military science, of its subdivisions, branches and classifications; 2d. Their ignorance of the nature of intellectual hierarchy in sciences; 3d. Those Congressional wiseacres proved how easily the West Point Engineers humbugged them. Congress consecrates the engineer as number one. Congress had better send a trustful man to Europe, to the continent, and find out what is considered as number one in the science of warfare. But every luminous body throws a shadow; the Academy of Sciences, and this number one, are the shadows thrown by that political body.

February 28.—Seldom, if ever, in history was the vital principle of a society, of a nation, of a Government, so bitterly assailed, and its destruction attempted by combined elements and forces of the most hellish origin and nature, as the vital principle of American institutions is now assailed. The enemies, the sappers, the miners, are the Union-Slavery-Saviours of all kinds and hues. But darkness cannot destroy light, nor cold overpower heat:—so the united conspiracy will not prevail against light and right and justice.

February 28.—The last batch of various generals sent for confirmation to the Senate, reflects and illustrates the manner in which promotion is managed, and military powers and capacity estimated at the White House.

Hooker and Heintzelman are made major generals because they brilliantly fought at Williamsburgh, and Sumner is likewise promoted for Williamsburgh, where, in pursuance of McClellan's orders, Sumner looked on when Heintzelman and Hooker were almost cut to pieces. The dignitaries of Halleck's pacific staff are promoted, and colonels who fight, and who, by their bravery and blood correct or neutralize the awful deadly blunders of Halleck and of his staff, such colonels are *not* promoted!

February 28. — Congress outlawed all foreign intervention, mediation! Catch it, foreign meddlers. Catch it, *Decembriseur* and your lackeys.

February 28.—Congress by its boldness, saved the immaculate Republican idea, saved the principle of self-government, and deserves the gratitude of all those from pole to pole, who have at heart the triumph of freedom, the triumph of light! To its last hours, this Congress had to overcome all the mean, petty appetites and cravings, which so often palsy, defile, or at the best, neutralize the noblest activity; Congress

had to overcome prejudices, narrow-mindedness and
bad faith. Many of the so called political friends—
vide, the great Republican press—are as troublesome,
as much nuisances, as are the Sewardites and the Copperheads. Others accuse the Congress for not having
done enough. Copperheads and Sewardites accuse
Congress of having done too much. And thus,
the majority of Congress marches on across impediments and abuses thrown in its way both by friends
and by enemies.

The *Tribune* bitterly and boldly attacks Dahlgren,
and trembling caves in before Seward. Of course!
Dahlgren can only send 11 and 15 inch shells to crush
the enemy; brother politician Seward can be useful
for some scheme.

Press—Ethics—President's Powers—Seward's Manifestoes—Cavalry—Letters of Marque—Halleck—Siegel—Fighting—McDowell—Schalk—Hooker—Etat Major-General—Gold—Cloaca Maxima—Alliance—Burnside—Halleckiana—Had we but Generals, how often Lee could have been destroyed, etc.

March 1.—Unprecedented is the fact in the history of constitutionally-governed nations, that the patriots of a political party in power, that its most devoted and ardent men, as a question of life or death, are forced to support and defend an Administration which they placed at the helm, and whose many, many acts they disapprove.

The soldiers in the hospitals die the death of confessors to the great cause. And the hair turns not white on the heads of those whose policy, helplessness, and ignorance, crowd the hospitals with the people's best children.

March 2.—The New-York *Times*—one among the great beacons and authorities in the country—the New York *Times* belies its title as the " little villain." Gigantically, Atlas-like, that sheet upholds Seward and Weed. The *Times* makes one admire the senile, compromising.

mediating, arbitrating, and, at times, stumbling *Tribune*, and the cautious but often ardent *Evening Post*.

The *Times* joins in the outcry against the radicals. It is Seward-Weed's watchword. It is the watchword of the *Herald*. It is the watchword of the most thickly coppered Copperheads. Genuine, pure convictions and principles are always radical. Christianity could not have been established were not the first Christians most absolute radicals. They compromised not with heathenism, compromised not with Judaism, which in every way was their father. Radicals—true ones—look to the great aim, forget their persons, and are not moved by mean interests and vanities.

The press in Europe, above all, on the Continent, is different. Its editors and contributors risk their liberty, their persons, their pockets, and sacrifice all to their convictions. They are not afraid to speak out their convictions, even if under the penalty to lose—subscribers; and that is all the risk run by an American newspaper. The *Herald*, the *World*, the *Express*, all organs of the evil spirit, through thick and thin, stand to their fetish, that McClellan; the Republican papers neither pitilessly attack the enemies, nor boldly and manfully support the friends, of the cause.

I nurse no personal likings or dislikings; the times are too mighty, too earnest for such pettiness. For me, men are agencies of principles: bad agencies of an intrinsically good principle are often more mischievous than are bad principles and their confessors. The eternal tendency of human elevation and purification is to eliminate, to dissolve, to uproot social evils, to neutralize or push aside bad men, in whatever skin they may go about. It is a slow and difficult, but nevertheless incessant work of our race. It is consecrated by all founders of religions, by legislators, by philosophers, by moralists; it is an article of human, social and political ethics. As far as I experienced, the European radical press more strictly observes that rule of political ethics than the American press is wont to do. And the press, bad or good, is the high pontifex of our times; more than any other social agency whatever, the press ought, at least, to be manly, elevated, indomitable, vigilant and straight-forward. I mean the respectable press.

March 3.—Senator Wilson's kind of farewell speech to the Copperheads was ringing with fiery and elevated patriotism. It re-echoed the sentiments, the notions, the aspirations of the people. The cobbler of Natick rose above the rhetors, above the deliverers of prosy, classical, polished, elaborated orations, above young and above gray-haired Athenians, high as our fiery and stormy epoch towers over the epochs of quiet, self-satisfied, smooth, cold, elaborate and soulless civilities.

March 4.—Mr. Lincoln hesitates—and, as many assert, is altogether opposed to use all the severity of the laws against the rebels. And shall not our butch-

ered soldiers be avenged ? It is sacrilegious to put in
the same scales the Union soldier and the rebels; it
is the same as to put on equal terms before justice
the incendiary and the man who stops or kills the criminal in *flagrante delicto.*

March 3.—After a tedious labor I waded through
the State papers. O, what an accumulation of ignorance ! Almost every historical and chronological
fact misplaced, misunderstood, perverted, distorted,
wrongly applied. And how many, many contradictions ! Only when Mr. Seward can simply—(very,
very seldom) point out to England that by *this* and
that fact and *act* England violates the international
laws and rules of neutrality and of good comity between two *friendly* governments and nations : then,
only, Mr. Seward's papers acquire historical and
political signification. But not his spread eagleism,
not his argumentation ; and, still less his broad and
inexhaustible and variegated information. Diplomatic
and statesmanlike character can not be conceded to
his State papers. Few, very few, will read them,
although foreign Courts, ministers, statesmen, princes,
and the so-called celebrated women are complimented
and deluged with them. The most pitiless critics of
these productions would be the smaller clerks in the
Deparments of Foreign Affairs in London and Paris.
Only they are not fools to waste their time on such
specimens of literature.

March 4.—Congress adjourned. This Thirty-Seventh

Congress marks a new era in the American and in the world's history. It inaugurated and directed a new evolution in the onward progress of mankind. The task of this Congress was by far more difficult and heavier than was the task of the revolutionary and of the constitutional Congresses. The revolutionary Congress had to fight an external enemy. The tories of that epoch were comparatively less dangerous than are now all kinds of Copperheads ; it had to overcome material wants and impediments, and not moral, nor social ones. That Congress was omnipotent, governed the country, and was backed by its virgin enthusiasm, by unity of purpose, and was not hampered by any formulas and precedents. The Thirty-Seventh Congress had to fight a powerful enemy, spread almost over two-thirds of the territory of the Union ; it had to fight and stand, so to speak, at home against inveterate prejudices, against such bitter and dangerous domestic enemies as are the Northern men with Southern principles. This Congress was manacled by constitutional formulas, and had to carry various other deadweights already pointed out. In the first part of the session, Pike, Member of Congress from Maine, laid down as the task for the Congress, *Fight*, *Tax*, *Emancipate*—and the Congress fulfilled the task. In a certain aspect the Thirty-Seventh Congress showed itself almost superior to the great immortal French Convention, which ruled, governed, administered, and legislated, while this Congress dragged a Lincoln, a

Seward, etc. This Congress accomplished noble and great things without containing the so-called "great" or "representative" men, and thus Congress thoroughly vindicated the great social truth of genuine, democratic self-government.

March 5.—The *good* press reduces the activity of the Thirty Seventh Congress to its own rather pigmy-like proportions.

Congress was powerless to purify the corrosive air prevailing in Washington, above all in the various official strata. Congress ardently wished to purify, but the third side of the Congressional triangle, the executive and administrative power, preferred to nurse the foul elements. Such doubtful, and some worse than doubtful officials, undoubtedly will become more bold, expecting the near-at-hand advent of the Copperhead Democratic Millennium.

March 6.—The Copperhead members of both the Houses have been very prolific and *scientific* about the inferiority of race. Pretty specimens of superiority are they, with their sham, superficial, at hap-hazard gathered, unvaluable small information, with their inveterate prejudices, with their opaque, heavy, unlofty minds! Give to any Africo-American equal chances with these props of darkness, and he very speedily will assert over them an unquestionable superiority. Are not the humble, suffering, orderly contrabands infinitely superior to the rowdy, unruly, ignorant, savage and bloody whites?

Southern papers are filled with accounts of the savage persecutions to which the Union men are exposed in the rebel region.   It is the result of what Mr. Seward likes to call his forbearing policy and of the McClellan and Halleck warfare of 1861—62.

March 7.—For the first time in the world's history, for the first time in the history of nations governed and administered by positive, well established, well organised, well defined laws—powers, such as those conferred by Congress on Mr. Lincoln, have been so conferred. Never have such powers been in advance, coolly, legally deliberated, and in advance granted, to any sovereign, as are forced upon Mr. Lincoln by Congress, and forced upon him with the assent of a considerable majority of the people.

Never has a nation or an honest political body whatever, shown to any mortal a confidence similar to that shown to Mr. Lincoln. Never in antiquity, in the days of Athens' and Rome's purest patriotism and civic virtue, has the people invested its best men with a trust so boundless as did the last Congress give to Mr. Lincoln.

The powers granted to a Roman dictator were granted for a short time, and they were extra legal in their nature and character; in their action and execution the dictatorial powers were rather taken than granted in detail. The powers forced on Mr. Lincoln are most minutely specified; they have been most carefully framed and surrounded by all the

sacred rites of law, according to justice and the written Constitution. These powers are sanctioned by all
formulas constituting the legal cement of a social
structure erected by the freest people that ever existed. These powers deliver into Mr. Lincoln's hand
all that is dear and sacred to man—his liberty, his
domestic hearth, his family, life and fortune. A well
and deliberately discussed and matured statute puts
all such earthly goods at Mr. Lincoln's disposal and
free use.

The sublime axiom, *salus populi suprema lex esto*
again becomes blood and life, and becomes so by the
free, deliberate will and decision of the foremost
standard-bearer of light and civilization, the first born
in the spirit of Christian ethics and of the rights of
man.—

The Cromwells, the Napoleons, the absolute kings,
the autocrats, and all those whose rule was unlimited
and not defined—all such grasped at such powers.
They seized them under the pressure of the direst
necessity, or to satisfy their personal ambition and
exaltation. The French Convention itself exercised
unlimited dictatorial powers. But the Convention
allowed not these powers to be carried out of the legis-
lative sanctuary. The Committee of Robespierre was a
board belonging to and emanating from the Convention ; the Commissaries sent to the provinces and to
the armies were members of the Convention and represented its unlimited powers. When the Committee

of Public Safety wanted a new power to meet a new emergency, the Convention, so to speak, daily adjusted the law and its might to such emergencies.

Will Mr. Lincoln realize the grandeur of this unparallelled trust? Has he a clear comprehension of the sacrifice thus perpetrated by the people? I shudder to think about it and to doubt.

The men of the people's heart—a Fremont, a Butler, are still shelved, and the Sewards, the Hallecks, are in positions wherein no true patriot wishes them to be. The Republican press had better learn tenacity from the Copperhead press, which never has given up that fetish, McClellan, and never misses the slightest occasion to bring his name in a wreath of lies before the public.

March 8.—A great Union meeting in New York. War Democrats, Republicans, etc., etc., etc. War to the knife with the rebels is the watchword. Of course, Mr. Seward writes a letter to the meeting. The letter bristles with stereotyped generalities and Unionism. The substance of the Seward manifesto is: "Look at me; I, Seward, I am the man to lead the Union party. I am not a Republican nor a Democrat, but Union, Union, Union."

The *I*, the No. 1, looks out from every word of that manifesto. With a certain skill, Mr. Seward packs together high-sounding words, but these his phrases, are cold and hollow. Mr. Seward begins by saying that the people are to confer upon him the highest honors. Mr. Seward enlightens, and, so to speak, *pedagogues* the people concerning what everybody ought to sacrifice. The twenty-two millions of people have already sacrificed every thing, and sacrificed it without being doctrined by you, O, great patriot! and you, great patriot, you have hitherto sacrificed NOTHING!

Let Mr. Seward show his patriotic record! To his ambition, selfishness, ignorance and innate insincerity he has sacrificed as much of the people's honor, of the people's interests, and of the people's blood as was feasible. History cannot be cheated. History will compare Mr. Seward's manifestoes and phrases with his actions!

March 8.—The cavalry horses look as if they came from Egypt during the seven years' famine. I inquired the reason from different soldiers and officers of various regiments. Nine-tenths of them agreed that the horses scarcely receive half the ration of oats and hay allotted to them by the government. Somebody steals the other half, but every body is satisfied. All this could very easily be ferreted out, but it seems that no will exists any where to bring the thieves to punishment.

March 8.—During weeks and weeks I watched Mc-Dowell's inquiry. What an honest and straight-forward man is Sigel. McDowell would make an excellent criminal lawyer. McDowell is the most cunning to cross examine; he would shine among all criminal catchers. The Know-Nothing West Point hatred is stirred up against Sigel. I was most positively assurred that at Pea Ridge a West Point drunkard and general expressly fired his batteries in Sigel's rear, to throw Sigel's troops into disorder and disgrace. But in the fire Sigel cannot be disgraced nor confused ; so say his soldiers and companions. Sigel would do a great deal of good, but the Know-Nothing-West Point-Halleck envy, ignorance and selfishness are combined and bitter against Sigel.

In this inquiry Sigel proved that he always fought his whole corps himself. So do all good commanders ; so did Reno, Kearney, so do Hooker, Heintzelman, Rosecrans, and very likely all generals in the West.

The McClellan-Franklin school, and very probably the Simon-pure West Pointers, fight differently. In their opinion, the commander of a corps relies on his generals of divisions ; these on the generals of brigades, who, in their turn rely on colonels, and thus any kind of *ensemble* disappears. Of course exceptions exist, but in general our battles seem to be fought by regiments and by colonels. O West Point ! At the last Bull Run two days' battles, McDowell fought his corps in the West-Point-McClellan fashion. His own statements show that his corps was scattered, that he had it not in hand, that he even knew not where the divisions of his corps were located ; and during the night of 29–30, he, McDowell, after wandering about the field in search of his corps, spent that night bivouacking amidst Sigel's corps !

March 9.—New York politicians behaved as meanly towards Wadsworth as if they were all from Seward's school.

March 9.—Hooker is at the Herculean work of reorganizing the army. Those who visited it assert that Hooker is very active, very just; and that he has already accomplished the magician's work in introducing order and changing the spirit of the army. Only some few inveterate McClellanites and envious, genuine West Pointers are slandering Hooker.

March 12.—Since the adjournment of Congress, everything looks sluggish and in suspense. The Administration, that is, Mr. Lincoln, is at work preparing measures, etc., to carry out the laws of Congress; Mr. Seward is at work to baffle them; Blair is going over to border-State policy; Stanton, firm, as of old; so is Welles; Bates recognises good principles, but is afraid to see such principles at once brought to light; Chase makes bonds and notes. We shall see what will come from all these preparations. But for Congress, Lincoln or the executive, would have been disabled from executing the laws. Congress, by its laws or statutes, aided the Executive branch in its *sworn duty*.

March 13.—The various Chambers of Commerce petition and ask that the president may issue letters of marque. It is to be supposed, or rather to be ad-

mitted, that the Chambers of Commerce know what is
the best for them, how our commerce is to be protected, how the rebel pirates swept from the oceans,
and how England, treacherous England, perfidious
Albion, be punished. But Sumner—of course—knows
better than our Chambers of Commerce, and our
commercial marine; with all his little might, Sumner
opposes what the country's interests demand, and demand urgently.   I am sure that already this general
demonstration of the national wish and will, the demonstrations made by our Chambers of Commerce,
etc., will impress England, or at least the English supporters of piracy.

Sumner will believe that his letters to English old
women will change the minds of the English semi-
pirates.   Sumner is a little afraid of losing ground
with the English guardians of civilization. Sumner is
full of good wishes, of generous conceptions, and is
the man for the millennium. Sumner lacks the keen,
sharp, piercing appreciation of common events.   And
thus Sumner cannot detect that England makes war
on our commerce, under the piratic flag of the rebels.

March 14.—The primitive Christians scarcely had
more terrible enemies, scarcely had to overcome
greater impediments, than are opposed to the principle of human rights, and of emancipation. All that is
the meanest, the most degraded, the most dastardly
and the most treacherous, is combined against us.

Many of the former confessors, many of our friends, many, unconscious of it—*Sewardise* and *Blairise.*

Mud is stirred up, flows, rises and penetrates in all directions. The *Cloaca Maxima* in Rome, during thirty centuries scarcely carried more filth than is here besieging, storming the departments, all the administrative issues, and all the so-called political issues.

I am sure that the enemies of emancipation, that Seward, Weed, etc., wait for some great victory, for the fall of Vicksburgh or of Charleston, to renew their efforts to pacify, to unite, to kiss the hands of traitors, and to save slavery. I see positive indications of it. Seward expects in 1864 to ride into the White House on such reconciliation. What a good time then for the Weeds, and for all the Seward-ites!

March 15.—Persons who seemed well informed, assured me that Weed got hold of Stanton, and secretly presides over the contracts in the War Department. If so, it is very secretly done ; as I investigated, traced it, and found out nothing. At any rate, Weed would never get at a Watson, a man altogether independent of any political influences. Watson is the incarnation of honest and intelligent duty.

Wilkes' *Spirit of the Times* is unrelenting in its haughty independence. It is the only public organ in this country of like character ; at least I know not another.

March 15.—It is so saddening to witness how all kinds of incapacities, stupidities, how meanness, hollowness, heartlessness, all incarnated in politicians, in trimmers, in narrow brained ; how all of them ride on the shoulders of the masses, and use them for their sordid, mean, selfish and ambitious ends. And the masses are superior to those riders in everything constituting manhood, honesty and intellect !

March 16.—Halleck wrote a letter to Rosecrans, explaining how to deal with all kinds of treason, and with all kinds of traitors. It looks as if Halleck improved, and tried to become energetic. What is in the wind ? Is Mr. Lincoln becoming seriously serious ?

March 16.—Genuine, social and practical freedom, is generated by individual rational freedom. If a man cannot, or even worse, if a man understands not to act as a free rational being in every daily circumstance of life during the week, then he cannot understand to behave on Sunday as a free man ; and act as a free man in all his political and social relations and duties. The North upholds that law of freedom against the slavocracy, and fights to carry and establish a genuine social organism where at present barbarity, oppression, lawlessness and recklessness, prevail and preside.

March 18.—I sent Hooker Schalk's *Summary of the Science of War.* It is the best, the clearest handbook ever published. About six months ago, when Banks commanded the defenses of Washington, I suggested to him to try and get Schalk into head-quarters, or into the staff. The ruling powers proffered to Schalk to make him captain at large, and this was proffered at a time when altogether unmilitary men became colonels, etc., at the head-quarters. I never myself saw Schalk, but he refused the offer, as years ago he was a captain in the Austrian army, is independent, and knows his own value. Any European government, above all when having on hand a great war, with both hands with military grades, would seize upon a capacity such as Schalk's. Here they know better. My hobby is that the president be surrounded by a genuine staff composed either of General Butler or any other capable American general, of Sigel, of Schalk, and of a few more American officers, who easily could organise a staff, *un etat Major genéral*, such as all European governments have. But West Point wisdom, engineers and routine, kill, murder, throttle, everything beyond their reach, and thus murder the people.

March 20.—Every week Mr. Seward pours over the fated country his cold, shallow Union rhetoric. But whoever reads it feels that all this combined phraseology gushes not from a patriotic heart; every one detects therein bids for the next Presidency.

Gold is at fifty-five per cent here; in Richmond, gold is four to six hundred per cent. The money bags, and all those who adjust the affairs of the world to the rise and to the fall of all kind of exchanges, they may base their calculations on the above figures, and find out who has more chances of success, the rebels or we!

Mud, stench on the increase, and because I see, smell and feel it, "*My friends scorn me, but my eye poureth* tears *into*" [Psalm] the noble American people.

March 21.—The *honest* Conservatives and the small church of abolitionists are equally narrow-minded, and abuse the last Congress. The one and the other comprehend not, and cannot comprehend the immense social and historical signification of the last Congress. It made me almost sick to find Edward Everett joining in the chorus. But he, too, is growing very old.

March 22.—What are generally called excellent authorities assert that an offensive and defensive alliance is concluded between Seward and Stanton. Further, I am told, that Senator Morgan, Thurlow Weed, and a certain Whiting, a new star on the politician's horizon, have been the attorneys of the two contracting powers. I cannot yet detect any signs of such an alliance, and disbelieve the story. A short time will be necessary to see its fruits. Until I see I wait!.... But were it true? Who will be taken in? I am sure it will not be Seward. Is Stanton dragged down by the infuriated fates?

March 23.—Burnside is to save Kentucky, almost lost by Halleck and Buell. Congress adjourned, and no investigation was made into Halleck's conduct after Corinth in 1862. The Western army disappeared; Buell commanded in Kentucky, and rebels, guerillas, cut-throats, murderers and thieves overflow the west, menaced Cincinnati. And all this when the Secretary of War in his report speaks about eight hundred thousand men in the field. But the Secretary of War provides men and means; great Lincoln, the still greater Halleck distribute and use them. This explains all. Burnside is honest and loyal, only give him no army to command. I deeply regret that Burnside's honesty squares not at all with his military capacity.

The Government is at a loss what to do with honest, ignorant, useless military big men, who in some way or other rose above their congenial but very low level. Already last year I suggested (in writing) to Stanton to gather together such intellectual military invalids and to establish an honorary military council, to counsel nothing. Occasionally such a council could direct various investigations, give its advice about shoes, pants, horses and horse-shoes. Something like such council really exists in Russia, and I pointed it out to Stanton for imitation.

March 25.—Stanton scorns the slander concerning his alliance with Seward and Weed. It is an invention of Blair, and based on the fact that Stanton sides with Seward in the question *of letters of marque*, opposed by Blair under the influence of Sumner the civiliser. I believe Stanton, and not my former informer.

Halleckiana. This great, unequalled great man
declared that ." it were better even to send McClellan
to Kentucky, or to the West, than to send there Fremont, as Fremont would at once free the niggers."

The admirers of poor argument, of spread-eagleism,
and of ignorant quotations stolen from history, make a
fuss about Mr. Seward's State papers. The good in
these papers is where Mr. Seward, in his confused
phraseology, re-echoes the will, the decision of the
people, no longer to be humbugged by England's perversion of international laws and of the rights and duties of neutrals; the will of the people sooner or later
to take England to account. (I hope it will be done,
and no English goods will ever pollute the American soil. It will be the best vengeance.) The repudi-
ation of any mediation is in the marrow of the people,
and Seward's muddy arguments only perverted and
weakened it. In Europe, the substance of Seward's
dispatch, is considered the passage where Seward's
highfalutin logomachy offers to the rebels their vacant
seats in the Congress.

March 26.—Had we generals, the rebel army in
Virginia ought to have been dispersed and destroyed
after the first Bull Run :

A. McClellan.—Any day in November and December, 1861.

B. McClellan.—Any day in January and February, 1862, at Centerville, Manassas.

C. McClellan.—At Yorktown, and when the rebels retreated to Richmond.

D. McClellan.—After the battle of Fair Oaks, Richmond easily could and ought to have been taken. (See Hurlbut, Hooker, Kearney and Heintzelman.)

E. McClellan.—Richmond could have been taken before the fatal change of base. (See January, Fitz John Porter.)

F. But for the wailings of McClellan and his stick-in-the-mud do-nothing strategy, McDowell, Banks and Fremont would have marched to Richmond from north, north-west, and west, when we already reached Stanton, and could take Gordonsville.

G. General Pope and General McDowell, the McClellan pretorians, at the August 1862, fights between the Rappahannock and the Potomac.

H. McClellan.—Invasion of Maryland, 1862. Go in the rear of Lee, cut him from his basis, and then Lee would be lost, even having a McClellan for an antagonist.

I. McClellan.—After Antietam battle, won by Hooker, and above all by the indomitable bravery of the soldiers and officers, and not by McClellan's generalship, Lee ought to have been followed and thrown into the Potomac.

K. McClellan.—Lay for weeks idle at Harper's Ferry, gave Lee time to reorganize his army and to take positions. Elections. Copperheads, French mediation.

L. McClellan.—By not cutting Lee in two when he was near Gordonsville, Jackson at Winchester, and our army around Warrenton.

M. Burnside.—By continuing the above mentioned fault of McClellan.

N. Burnside.—By his sluggish march to Fredericksburgh, (see Diary, December.)

O. Halleck, Meigs, etc. The affair of the pontoons.

P. Burnside, Franklin.—The attack of the Fredericksburg Heights.

March 28.—From the day of Sumter, and when the Massachusetts men hurrying to the defence of the Union, were murdered by the Southern *gentlemen* in Baltimore, this struggle in reality is carried on between the Southern gentlemen, backed by abettors in the North, (abettors existing even in our army,) all of them united against the Yankee, who incarnates civilization, right, liberty, intellectual superior devolopment, and therefore is hated by the *gentleman*—this genuine Southern growth embodying darkness, violence, and all the virtues highly prized in hell. The Yankee, that is, the intelligent, laborious inhabitant of New England and of the Northern villages and towns, represents the highest civilization : the best *Southern gentleman*, that lord of plantations, that cotton, tobacco and slavemonger, at the best is somewhat polished, varnished ; the varnish covers all kinds of barbarity and of rottenness. It is to be regretted that our army contains officers modelled on the Southern pattern, to whom human rights and civilization are as distasteful as they are to any high-toned slave-whipper in the South.

March 29.—The destruction of slavery, the triumph of self government ought not to be the only fruit of this war. The politician ought to be buried in the offal of the war. The crushing of politicians is a question as vital as the crushing of the rebellion and of treason. All the politicians are a nuisance, a curse, a plague worse than was any in Egypt. All of them are equal, be they Thurlow Weeds or Forneys, or etc. etc. etc. A better and purer race of leaders of the people will, I hope, be born from this terrible struggle. Were I a stump speaker I should day and night campaign against the politician, that luxuriant and poisonous weed in the American Eden.

March 30.—Glorious news from Hooker's army. Even the most inveterate McClellanites admire his activity and indeed are astonished to what degree Hooker has recast, reinvigorated, purified the spirit of the army. To reorganise a demoralised army requires more nerve than to win a battle. Hooker takes care of the soldiers. And now I hope that Hooker, having reorganised the army, will not keep it idly in camp, but move, and strike and crush the traitors. Hooker! *En avant! marchons!*

March 31.—Some newspapers in New York and the National Intelligencer here in Washington, the paid organ of Seward and likewise organ of treason gilded by Unionism—all of them begin to discuss the necessity of a staff.　All of them reveal a West Point knowledge of the subject; and the staff which they demand or which they would organise, would be not a bit better than the existing ones.

APRIL, 1863.

Lord Lyons—Blue book—Diplomats—Butler—Franklin—Bancroft—Homunculi
—Fetishism — Committee on the Conduct of the War — Non-intercourse—
Peterhoff— Sultan's Firman — Seward — Halleck—Race — Capua—Feint —
Letter writing — England — Russia — American Revolution — Renovation —
Women—Monroe doctrine, etc., etc., etc.

April 1.—The English Blue Book reveals the fact that Lord Lyons held meetings and semi-official, or if one will, unofficial *talks* with what he calls "the leaders of the Conservatives in New York;" that is, with the leaders of the Copperheads, and of the slavery and rebellion saviours. The Despatches of Lord Lyons prove how difficult it is to become familiar with the public spirit in this country, even for a cautious, discreet diplomat and an Englishman. But perhaps we should say, *because* an Englishman, Lord Lyons became confused. Lord Lyons took for reality a bubble emanating from a putrescent fermentation. I am at a loss to understand why Earl Russell divulged the above mentioned correspondence, thus putting Lord Lyons into a false and unpleasant position with the party in power.

As for the fact itself, it is neither new nor unwonted.   Diplomacy and diplomats meddle with all parties; they do it openly or secretly, according to circumstances.   English diplomacy was always foremost in meddling, and above all it has been so during this whole century.   The English diplomat is not yet born, who will not meddle or intrigue with all kinds of parties, either in a nation, in a body politic, in a cabinet or at court.

When a nation, a dynasty, a government becomes entangled in domestic troubles, the first thing they have to do is to politely bow out of the country all the foreign diplomacy and diplomats, be these diplomats hostile, indifferent, or even friendly.   And the longer a diplomat has resided in a country, the more absolutely he ought to be bowed out with his other colleagues; to bow them all in or back, when the domestic struggle is finished.

History bristles with evidences of the meddling of diplomats with political parties, and bears evidence of the mischief done, and of the fatal misfortunes accruing to a country that is victimised by foreign diplomacy and by diplomats.   Without ransacking history so far back as to the treaty of Vienna, (1815) look to Spain, above all, during Isabella I.'s minority, to Greece, to Turkey, etc.   And under my eyes, Mexico is killed by diplomacy and by diplomats.

Diplomatic meddlings become the more dangerous when no court exists that might more or less control them, to impress on them a certain curb in their semi-official and non-official conduct.   But at times it is difficult, even to a sovereign, to a court, to keep in order the intriguing diplomats, above all to keep them at bay in their semi-official social relations.

In principle, and *de facto*, a diplomat, and principally a diplomat representing a powerful sovereign or nation, has no, or very few, private, inoffensive, social, worldly, parlor relations in the country, or in the place to which he is appointed, and where he resides. Every action, step, relation, intimacy of a diplomat has a signification, and is watched by very argus-like eyes ; alike by the government to which he is accredited, and by his colleagues, most of whom are also his rivals.   Not even the Jesuits watch each other more vigilantly, and denounce each other more pitilessly, than do the diplomats—officially, semi-officially and privately.

It requires great tact in a diplomat to bring into harmony his official and his social, and non-official conduct.   Lord Lyons generally showed this tact and adroitly avoided the breakers.   At times such want of harmony is apparent and is the result of the will, or of the principles of the court and of the sovereign represented by a diplomat.   Thus, after the revolution of July, 1830, the sovereign and the diplomats in the Holy Alliance, of Russia, Austria, and Prussia recognised Louis Phillipe's royalty as a fact but not as a principle.   Therefore, in their social relations the Ambas-

sadors of Russia, Austria, and Prussia, most emphatically sided with the Carlists, the most bitter and unrelenting enemies of the Orleans and of the order of
things inaugurated by the revolution of July, and Carlists always crowded the saloons of the Holy Alliance's
diplomats. The Duke d'Orleans, Louis Phillipe's son,
scearcely dared to enter the brilliant, highly aristocratic, and purely legitimist saloon of the Countess Ap-
pony, wife of the Austrian Ambassador. Of course
the conduct of the Count and Conntess was approved,
and applauded, in Vienna. But at times, for some
reason or other, a diplomat puts in contradiction his
official and non-official conduct, and does it not only
without instructions or approval of his sovereign and
government, but in contradiction to the intentions of
his master and in contradiction to the prevailing opinion of his country. And thus it happens, that a diplomat presents to a government in trouble the most sincere and the most cheering official expressions of
sympathy from his master; and with the same hand
the diplomat gives the heartiest shakes to the most
unrelenting enemies of the same government.

The Russian, skillful, shrewd and proud diplomacy,
generally holds an independent, almost an isolated
position from England and from France. The Russian
diplomacy goes its own way, at times joined or joining
according to circumstances, but never, never following
in the wake of the two rival powers. During this our
war, and doubtless for the first time since Russian

diplomacy has existed, a Russian diplomat semi and non-officially, seemingly, limped after the diplomats of England and of France. But such a diplomatic *mistake* can not last long.

April 2.—Official, lordish, Toryish England, plays treason and infamy right and left. The English money lenders to rebels, the genuine owners of rebel piratical ships, are anxious to destroy the American commerce and to establish over the South an English monopoly. All this because *odiunt dum metuant* the Yankee. You tories, you enemies of freedom, your time of reckoning will come, and it will come at the hands of your own people. You fear the example of America for your oppressions, for your rent-rolls.

April 3.—The country ought to have had already about one hundred thousand Africo-Americans, either under arms, in the field, or drilling in camps. But to-day Lincoln has not yet brought together more than ten to fifteen thousand in the field ; and what is done, is done rather, so to speak, by private enterprise than by the Government. Mr. Lincoln hesitates, meditates, and shifts, instead of going to work manfully, boldly, and decidedly, Every time an Africo-American regiment is armed or created, Mr. Lincoln seems as though making an effort, or making a gracious concession in permitting the increase of our forces. It seems as if Mr. Lincoln were ready to exhaust all the resources of the country before he boldly strikes the

Africo American vein.   How differently the whole affair should have been conducted !

April 4.—Almost every day I hear very intelligent and patriotic men wonder why every thing is going on so undecidedly, so sluggishly ; and all of them, in their despondency, dare not or will not ascend to the cause. And when they finally see where the fault lies, they are still more desponding.

Europe, that is, European statesmen, judge the country, the people, by its leaders and governors. European statesmen judge the events by the turn given to them by a Lincoln, a Seward ; this furnishes an explanation of many of the misdeeds committed by English and French statesmen.

April 4.—The people at large, with indomitable activity, mends, repairs the disasters resulting from the inability and the selfishness of its official chiefs. One day, however, the people will turn its eyes and exclaim :

"*But thou, O God ! shalt bring them down into the pit of destruction ; bloody and deceitful men shall not live out half their days.*"

April 4.—General Butler's speech in New York, at the Academy of Music, is the best, nay, is the paramount exposition of the whole rebellion in its social, governmental and military aspects. No President's Message, no letter, no one of the emanations of Seward's letter and dispatch-writing, corrosive disease, not an article in any press compares with Butler's speech

for lucidity, logic, conciseness and strong reasoning.
Butler laid down a law, a doctrine—and what he lays
down as such, contains more cardinal truth and reason
than all that was ever uttered by the Administration.
And Butler is shelved and bartered to France by Seward as long since as 1862 ; and the people bear it, and
the great clear-sighted press subsides, instead of day
and night battering the Administration for pushing
aside the *only man*, emphatically the ONLY MAN who
was always and everywhere equal to every emergency—who never was found amiss, and who never for-
got that an abyss separates the condition of a rebel, be
he armed or unarmed, (the second even more dangerous,) from a loyal citizen and from the loyal Government.

April 4.—The annals of the Navy during this war
will constitute a cheering and consoling page for any
future historian. If the Navy at times is unsuccessful, the want of success can be traced to altogether
different reasons than many of the disasters on land.
Nothing similar to McClellanism pollutes the Navy—
and want of vigilance and other mistakes become virtues when compared with want of convictions, with
selfishness, and with intrigue. I have not yet heard
any justified complaint against the honesty of the
Navy Department; I feel so happy not to be disappointed in the tars of all grades, and that Neptune
Welles, with his Fox, (but not a red-haired, thieving
fox,) keep steady, clean, and as active as possible.

April 5.—Senator Sumner pines and laments, Jeremiah-like, on the ruins of our foreign policy, and accuses Seward of it—behind his back.   Why has not *pater conscriptus* uttered a single word of condemnation from his Senatorial *fauteuil*, and kept mute during three sessions? *Sunt nobis homunculi sed non homines.*

April 5.—A letter in the papers, in all probability written under the eye of General Franklin, tries to exculpate the General from all the blood spilt at Fredericksburgh.   It will not do, although the writer has in his hands documents, as orders, etc.   Franklin orders General Meade to attack the enemy's lines at the head of 4500 men, (he ought to have given to Meade at least double that number); brave and undaunted Meade breaks through the enemy ; and Franklin's excuse for not supporting Meade is, that he had no orders from head-quarters to do it.   By God !   Those geniuses, West Point No. Ones, suppose that any dust can be thrown to cover their nameless—at the best—helplessness.   Franklin commanded a whole wing, sixty thousand men ; his part in the battle was the key to the whole attack.   Franklin's eventual success must decide the day.   Meade was in Franklin's command, and to support Meade, Franklin wants an order from head-quarters.   Such an excuse made by a general at the head of a large part of the army —or rather such a crime not to support a part of his own command engaged with the enemy, because no special orders from head-quarters prescribed his doing so—such a case or excuse is almost unexampled in the history of warfare. And when such cases happened, then the guilty was not long kept in command. Three bloody groans for Franklin !

April 6.—George Bancroft has the insight of a genuine historian. Few men, if any, can be compared to him for the clearness, breadth, and justness with which in this war Bancroft comprehends and embraces events and men. Bancroft's judgment is almost faultless, and it is to be regretted that bancroft, so to speak, is outside of the circle instead of being inside, and in some way among the pilots.

April 6.—The Report of the Committee on the Conduct of the War will make the coming generation and the future historian shudder. No one will be able to comprehend how such a McClellan could have been thus long kept in the command of an army, and still less how there could have existed men claiming to have sound reason and heart, and constitute a McClellan party. McClellan is the most disgusting psychological anomaly. It is an evidence how a mental poison rapidly spreads and permeates all. As was repeatedly pointed out in this DIARY, individuals who started the McClellan fetishism, were admirers of the *Southern gentlemen*, were worshippers of slavery, were secret or open partisans of rebellion. Many such subsequently appear as Copperheads, peace men, as Union-men, as Conservatives. The other stratum of McClellanism is composed of intriguers. These combined forces, supported by would-be wise ignorance, spread the worship, and poisoned thousands and tens of thousands of honest but not clear-sighted minds. The Report, or rather the investigation was conducted with the utmost fairness; of course Ben Wade could not act otherwise than fairly and nobly. Some critics say that McClellan's case could have been yet more strongly brought out, and the fetish could have been shown to the people in his most disgustingly true nakedness.

April 6.—The people feel how the treason of the English evil-wishers slowly extends through its organs. By Butler, Wade, Grimes and others, the people ask for non-intercourse with the English assassin, who surreptitiously, stealthily under cover of darkness, of legal formality, deals, or attempts to deal, a deadly blow. The American sentimentalists strain to the utmost their soft brains, to find excuses for English treason.

English lordlings, scholars, moralists of the Carlyleian mental perversiom comment Homer, instead of being clear sighted commentators of what passes under their noses. The English phrase-mongering philanthropists all with joy smacked their bloody lips at the, by them ardently wished and expected downfall of a noble, free and self-governing people. Tigers, hyenas and jackals! clatter your teeth, smack your lips! but you shall not get at the prey.

April 7.—The President visits the Potomac army at Falmouth. Seward wished to be of the party, offering to make a stirring speech to the soldiers—that is, to impress the heroes with the notion that in Seward they beheld a still greater hero, a patriot reeking with Unionism and sacrifices, and eventually prepare their votes for the next presidential election. Certain influences took the wind out of Seward's sails, and as a naughty, arrogant boy, he was left behind to bite his nails, and to pour out a logomachy.

April 7.—I am very uneasy about Charleston. It seems that something works foul. Either they have not men enough, or brains enough. A good artillerist, having confidence in the guns, and having the needed insight how and where to use them, ought to command our forces. Will the iron-clads resist the concentric fire from so numerous batteries ?

The diplomats of the *prospective mediation* and their tails are scared by the elections in Connecticut. Others, however, of that illustrious European body are out-spoken friends of Union and of freedom. The representatives of the American republics are to be relied upon. St. Domingo, Mexico sufficiently teaches all races, *latin* (?) as well as non-latin, that honey-mouthed governmental Europe is an all-devouring wolf under a sheep's skin.

Non-intercourse! no intercourse with England and with France as long as France chooses to be ridden by the *Decembriseur !*   Such ought to be the watch-word for a long, long time to come.

April 8.—The New York *Times* is now boiling with patriotic wrath against McClellan.   Very well. But when McClellan captured maple guns at Center-ville and Manassas, when he digged mud and graves for our soldiers before Yorktown, and in the Chicka-hominy, the *Times* was extatic beyond measure and description, extatic over the matured plans, the gigantic strategy of McClellan—and at that epoch the *Times* powerfully contributed to confuse the public opinion.

April 8.—A Mr. Ockford, (or of similar name,) who for many years, was a ship broker in England, advised our government and above all, Mr. Seward, to insti-tute procedings before the English courts against the building and arming of the iron-clads for the rebels. Seward, of course, snubbed him off with the Seward-ian verdict that the jury in England will give or pro-nounce no verdict of guilty, in our favor, as our jury would not find any one guilty of treason.   Good for a Seward.

Patriots from various States, among them Boutwell, how member of Congress from Massachusetts, urged the Cabinet ; 1st, to declare peremptorily to the Eng-lish Government that if the rebel iron-clads are allowed to go out from English ports, our government will consider it as being a deliberate and willful act of hostility ; 2d, to publish at once the above declaration,

that the English people at large may judge of the affair.
Seward opposed such a bold step—Sumner ditto.

April 9.—I am at a loss to find in history, any government whatever that so little took or takes into account the intrinsic and intellectual fitness of an individual for the office entrusted to him, as does the government of Mr. Lincoln. I cannot imagine that it could have been always so, under previous administrations. It seems that in the opinion of the Executive, not only geniuses, but men of studies, and of special and specific preparation and knowledge run in the streets, crowd the villages and states, and the Executive has only to stretch his hand from the window, to take hold of an unmistakable capacity, etc. The Executive ought to have some experience by this time; but alas, *experientia non docet* in the White House.

April 10.—Agitated as my existence has been, I never fell among so much littleness, meanness, servility as here. To avoid it, and not to despair, or rage, or despond, several times a day, it is necessary to avoid contact with politicians, and reduce to few, very few, all intercourse with them. I cannot complain, as I find compensation — but nevertheless, I am afraid that the study and the analysis of so much mud and offal may tell upon me. Physical monstrosities are attractive to physiologists or rather to pathologists. But an anthropologist prefers normal nobleness of mind, and shudders at sight and contact with intellectual and moral crookedness.

April 11.—Sumter day. Two years elapsed, and treason not yet crushed ; Charleston not yet ploughed over and sown with salt; Beauregard still in command, and the snake still keeping at bay the eagle. And all this because in December, 1861, and in January, 1862, McClellan wished not, Seward wished not, and Mr. Lincoln could not decide whether to wish that Charleston and Savannah—defenceless at that time—be taken after the fall of Port Royal. Two years ! and the people still bleed, and the exterminating angel strikes not the malefactors, and the earth bursts not, and they are not yet in Gehenna's embrace.

Old patriot Everett made an uncompromising speech. That is by far better than to make a hero out of a McClellan. But the misdeeds of the Administration easily confused such impressionable receptive minds as is Edward Everett's.

April 11.—The Report of the Committee on the Conduct of the War, discloses how McClellan deliberately ruined General Stone, and I have little doubt that McClellan ruined Fitz-John Porter.

April 12.—Our navy makes brilliant prizes of Anglo-rebel flags and ships. But Mr. Seward does his utmost to render the labor of our cruisers as difficult and as dangerous as possible. Of course he does it not intentionally, only because he so *masterly masters* the international laws, the laws and rules of search, the rights and duties of neutrals, etc., and as a genuine incarnation of *fiat justitia*, he is indifferent to national interests and to the national flag.

I am curious to learn whether the truth will ever be generally known concerning the seizure of the Anglo-rebel steamer Peterhoff. Then the people would learn how old Welles bravely defended what *turpe* Seward had decided to drag in the mire. The people would learn what an utterly ignorant impudence presided over the restoring to England of the Peterhoff's mail bag of a vessel a contrabandist, a blockade runner, and a forger. The people would know how Mr. Seward, aided by Mr. Lincoln, has done all in his power to make impossible the condemnation of the Anglo-rebel property. The people would know how *turpe* Seward tried to urge and to persuade Neptune Welles to violate the statutes of the country ; how the great Secretary of State declared that he cared very little for law, and how he and Lincoln, by a Sultan's firman, directed the decision of the Judge on his bench.

April 14.—My gloomy forebodings about the attack on Charleston are already partly realized. Beaten off! that is the short solution of a long story. But of course nobody will be at fault. This attack on Charleston to some extent justifies : *parturiunt montes*, etc.

De profundis clamavi for light and some inklings of sense and energy. But to search for sense and energy among counterfeits!.... The condition here vividly brings to mind Ovid's

.... quem dixere chaos !

April 14.—In a letter to the Loyal League of New York, Mr. Seward is out with his—at least—one hundred and fiftieth prophecy. As fate finds a particular pleasure in quickly giving the lie to the inspired prophet, so we have the affair of Charleston, and some other small disasters. Oh, why has Congress forgotten to pass a law forbidding Seward, for decency's sake, to make himself ridiculous? Among others, hear the following query: *Whether this unconquerable and irresistible nation shall suddenly perish through imbecility?* etc. O Mr. Seward! how can you thus pointedly and mercilessly criticise your own deeds and policy? Seward squints toward the presidency that he may complete that masterly production.

Oh! how the old hacks turn their dizzy heads towards the White House. It would be ludicrous, and the lowest comedy of life, were not the track running through blood and among corpses. I am told that even Halleck squints that way. And why not? All is possible; and Halleck's nag has as long ears as have the nags and hacks of the other race-runners.

April 14.—Halleck consolidates the regiments and incidentally deprives the army of the best and most experienced officers. The numerically smaller regiment is dissolved in the larger one. But most generally the smaller regiment was the bravest and has seen more fire which melted it. Thus good officers are mustered out and thrown on the pavement, and the enthusiasm for the flag of the regiment destroyed, for its victorious memories, for the recollections of common hardships and all the like noble cements of a military life. Certainly, great difficulty exists to remount or to restore a regiment. But O, Hallecks! O, Thomases! O, McDowells! all of you, genii, or genuises, surmount difficulties.

April 14.—In a public speech in New York, General Fremont has explained the duty and the obligations of a soldier in a republic. Few, very few, of our striped and starred citizens, and still less those educated at West Point have a comprehension of what a Republican citizen soldier is.

April 14.—Halleck directly and indirectly exercises a fatal influence on our army. I learn that his book on military not-science largely circulates; above all, in the Potomac Army.

April 14.—It is the mission of the American people to make all the trials and experiences by which all other nations will hereafter profit. So the social experiment of self-government; the same with various mechanical and comercial inventions. The Americans experiment in political and domestic economy, in the art provided for man's well-being and in the art of killing him. New fire-arms, guns, etc., are now first used.

The until now undecided question between batteries on land and floating ones will be decided in Charleston harbor. Who will have the best, the Monitors or the batteries?

April 15.—I wrote to Hooker imploring him for the sake of the country, and for the sake of his good name, to put an end to the carousings in his camp, and to sweep out all kind of women, be they wives, sisters, sweethearts or the promiscuous rest of crinolines.

April 15.—Certain Republican newspapers perform now the same capers to please and puff Seward and Halleck, as they did before to puff McClellan when in power.

April 16.—Night after night the White House is serenaded. And why not?....From all sides news of brilliant victories on land and on sea; news that Seward's foreign policy is successful; everywhere Halleck's military science carries before it everything, and lickspittles are numberless.

> Wild jauchtzend schleudert selbst der Gott der Freude,
> Den Pechkrantz in das brenene Gebaüde!

My veins and brains almost bursting to witness all this. But for .... it would be all over.

> ...... tibi desinet.

April 17.—I met one of the best and of the most radical ex-members of Congress. He was very desponding, almost despairing at the condition of affairs. He returned from the White House, and notwithstanding his despair, tried to explain to me how Mr. Lincoln's eminent and matchless civil and military capacities finally will save the country. *Et tu, Brute,* exclaimed I, without the classical accent and meaning. The ex-honorable had in his pocket a nomination for an influential office.

April 17.—Immense inexhaustible means in men, money, beasts, equipment, war material devoured and disappearing in the bottomlesss abyss of helplessness. The counterfeits ask for more, always for more, and more of the high-minded people grudge not its blood.

Labitur ex oculis ...... gutta meis.

A Forney puffs Cameron over Napoleon! A true American gentlewoman as patriotic as patriotism itself, quivering under the disastrous condition of affairs at home and abroad, exclaimed: " that at least the Southern leaders redeem the honor of the American name by their indomitable bravery, their iron will and their fertility of resources." What was to be answered ?

April 18.—As long as England is ruled by her aristocracy, whether Tories or Whigs, a Hannibalian hate ought to be the creed of every American. Let the government of England pass into the hands of JOHN S. MILL, and into those of the Lancashire working classes, and then the two peoples may be friends.

April 18.—Hooker is to move. If Hooker brings out the army victorious from the bad strategic position wherein the army was put by Halleck-Burnside, then the people can never sufficiently admire Hooker's genius. Such a manœuvre will be a revelation.

April 18.—I learn that General Hunter has about seven thousand disposable men in his whole department, for the attack of Charleston.   If he is to storm the batteries by land, then Hunter has not men enough to do it; it is therefore folly and crime to order, or to allow, the attack of the defenses of Charleston.

April 18.—Mr. Seward has not at all given up his firm decision to violate the national statutes and the international rules, by insisting upon the restoration to England of the mails of that Anglo-Piratic vessel, the Peterhoff.   A mail on a blockade-runner enjoys no immunity, since regular mail steamers, or at least mail agents and carriers are established by England. Even previously, neutral private vessels could not always claim the immunity for the mail, when they are caught in an unlawful trade.   But, of course, the State Department knows better.

In the case of the ship Labuan, an English blockade-runner, Mr. Seward, backed by Mr. Lincoln, ordered the judge how to decide, ordered the judge to give up the prize, and Mr. Seward urged the English agents not to lose time in prosecuting American captors for costs and damages.   The Labuan was a good prize, but Mr. Seward is the incarnation of wisdom and of justice !

April 20.—The not quite heavenly trio—Lincoln, Seward and Halleck—maintain, and find imbeciles and lickspittles enough to believe them, that they, the trio, could not as yet, act decidedly in the Emancipation question, they being in this, as in other questions, too far in advance of the people. What blasphemy! Those *lumina mundi* believe that the people will forget their records. To be sure, the Americans, good-natured as they are, easily forget the misdeeds of *yesterday*, but this *yesterday* shall be somehow recalled to their memory.

If all the West Pointers were like Grant, Roscerans, Hooker, Barnard and thousands of them throughout all grades, then West Point would be a blessing for the country. Unhappily, hitherto, the small, bad clique of West Point engineers No. one, exercised a preponderating, influence on the conduct of the war, and thus West Point became in disrespect, nay, in horror. I believe that the good West Pointers are more numerous than the altogether bad ones, but they often mar their best qualities by a certain, not altogether admirable, *esprit du corps*.

April 20.—The generation crowding on this fogyish one will sit in court of justice over the evil-doers, over the helpless, over the egotists who are to-day at work. That generation will begin the assizes during the lifetime of these great leaders in Administration, in politics, in war.

Discite justitiam moniti nec temere divos !

April 20.—Yesterday, April 19th, Mr. Lincoln and his Aide, Halleck, went to Acquia Creek to visit

Hooker, to have a peep into his plans, and, of course to babble about them. I hope Hooker will most politely keep his own secrets.

April 21.—The American people never will and never can know and realize the whole immensity of McClellan's treasonable incapacity, and to what extent all subsequent disasters have their roots in the inactivity of McClellan during 1861–62. Whatever may be the official reports, or private investigations, chronicles, confessions, memoirs, all the facts will never be known. Never will it be known how almost from the day when he was intrusted with the command, McClellan was without any settled plans, always hesitating, irresolute ; how almost hourly he (deliberately or not, I will not decide) stuffed Mr. Lincoln with lies, and did the same to others members of the Cabinet. The evidences thereof are scattered in all directions, and it is impossible to gather them all. Mr Lincoln could testify—if he would. Almost every day I learn some such fact, but I could not gather and record them all. Seward mostly sided with McClellan, and so did Blair, *par nobile fratrum*.

Few, if any, detailed reports of the campaigns and battles fought by McClellan have been sent by him to the President or to the War Department. Such reports ought to be made immediately ; so it is done in every well regulated government. It is the duty of the staff of the army to prepare the like reports. But McClellan did in his own way, and his reports, if ever he sends them, would only be disquisitions elaborated *ex post*, and even apart from their truthfulness—null.

All kinds of lies against Stanton have been elaborated by McClellan and his partisans, and circulated in the public. The truth is, that when Stanton became McClellan's superior, Stanton tried in every friendly and devoted way to awake McClellan to the sense of honor and duty, to make him fight the enemy, and not dodge the fight under false pretenses. Stanton implored McClellan to get ready, and not to evade from day to day ; and only when utterly disappointed by McClellan's hesitation and untruthfulness, Stanton, so to say, in dispair, forced McClellan to action. Stanton was a friend of McClellan, but sacrified friendship to the sacred duty of a patriot.

April 21.—England plays as false in Europe as she does here. England makes a noise about Poland, and after a few speeches will give up Poland. More than forty years of experience satisfied me about England's political honesty. In 1831, Englishmen made speeches, the Russian fought and finally overpowered us. England hates Russia as it hates this country, and fears them both. I hope a time will come when America and Russia joining hands will throttle that perfidious England. Were only Russia represented here in her tendencies, convictions and aspirations ! What a brilliant, elevated, dominating position could have been that of a Russian diplomat here, during this civil war. England and France would have been always in his *ante-chambre.*

April 21.—Letter-writing is the fashion of the day. Halleck treads into Seward's footsteps or shoes. Halleck thunders to Union leagues; to meetings; it reads splendidly, had only Halleck not contributed to increase the " perils " of the country. Letter-writitg is to atone for deadly blunders.   The same with Seward as with Halleck. If Halleck would not have been fooled by Beauregard, if Halleck had taken Corinth instead of approaching the city by paralells distant *five miles*; the " peril" would no longer exist.

April 21.—Foreign and domestic papers herald that the honorable Sanford, United States Minister to Belgium, and residing in Brussels, has given a great and highly admired diplomatic dinner, etc., etc. I hope the Sewing machine was in honor and exposed as a *surtout* on the banquet's table, and that only the guano-claim successfully recovered from Venezuela, and other equally innocent pickings paid the piper. *Vive la bagatelle,* and Seward's *alter ego* at the European courts.

April 22.—I so often meet men pushed into the background of affairs; men young, intelligent, active, clearsighted, in one word, fitted out with all mental and intellectual requisites for commanders, leaders, pilots and helmsmen of every kind ; and nevertheless twenty times a day I hear repeated the question: " Whom shall we put? we have no men."—It is wonderful that such men cannot cut their way though the apathy of public opinion, which seems to prefer old hacks for dragging a steam engine instead of putting to it good, energetic engineers, and let the steam work. Young men! young men, it is likewise your fault; you ought to assert yourselves; you ought to act, and push the fogies aside, instead of subsiding into useless criticism, and useless consideration for *experienced* narrow-mindedness, for ignorance or for helplessness. In times as trying as ours are, men and not counterfeits are needed.

April 22.—In Europe, they wonder at our manner of carrying on the war, at our General-in-Chief, who, in the eyes and the judgment of European generals, acts without a plan and without *an ensemble;* they wonder at the groping and shy general policy, and nevertheless a policy full of contradictions. The Europeans thus astonished are true friends of the North, of the emancipation, and are competent judges.

Ayril 22.—I hear that Hooker intends to make a kind of feint against Lee. Feints are old, silly tricks, almost impossible with large armies, and therefore very seldom feints are successful. Lee is not to be caught in this way, and the less so as he has as many spies as inhabitants, in, and around Hooker's camp. To cross the river on a well selected point, and, Hooker-like, attack the surprised enemy is the thing.

April 22.—"Loyalty, loyalty," resounds in speeches, is re-echoed in letters, in newspapers. Well,

Loyalty, but to whom? I hope not to the person of any president, but to the ever-living principle of human liberty. Next eureka is, "the administration must be sustained." Of course, but not because it intrinsically deserves it, but because no better one can be had, and no radical change can be effected.

April 22.—The English Cabinet takes in sails, and begins to show less impudence in the violation of neutral duties. Lord John Russell's letter to the constructors of the piratical ships. Certainly Mr. Seward will claim the credit of having brought England to terms by his eloquent dispatches. Sumner may dispute with Seward the influence on English fogies. In reality, the bitter and exasperated feeling of the people frightened England.

April 24.—It is repulsive to read how the press exults that the famine in the South is our best ally. Well! I hate the rebels, but I would rather that the superiority of brains may crush them, and not famine. The rebels manfully supporting famine, give evidence of heroism; and why is it in such disgusting cause!

April 23.—Senator Sumner empatically receives and admits into church and communion, the freshly to emancipation converted General Thomas, Adjutant General, now organizing Africo-American regiments in the Mississippi valley. Better *late than never*, for such Thomases, Hallecks, etc., only I doubt if a Thomas will ever become a Paul.

April 24.—Our State Department does not enjoy a

high consideration abroad.   I see this from public diplomatic acts, and from private letters.   I am sure that Mr. Dayton has found this out long ago, and I suppose so did Mr. Adams.   Of course not a Sanford. If the State Department had not at its back twenty-two millions of Americans, foreign Cabinets would treat us—God, alone, knows how.

April 24.—I hope to live long enough to see the end of this war, and then to disentangle my brains from the pursuits which now fill them.   Then good-bye, O, international laws, with your customs and rules.   England handled them for centuries, as the wolf with the lamb at the spring.   When I witness the confusion and worse, here, I seem to see—*en min-iature*—reproduced some parts of the Byzantine times. All cracks but not the people, and to ——— I am in-debted that my brains hold out.

April 24.—What a confusion Burnside's order No. 8 reveals ; the president willing, unwilling, shifting, and time rapidly running on.

April 24.—Senator Sumner, without being called as he ought to have been—to give advice, discovered the Peterhoff case.   The Senator laid before the Pres-ident, all the authorities bearing on the case, showed by them to the President, that the mail was not to be returned to the English Counsul, but lawfully ought to be opened by the Prize Court.   The Senator so far convinced the President, that Mr. Lincoln, next morn-ing at once violated the statutes, and through Mr.

Seward, instructed the District Attorney to instruct the Court to give up the mail unopened to England.

Brave and good Sumner exercises influence on Mr. Lincoln.

April 24.—Every one has his word to say about civilized warfare, about international warfare, laws of war, etc. In principle, no laws of public war are applicable to rebels, and if they are, it is only on the grounds of expediency or of humanity. Laws of international warfare are applicable to independent nations, and not to rebels. Has England ever treated the Irish according to the laws of international warfare? Has England considered Napper Tandy and his aids as belligerents? The word *war* in its legal or international sense ought to have been suppressed at the start from the official, national vocabulary; to suppress a rebellion is not to *wage a war*.

April 25.—When the bloody tornado shall pass over, and the normal condition be restored, then only will begin to germinate the seeds of good and of evil, seeds so broadcast sown by this rebellion. All will become either recast or renovated, the plough of war having penetrated to the core of the people. Customs, habits, notions, modes of thinking and of appreciating events and men, political, social, domestic morals will be changed or modified. The men baptized in blood and fire will shake all. Many of them endowed with all the rays of manhood, others lawless and reckless. Many domestic hearths will be upturned, extinct, destroyed ; the women likewise passing through the terrible probation. Many women remained true to the loftiest womanhood, others became carried away by the impure turmoil. All this will tell and shape out the next generations.

I ardently hope that this war will breed and educate a population strong, clearsighted, manly, decided in ideas and in action ; and such a population will be scattered all over this extensive country. Men who stood the test of battles, will not submit to the village, township, or to politicians at large, but will judge for themselves, and will take the lead. These men went into the field a common iron ore, they will return steel. The shock will tear the scales from the people's eyes, and the people easily will discern between pure grain and chaff. I am sure that a man who fought for the great cause, who brought home honorable wounds and scars, whose limbs are rotting on fields of battle ; such a man will become an authority ; and death-knell to the abject race of politicians ; the days of shallow, cold, rhetors are numbered, and vanity and selfishness will be doomed. *Non vobis, non vobis—sed populo....*

April 25.—Nr. Seward is elated, triumphant, grand. Emigration from Europe, evoked, beckoned by him is to replace the population lost in the war.

What is to be more scorned ? Seward's heartless cruelty or his reckless ignorance, to believe that such a numerous emigration will pour in, as to at once make

up for those of whom at least one third were butchered by flippancy of Mr. Seward's policy to which
Lincoln became committed.

April 26.—The people are bound onwards *per aspera
ad astra:* the giddy brained helmsmen, military and
civil chiefs and commanders may hurl the people in
an opposite direction.

April 26.—Whoever will dispassionately read the
various statutes published by the 37th Congress; will
speak of its labors as I do, and the future historian
will find in those statutes the best light by which to
comprehend and to appreciate the prevailing temper
of the people.

April 27.—Rhetors and some abolitionists of the
small church—not Wendell Phillips—still are satisfied
with mistakes and disasters, because *otherwise slavery
would not have been destroyed.* If they have a heart,
it is a clump of ice, and their brains are common jelly.
With men at the head who would have had faith and
a lofty consciousness of their task, the rebellion and
slavery could have been both crushed in the year 1861,
or any time in 1862. Any one but an idiot ought to
have seen at the start, that as the rebels fight to maintain slavery, in striking slavery you strike at the rebels. The blood spilt because of the narrow-mindedness of the leaders, that blood will cry to heaven,
whatever be the absolution granted by the rhetors and
by the small church.

April 27.—Mr. Seward went on a visit to the army,

dragging with him some diplomats. The army was not to forget the existence of the Secretary of State, this foremost Union-saviour, and the candidate for the next Presidency. Others say that Seward ran away to dodge the Peterhoff case.

April 27.—How the politicians of the *Times* and of the *Chronicle* lustily attack—now—McClellan. If I am well informed, it was the editor of the *Chronicle*, himself a leading politician, and influential in both Houses, who instigated Lovejoy, Member of Congress, to move resolutions in favor of McClellan for the battle at Williamsburgh, where McClellan did what he could to have his own army destroyed.

April 28.—Mr. Seward elaborated for the President a paper in the Peterhoff case—and, *horribile dictu,* as I am told—even the President found the argument, or whatever else it was, very, very light. The President sent for the chief clerk to explain to him the unintelligible document—and more darkness prevailed. Bravo, Mr. Seward! your name and your place in the history of the times are firmly nailed!

April 28.—The time will come, and even I may yet witness it, when these deep wounds struck by the rebellion will be healed; when even the scars of blows dealt to the people by such Lincolns, Sewards, McClellans, Hallecks, the other *minor gens,* will be invisible—and this great people, steeled by events, will be more powerful than it ever was. Then the Monroe doctrine will be applied in all its sternness and rigor, and from pole to pole no European power will defile this continent. The so-called America-Hispano-Latin races humbugged by Europe, will have found how cursed is *any whatever* European influence. The main land and the Isles must be purified therefrom. Will any European government, power, or statesman permit the United States to acquire even the most barren rock on the European continent? The American continent is equal, if not more to Europe, and the degrading stigma of European colonies and possessions must be blotted from this American soil.

April 29.—The President appoints a day of fasting and prayer. Well! it is not for the people to fast and to pray, but for the evil-doers. Lead on, Mr. Lincoln, attended by Seward and Halleck—all in sackcloth and ashes.

April 29.—The President's and General Martindale's proclamations officially recognize the existence of God. It is consoling, and knocks down the far-famed *Deo erexit Voltaire.*

April 29.—To the right and to the left I hear praise of Mr. Chase as the great financier. Well he may be praised, having in his hand thousands and thousands of cows to be milked. The *financier* is the people, and prevents Chase from ruining the country.

April 29.—A Richmond paper calls McClellan a compound of lies and of cowardice. McClellan, the fetish of Copperheads and of peace-makers. The Richmond paper must have some special reasons which justify this stern appreciation.

April 30.—The *World*, a paper born in barter, in mud and in shamelessness, condemns General Wadsworth's name to eternal infamy. What a court of honor the *World's* scribblers ! The one a hireling of the brothers Woods, and sold by them in the lump to some other Copperhead financier ; the other a pants and overcoats stealing beau. The rest must be similar.

April 30.—The abomination of slavery makes such a splendid field to any rhetor attacking that curse. Were it not so, how many rhetors would be abolitionists ?

MAY, 1863.

Advance—Crossing—Chancellorsville—Hooker—Staff—Lee—Jackson—Stunned
—Suggestions—Meade—Swinton—La Fayette—Intrigues—Happy Grant—
Rosecrans—Halleck—Foote—Elections—Re-elections—Tracks—Seward—413
—etc., etc., etc.

May 1.—General anxiety about Hooker. If he successfully crosses the river, this alone will count among the most brilliant actions in military history. To cross a river with a large army under the eyes, almost under the guns of an enemy, concentrated, strong, vigilant, and supported by the population, would honor the name of any world-renowned captain.

May 2.—Mr. Seward forces upon the Department of the Navy, instructions for our cruizers that are so obviously favorable to blockade-runners, that our officers may rather give up capturing. Mr. Seward's instructions concede more to England, than was ever asked by England, or by any neutral from a belligerent of a third class power.

May 2.—How could Mr. Adams to that extent violate all the international proprieties, and deliver a .kind of pass to a vessel loaded in England with arms and ammunition for Matamoras. It is an offence against England, and a flagrant violation of neutrality to France. Not yet time to show our teeth to them. And all this in favor of that adventurer and almost pickpocket Zermann, this mock-admiral, mock-general, whom twice here they put up for a general in our army. But for me they would have made him one, and disgraced the American uniform. This police malefactor was patronised by some New Yorkers, by Senator Harris and from Mr. Seward may have got strong letters for Mr. Adams. It is probable that Zermann sold Mr. Adams to secessionists who may have wished to stir up trouble by this passport business. I am sure the affair will be hushed up and entirely forgotten.

May 2.—Glorious! glorious. Hooker crossed—and successfully. The rebels, caught napping, disturbed him not. Now at them, at them, without loss of an hour! The soldiers will perform wonders when in the hands of true soldiers for commanders, when led on by a true soldier.

O heaven! Why does Hooker publish such a proclamation? It is the merest nonsense. To thank the soldiers, few words were needed. But to say that the enemy must come and fight us on our own ground. O heaven! Hooker ought not to have had time to write a proclamation, but ought to pitch into the rebels, surprise and confuse them, and not wait for them. What is the matter? I tremble.

May 3.—Rumors, anxiety. The patriots feverish. One might easily become delirious.....Copperheads, Washington secessionists, spread all kinds of disastrous rumors. The secessionists here in Washington, are always invisible when any success attends our arms; but when we are worsted, they are forth coming on all corners, as toads are after a shower of rain.

May 4.—Confused news, but it seems that Hooker is successful. Still not so complete as was expected. Hooker's manœuvreing seems heavy, slow.

The Copperheads more dangerous and more envenomed than the secessionists. And very natural. The secesh risks all for a bad cause and a bad creed. But the *World* has no conviction, only envy and mischief, and risks nothing.

May 5.—Nothing decided; nothing certain. From what I can gather, the new generation or stratum of of generals fights differently from the style of the Simon-pure McClellan tribe. They are in front, and not in the rear according to regulations.

Halleck digs, digs entrenchments around Washington. I meet battalions with spades. Engineers show their poor skill! and Mr. Lincoln is comforted to be strongly defended!

May 5.—Night, storm, rain. News rather doubtful. Stanton said to me that he belives in Hooker,

even if Hooker be unsuccessful. Bravo! Not want
of success condemns a general, but the way and manner in which he acted ; and how he dealt with events.

May 6.—Seward is bitterly attacked by the *World*,
and by other Copperheads. I could not unite with a
World and with Copperheads to attack even a Seward. They are too filthy.—*Arcades ambo.*

May 6.—Hooker retreats and recrosses the river.
Say now what you will to make it swallow, at the best
it is an unsuccessful affair, if not an actual disaster.
I believe not in the swelling of the river. Bosh! in
three days these rivers fell. Have any generals
Franklinized? I dare ' not ask ; I most wish not to
know anything.

May 7.—*Nocte pluit tota* (*not*) *redeunt spectacula
mane ;* grim, dark, cold, rainy night. Are the Gods
against us? Or has imbecility exasperated even the
merciful but rational Christian God to that extent,
that God turns his back upon us ?

May 7.—Hiob's news come in, confused to sure,
but still one finds something like a foothold. I am
thunder-struck, annihilated. I listened to Hooker's
best friends but can hardly help crying. Hooker is a
failure as a commander of a large army. Hooker is
good for a corps or two, but not for the whole command and responsibility. From all that I can learn,
Hooker fights well, courageously, but he, like the
others, *has not the greatest and truest gift* in a commander : *Hooker cannot manœuvre his army.*   All

that I hear up to this moment strengtheneth my conclusion, and I am sure that the more the details come in, the stronger the truth will come out. Hooker can not manœuvre an army. Hooker may attack vigorously, stand as a rock, but cannot manœuvre.

Hooker seems to have committed the same faults and mistake as his predecessors did. He kept more men out of the fire than in the fire. And this from Hooker who accused his former chiefs of that very fault. But poor Hooker was unsupported by a good staff. This check may turn out to be a great disaster. At any rate, a whole campaign is lost, and one more commander may go overboard. Hooker will raise against him a terrible storm. God grant that Hooker could be honestly defended.

—*La critique est aisée, mais l' art est difficil* is perhaps again illustrated by Hooker. If Hooker is in fault, then he ought not to survive this disaster. After all that he said, after all that we said and repeated in his favor, to turn out an awful mistake!

May 8.—Worse and worse. 1 do not learn one single fact exculpating Hooker. I scarcely dare to look in the people's faces. The rain is no justification. Hooker showed no vigor before the rain. After he crossed, and had his army in hand, instead of attacking, he subsided, seemingly trying to find out the plans of the rebels instead of acting so as not to give them time to make plans or to execute them.

Tel brille au second rang qui s'éclipse au prèmier,

is almost all to be said in Hooker's defense. I tremble to know all the minute details. A paroled prisoner returned from Richmond said to me that terror was terrible in Richmond — that Lee and his army had no supplies. No troops in Richmond—Stoneman cut the bridges. The rebels were one the brink of a precipice, and extricated themselves.

May 8.—Boutwell, Member of Congress, told me that the district of St. Louis paid more new taxes to January than any other district in the United States. Bravo, Missourians. That is loyalty.

May 8 : *Evening*—More details about this unhappy Chancellorsville. Lee and the rebel generals have been decidedly surprised—in the military sense—by the crossing of the river, and by Hooker coming thus in part in their rear. But we lost time, they retrieved and *manœuvred* splendidly ; better than they ever have done before. Lee showed that he has learned something. Lee showed that, by a year's practice, he has at length acquired skill in handling a large army. The apprenticeship on our side is not so successful ; our generals have no experience therein, and McClellan was worse at Harper's Ferry in November than at Williamsburg in the spring. McClellan learned nothing. Will it be possible to find among our Potomac generals one in whom revelation will supply experience ?

The more I learn about that affair the more thoroughly I am convinced that Hooker's misfortune had the same cause and source as the misfortunes of those before him.   No military scientific staff and chief-of-staff.   Butterfield was not even with Hooker, but at Falmouth at the telegraph.   If it is so, then no words can sufficiently condemn them all.

If Kepler, or Herschel, or Fulton, or Ericcson had violated axioms and laws of mathematics and dynamics, their labors would have been as so much chaff and dust.   War is mechanism and science, inspiration and rule; a genuine staff for an army is a scientific law, and if this law is not recognized and is violated, then the disasters become a mathematically certain result.

May 8.—The defenders of Hooker call the result a drawn battle.   Mr. Lincoln calls it a lost battle.   I call it a miscarried, if not altogether lost, campaign.

May 9.—The poorest defence of Hooker is that the terrain was such that he could not manœuvre.   If the terrain was so bad, Hooker ought to have known it beforehand, and not brought his army there.   The rebels have not been prevented from marching and manœuvreing on the same ground, and not prevented from attacking Hooker, all of which ought to have been done by our army.

May 9.—All is again in unspeakable confusion. All seems to crack.   This time, more than ever, a powerful mind is necessary to disentangle the country.   If all is confirmed concerning Hooker's incapacity, then it is a crime to keep him in command; but who after him? It becomes now only a guess, a lottery.

The acting Chief-of Staff on the battle-field was General Van Alen. Brave and devoted; but Van Alen saw the fire for the first time, and makes no claims to be a scientific soldier.

May 10.—I wrote to Stanton to call his attention to, and explain the reasons of Hooker's so-called miscarriage. The insufficiency, the inadequacy of his staff and of chief-of-staff. Hooker attempted what not even Napoleon would have dared to attempt, to fight an army of more than one hundred thousand men, literally without a staff, or without a thorough, scientific and experienced chief-of-staff. I directed Stanton's attention to evidences from military history. Persons interested in such questions read Battle of Ligny and Waterloo, by Thiers.

Cobden, Cobden the friend of the Union, can no more stand Mr. Seward's confused logomachy, and in a speech sneers at Mr. Seward's dispatches. The New York *Times dutifully* perverts Cobden's speech; other papers *dutifully* keep silent.

May 10.—To extenuate Hooker's misconduct, his supporters assert that he was struck, stunned, and his brains affected. Hooker was stunned on Friday, and his campaign was already lost on Tuesday before, when he wrote his silly proclamation, when he subsided with the army in a *semi-lunar* (the worst form of all) camp, and challenged Lee to come and fight him.

Lee did it. Hooker was intellectually stunned on Tuesday. Further: the results of the material stunning on Friday could never have been so fatal if the army had been organized on the basis of common sense, as are all the armies of intelligent governments in Europe. The chief-of-staff elaborates with the commander the plan of the action; he is therefore familiar with the intentions of the commander. When the commander is disabled, the chief-of-staff continues the action. At the storming of Warsaw, in 1831, Prince Paschkewitsch, the commander, was disabled or stunned, and his chief-of-staff, Count Toll, directed the storm for two days, and Warsaw fell into Russian hands.

No more effective is the defence of the defeat, by throwing the fault on the Eleventh Army Corps. The Eleventh Corps was put so much in advance of a very foggishly—if not worse—laid out camp, that it was temptingly exposed to any attack of the enemy. The Eleventh Corps was separated from the rest of the army, as was Casey's division in the Chickahominy. The laying of a camp, the distribution of the corps, in a well organized army, is the work of the staff and of its chief; but Butterfield was not even then in Chancellorsville. Lee, who if caught napping, quickly awoke, wheeled his army as if it were a child's toy, cut his way through woods which amazed Hooker, and arrived before Hooker's semi-lunar camp. We, all the time, as it seems, were ignorant of Lee's movements. A good staff, and what Lee did, we would have accomplished. Lee quietly found out our vulnerable point; and struck the blow. That, if you please, *was* a stunner. Finally: the Eleventh Corps was eleven or twelve thousand strong. The weakest in the army, equal to a strong division in a European army of one hundred thousand men. The breaking of a division or of twelve thousand men posted at the extreme flank, ought not and could not have been so fatal to the whole campaign. A true captain would have been prepared for such eventuality. Battles are recorded in history when a whole wing broke down and retreated, and nevertheless the true captain restored order and fortunes, and won the battle.

I am told that the rebels attacked in columns, and not in lines. The rebels learn and learned, and are not conceited. The terrain here in Virginia is specially fit for attacks in columns, according to continental European tactics. We will not learn, we know all, we have graduated—at West Point.

May 11.—I have it from a very reliable source, that Mr. Lincoln considers Sumner to be not very entertaining.

May 11.—The confusion is on the increase. Statesmen, politicians, honest, dishonest, stupid and intelligent, all huddled together. Their name is legion—and what a stench. It is abominable! And many think, and many may think, that I find pleasure in dwelling on such events, on such men as are here.

When I was a child, my tutor ingrained into my memory the *Cum stercore dum certo*, etc. But at any cost, I shall try to preserve the true reflection of events, of times, and of the actors.

May 12.—Jackson dead. Dead invincible! and therefore fell in time for his heroic name. Jackson took a sham, a falsehood, for faith and for truth—but he stood up faithfully, earnestly, devotedly to his convictions. Whatever have been his political errors, Jackson will pass to posterity, the hero of history, of poetry, and of the legend. His name was a terror, it was an army for friend and for enemy. For Jackson

O selig der, dem er in Siegesglantze,
Die blutigen Lorbeer'n um die Schlaefe windet.

May 12.—*Sewardiana.* Lord Lyons, or rather the English government, objects and protests against the instructions given to our cruisers, which instructions are intrinsically faultless. Mr. Lincoln jumps up and writes a clap-trap dispatch, wholly contrary to our statutes. Mr. Seward promises what he cannot perform, and this time the upshot is that his dispatch came before the Cabinet and was quashed, or, at least, recast.

The Morning *Chronicle*, of Washington—*magnum* Administration's *excrementum*—attacks SCHALK and his military reasonings. Oh! great politician.

Sus Minervam docet.

May 13.—The defenders of Hooker affirm that Sedgwick was in fault, and disobeyed orders.

1st. I have good reasons firmly to believe that Sedgwick heroically obeyed and executed orders sent to him. No doubt can exist about it.

2d. The orders written by *such* a staff as Hooker's might have been written in *such* a way as to confuse the God Mars himself. Marshal Soult could fight, but as a chief of Napoleon's staff at Waterloo, could not write intelligible orders.

3d. Setting aside Sedgwick's disobedience of orders, it does not in the least justify Hooker in hearing the roar of cannon, and knowing what was going on, and at the head of eighty thousand men allowing Sedgwick to be crushed; and all this within a few miles. Fitz-John Porter was cashiered for a similar offense. Hooker's action is by far worse, and thus Hooker deserves to be shot.

May 13.—Rumors that Halleck is to take the command of the army, together with Hooker. I almost believe it, because it is nameless, and here all that is illogical is, eventually, probable.

Poor Hooker. Undoubtedly, he had a soldier's spark in him. But adulation, flunkeyism, concert, covered the spark with dirt and mud. I pity him, but for all that, down with Hooker!

If Hooker or Halleck commands the army, Lee will have the *knack* to always whip them.

May 14.—Wrote a paper for Senators Wade and

Chandler, to point out the reasons of Hooker's failure. Did my utmost to explain to them that warfare to-day is not empiricism, but science, and that empiricism is only better when sham-science has the upper hand. Hooker's staff was worse than sham-science, and was not even empiricism.

I explained that such evils, although very deeply rooted, can, nevertheless, be remedied. An energetic government can, and ought to look for and find, the remedy. The army, as it is, contains good materials for every branch of organization ; it is the duty of the government to discover them and give them adequate functions.

Further: I suggested to these patriotic Senators that as in the present energency, it is difficult to put the hand on any general inspiring confidende, the President, the Secretary of War and the Senators, ought immediately to go to the army, and call together all the commanders of corps and of divisions. The President ought to explain to the difficulty, nay, the impossibility of making a new choice. But as the generals are well aware that there must be a commander, and that they know each other in the fire, the President appeals to their patriotism, and asks them to elect, by secret ballot on the spot, one from among themselves.

May 14: *One o'clock, P. M.*—The President, Halleck and Hooker in secret conclave. Stanton, it seems, is excluded. If so, I am glad on his account.

God have mercy on this wronged and slaughtered people. No holy spirit will inspire the Conclave.

May 15.—The English Government shelters behind the Enlistment Act. The Act is a municipal law, and a foreign nation has nothing to do with it. We are with England on friendly terms, and England has towards us duties of friendly comity, whatever be the municipal law. To invoke the Enlistment Act against us, is a mean pettifogger's trick.

A good-natured imbecile, C———, everybody's friend, and friend of Lincoln, Seward and the Administration in the lump, C——— asked me what I want by thus bitterly attacking everybody.

"I want the rebellion crushed, the slaves emancipated; but above all I want human life not to be sacriligiously wasted; I want men, not counterfeits."

"Well, my dear, point out where to find them?" answered everybody's friend.

May 15.—On their return from Falmouth, the patriotic Senators told me that they felt the ground for my proposed election of a commander by his colleagues, and that General Meade would have the greatest chance of being elected. *Va pour Meade.* Some say that Meade is a Copperhead at heart. Nonsense. Let him be a Copperhead at heart, and fight as he fought under Franklin, or fight as he would have fought at Chancellorsville if Hooker had not been trebly *stunned.*

May 15.—Much that I see here reminds me of the

debauched times in France ; on a microscopic scale, however; as well as of the times of the *Directoire.* The jobbers, contractors, lobbyists, etc., here could perhaps carry the prize even over. the supereminently infamous jobbers, etc., during the *Directoire.*

May 15.—"Peel of Halleck, Seward and Sumner," exclaims Wendell Philips, the apostle. Wendell Samson shakes the pillars, and the roof may crush the Philistines, and those who lack the needed pluck.

May 16.—The President visited Falmouth, consoled Hooker and Butterfield, shook hands with the generals, told them a story, and returned as wise as he went concerning the miscarriage at Chancellorsville. The repulse of our army does not frighten Mr. Lincoln, and this I must applaud from my whole heart. It is however another thing to admire the cool philosophy with which are swallowed the causes of a Fredericksburgh and a Chancellorsville — causes which devoured about twenty thousand men, if not more.

May 16.—Strange stories, and incredible, if any thing now-a-days is incredible. Mr. Lincoln, inspired by Hitchcock and Owen, turns spiritualist and rapper. Poor spirits, to be obliged to answer such calls !

May 17.—A high-minded, devoted, ardent patriot, a general of the army, had a long conversation with the President, who was sad, and very earnest. The patriot observed that Mr. Lincoln wanted only encouragement to take himself the command of the Army of the Potomac. As it stands now, this would be even better than any other choice. I am sure that once with the army, separated from Seward & Co., Mr. Lincoln will show great courage. If only Mr. Lincoln could then give the *walking papers* to General Halleck!

On the authority of the above conversation, I respectfully wrote to the President, and urged him to take the army's command, but to create a genuine staff for the army around his person.

I submitted to the President that the question relating to a staff for the Commander-in-chief of the Army and Navy [the President] and for the commander-in-chief of the Army, Major-General Halleck, has been often discussed by some New York, Boston and Washington dailies, and the wonted amount of confusion is thereby thrown broadcast among the public. The names of several generals have been mentioned by the press as a staff of the President. I doubt if any of them are properly qualified for such an important position. They are rather fitted for a military council *ad latus* to the President. Such a council exists in Russia near the person of the emperor; but it has nothing in common with a staff, with staff duties, or with the intellectual qualification for such duties. The project of such a council here was many months ago submitted to the Secretary of War. A Commander-in-chief, as mentioned above—one fighting and manœuvering on paper—making plans in his office, unfamiliar with every thing constituting a genuine military, scientific or practical soldier—to whom field and battle are uncongenial or improper—to whom grand and even small tactics are a *terra incognita*—such a chief is at best but an imitation of the English military organization, and certainly it is only in this country that obsolete English routine is almost uniformly imitated. Such a Commander-in-chief might have been of some small usefulness when our Army was but thirteen thousand to sixteen thousand strong, was scattered over the country, or warred only with Indians on the frontier. But all the great and highly perfected military powers on the continent of Europe consider such a commander a wholly unnecessary luxury, and not even Austria indulges in it now.

During the campaign against Napoleon in 1813–14 the allies were commanded by a generalissimo, the Prince Schwartzenberg; but he moved with the army, actively directed that great campaign.

The Continental sovereigns of Europe are born Commanders-in chief of their respective land and naval forces. As such, each of them has a personal staff; but such a personal staff must not be confused with a general, central staff, the paramount necessity of which for any military organization is similar to the nervous system and the brain for the human body. Special extensive studies as well as practical familiarity with the use of the drill and the tactics of infantry, cavalry and artillery, constitute absolutely essential requirements for an officer of such a staff. The necessary military special information also, as well as the duties, are very varied and complicated (see "*Logistics*," by Jomini and others.) This country has no such school of staff. West Point neither instructs nor provides the Army with officers for staff duties; and of course the difficulty now to obtain efficient officers for a staff, if not insurmountable, is appalling, and is only to be mastered by a great deal of good will, by insight and by discernment.

Many months ago, I pointed out, in the press, this paramount deficiency in the organization of the Federal Army. The Prince de Joinville ascribes General McClellan's military failures to the paramount inefficiency of that General's staff. Any one in the least familiar with military organization and military science is thunderstruck to find how the Federal military organization deal with staffs, and what is their comprehension of the qualification for staff duties.

It deserves a mention, that engineers and engineering constitute what is rather a secondary element in the organization of a special or of a general central staff.

Plans of wide comprehensive campaigns are generally elaborated by such general staffs. In the campaigns of 1813–14, the sovereigns of Russia and Prussia were surrounded by their repective general, and not only personal staffs. With the Colonels Dybitsch and Toll, of the Russian general staff, originated that bold, direct march on Paris, whose results changed the destinies of Europe. Other similar, although not so mighty facts are easily found in general military history.

Finally, I pointed out to the President, the names of Generals Sedgewick, Meade, Warren, Humphries, and Colonel J. Fry as fit for, and understanding, the duties of the staff.

May 17.—I record a rumor, which I supposed, and found out to be, without much foundation; it is nevertheless worth recording.

The rumor in question says that the President wished to dismiss Stanton and to take General Butler; that Mr. Seward was to decide between the two, and that he declined the responsibility. Seward and Butler in the same sack! Butler would have swallowed Seward, hat, international laws and all—and of course Seward declined the responsibility.

But now a story comes, which is a sad truth. William Swinton, military reporter for the *Times*, a young man of uncommon ability and truthfulness, prepared for his paper a detailed article about the whole of Hooker's Chancellorsville expedition. Before being published, the article was shown to Mr. Lincoln; and it was telegraphed to New York that if the article comes out, the author may accidentally find himself a boarder in Fort Lafayette. Almost the same day the President telegraphed to a patriot to whom Mr. Lincoln unbuttoned himself, not to reveal to anybody the conversation. Both these occurrences had in view only one object—it was to keep truth out of the people's knowledge. Truth is a dangerous weapon in the hands of a people.

May 19.—The President repeatedly refuses to make General Butler useful to the country's cause, notwithstanding the best men in the country ask Butler's appointment. I am only astonished that the best men can hope and expect anything of the sort; for, when a Butler will come up, then Sewards and Hallecks easily may go down—but—*pia desideria*.

May 20.—From many, many and various quarters, continually unholy efforts are made to excuse Hooker and Butterfield; the President seemingly listens and excuses. Well, I know what a Napoleon, or any other even unmilitary sovereign, would do with both.

May 21.—O, for light! for light! O, to find a man! one to prize, to trust, to have faith in him! It is so sickening to almost hourly dip the pen in—mud! I regret now to have started this *Diary*. I go on because it is started, and because I wish to contribute, even in the smallest manner, towards rendering justice to a great people, besides being always on the watch, always expecting to have to record a chain of brilliant actions, accomplished by noble and eminent men. But day after pay passes by, page heaps on page, and I must criticise, when I would be so happy to prize.

As a watchdog faithful to the people's cause, I try to stir up the shepherds—but alas! alas....

May 22.—Wrote a letter to Senator Wade explaining to him how incapable is Hooker of commanding a large army, how his habits and associations are contaminating and ruinous to the spirit of the army, and that Hooker is to return to the command of a corps or two.

May 23.—Vainly! vainly in all directions, among the helmsmen, leaders and commanders I search for a man inspired, or, at least, an enthusiast wholly forgetting himself for the holiness of the aim. Enthusiasm is eliminated from higher regions; is outlawed, is almost spit upon. Enthusiasm! that most powerful stimulus for heart and reason, and which alone expands, purifies, elevates man's intellectual faculties. Here the people, the unnamed, have enthusiasm, and to the people belong those noble patriots so often mentioned. But the men in power are cold, and extinguished as ashes. Jackson the President, Jackson the general, was an enthusiast. Enthusiasts have been the founders of this Republic.

Whatever was done great and noble in this world, was done by enthusiasts. The whole scientific progress of the human mind is the work of enthusiasm!

May 24.—Grant and the Western army before Vicksburgh unfold endurance, and fertility of resources, which, if shown by a McClellan and his successors, having in their hands such a powerful engine as was and is the Potomac Army, would have made an end to the rebellion. Happy Grant, Rosecrans and their armies! to be far off from the deleterious Washington influences and adulations. Influences and adulations ruined the commanders and many among the generals of the Potomac army. Adulations, intrigue, and helplessness fill, nay constitute the generals atmosphere. In various ways every body contributes to that atmosphere—participates in it. Every body influences or intrigues in the army. The President, the various Secretaries, Senators, Congressmen, newspapers, contractors, sutlers, jobbers, politicians, mothers, wives, sisters, sweethearts and loose crinolines. Jews, publicans, etc., and the rest of social leprosy. All this cannot thus immediately and directly reach the Western armies, the Western commanders, when it reaches, it is already—to some extent — weakened, oxygenated, purified. Add to it here the direct influence and meddling of the headquarters. I pity this fated army here, and at times I even pity the commanders and the generals.

May 25.—Grant is an eminent man as to character and as to capacity. To Admiral Foote and to him are due the victories at Fort Henry, of Donelson, and the bold stroke to enter into the interior of Secessia. Had Halleck not intervened, had Halleck and Buell not taken the affairs in their hands, *Foote* and *Grant* would have taken Nashville early in the spring of 1862, and cleared perhaps half of the Mississippi. After the capture of Fort Donelson, Foote demanded to be allowed at once to go with his gunboats to Nashville, to clear the Tennessee ; but Halleck caved in, or rather comprehended not. Grant and Rosecrans restored what Halleck and Buell brought to the brink of ruin.

May 28.—Mr. Seward, omnipotent in the White House, tries to conciliate the public, and in letters, etc., whitewashes himself from arrests of persons, etc. Mr. Seward is therefore innocent, thereof, as a lamb. But who inaugurated and directed them in 1861 ? I know the necessities of certain times, and am far from accusing ; but how can Seward attempt to throw upon others the first steps made in the direction of arrests ?

May 28.—Hooker still in command, and not even his staff changed. I am certain that Stanton is for the change in the staff.

May 28.—I am assured that the Blairs (I am not sure if General Blair is counted in) are the pedlars for Mr. Lincoln's re-election, as stated by the New York *Herald*. If Mr. Lincoln is re-elected, then the self-government is not yet founded on reason, intellect, and on sound judgment.

May 31.—I am assured by a diplomat that four hundred and thirteen is the last number of the correspondence between the Department of State and Lord Lyons. Oh, how much ink and paper wasted, and what a writing dysentery on both sides. The diplomat in question added that it was only from January first —of course it was a joke.

JUNE, 1863.

Banks—"The Enemy Crippled"—Count Zippelin—Hooker—Stanton—"Give
Him a Chance"—Mr. Lincoln's Looks—Rappahannock—Slaughter—North
Invaded—"To be Stirred up"—Blasphemous Curtin—Banquetting—Desperate
—Groping—Retaliation—Foote—Hooker—Seward—Panama—Chase—Re-
lieved—Meade—Nobody's fault—Staffs, etc., etc., etc.

June 1.—For some time Banks seems to move in
the right direction. Banks no more intends to destroy
slavery, and not thereby to hurt the slaveholders. So
Banks has become himself again, and the Sewardean
creed is evaporated. Banks has under him very good
officers, and intelligent, fighting generals; some of
them left by Butler, others, as for instance, Generals
Augur, Stone, etc., who embarked with Banks.

June 2.—I hear it reported that Hooker maintains
that he has worsted and crippled the enemy more than
if he had taken Richmond.

If the enemy in reality was worsted to that extent,
it was not in the least done by Hooker, Butterfield &
Co.'s generalship, but this time, as always, it was done
by the bravery of the troops, notwithstanding the bad
generalship, not by, but *in spite* of, that bad generalship.

June 3.—Count Zeppelin, an officer of the staff and aide to the King of Wurtemberg, came here to observe and to learn how *not* to do it! The Count visited the army at Falmouth. He was horror-struck at the prevailing disorder, and at the general and special miscomprehension of the needed knowledge and of the duties prevailing in the staff of the army. The Count says that if this confusion continues, the rebels may dare almost every thing. Count Zeppelin is what would be called here, a thorough Union man. He revolted greatly at witnessing the *nonchalance* with which human life is dealt with in the army, and the carelessness of commanders about the condition of soldiers ; the latter he most heartily admires, and therefore the more pities their fate. He assured me that rebel agents scattered in Germany tried their utmost to secure for the rebel army officers of the various arms. This explains the organization and the brilliant manœuvrings of the celebrated Stuart's cavalry, the novel rebel tactics in the use of artillery, and the attack by columns at Chancellorsville.

June 3.—Hooker, they say, waits to see what Lee will do. In other words, we are on the defensive, after such efforts and so much blood wasted. O, Ezekiel! O, Deuteronomy! help me to bless the leaders and the chiefs of this people.

I am told by a very good authority, that Mr. Lincoln takes a special care of his fellow-townsmen in Springfield. What a good, honest, neighborly sentiment, provided always that the public good is not suffering by it!

June 3.—A senator, who urged Mr. Lincoln to dismiss Halleck, was answered, that " as Halleck has not a single friend in the country, Mr. Lincoln feels himself in duty bound to stand by him." Admirable, but costly stubbornness.

June 3.—Poor Hooker! He is now the laughing-stock of Europe. I wish he may recover what he has lost or squandered. But alas! even now Hooker makes no attempt to surround himself with a genuine staff.

I wrote to Stanton, imploring him for the country's and for his own sake, to compel Hooker to reform his staff, and not to allow science to be any longer trodden under foot. I implored Stanton that either the President or he would select and nominate a chief-of-staff for Hooker, or rather for the Potomac army, as it is done in Europe. Stanton understands well the disastrous deficiency, and if he could, he would immediately go at it and change. But, first, the statutes or regulations, obligatory here, leave it with the commander to appoint his own staff and its chief. Stupid, rusty, foggyish and fogyish regulations, so perfectly in harmony with the general ignorance of what ought to be the staff of an army! Second, Stanton must yield to another will, and to what is believed here to be the higher knowledge of military affairs.

June 3.—" Give to Hooker one chance more," says

Mr. Lincoln, and so say several members of the Cabinet; "McClellan had so many."—Because they allowed McClellan to waste human life and time, it surely is no reason to repeat the sacrilegious condescension. A general may be unfortunate, lose a battle, or even lose a campaign; all this without being damnable when he has shown capacity, when he did his utmost, but could not conciliate *fatum* on his side. But such is not the case with Hooker, and such *emphatically* was *not* the case with McClellan and with Burnside.

June 3.—During these last fourteen days, the *big men* have been expecting a raid on Washington. More fortifications are constructed, and rifle pits dug. This time the Administration is perfectly right. All is probable and possible when capacity, decision, and lightning-like execution are on the one side, and on the other sham-science, want of earnestness, slowness and indecision.

June 5.—A very reliable and honorable patriot tells me that *grandissimo* Chase *looks down* upon any advice, suggestion, or warning. O, the great man! A time must come when all these great men will be held to a terrible account, will shed tears of blood, and their names will be scorned by coming generations, and the track to the White House may become also the track to the Tarpeian rock.

June 5.—I often meet Mr. Lincoln in the streets. Poor man! He looks exhausted, care-worn, spiritless, extinct. I pity him! Mr. Lincoln's looks are those of a man whose nights are sleepless, and whose days are comfortless. That is the price for a greatness to which he is not equal. Yet Mr. Lincoln, they say, wishes to be re-elected!

June 5.—Mr. Seward makes a speech to the volunteers of Auburn. All the same logomachy, all the same cold patriotism, all the same *I*, and all the same squint towards the next presidential election.

June 6.—Lincoln cannot realize to what extent Seward is and has been his evil spirit. Even the nearest in blood and heart to Lincoln know it, feel it, are awe-struck by it, warn him, and he is insensible.

June 7.—How I sympathize with Stanton, and admire his rude—others call it coarse—contempt of all that is said about him. That impure, lying, McClellan-copperhead motley crew, accuse Stanton of all the numberless criminal mistakes committed in the conduct of the war—committed by the generals, etc. Stanton never interferes with Mr. Lincoln nor with Halleck in matters that exclusively relate to pure warfare, as where and how to march the respective armies, how and in what way to attack the enemy, etc.

Reliable patriots coincide with me, that Stanton as clearly sees every thing to-day, as he saw it when entering on his thorny duty. I only wonder that he holds out in such an atmosphere. Stanton's energy is indomitable. Blair's party says that "Stanton goes off at half-cock." It is not true; but even if true, better to go off at half-cock than not at all.   Many say that Stanton ought to retire, if he is hampered by others in the exercise of his duties.   But if he were to retire, he could not at this moment reveal to the people the causes of such a step, and by remaining at his post, Stanton prevents still greater disasters and disgraces. He never asks any of his friends to say or to write a word in his defence, or rather to dispel the lies with which McClellanites and copperheads poison the atmosphere all around them.

June S.—Alexandria fortified, rifle-pits dug, etc. The third year of the war is the third terror upon Washington, and upon those counterfeit penates.

June 8.—What for—for heaven's or devil's sake—Hooker throws a division of cavalry across the Rappahannock, right in the dragon's jaw!   All the rebel army is on the other side, and this, our division, can never be decidedly supported.   It cannot be a *reconnoissance*—of what?   It cannot be a stratagem to surprise Lee.   If Lee wants to march anywhere north or west, this demonstration of Hooker's will not for a minute arrest Lee.

June 9.—The great Henry Ward Beecher emigrates for a time to Europe.   His parish richly supports him for the trip, and the preacher sells his choice, and as it is said, beloved picture gallery.   It is not for want of money.   Strange!   What a curious manifestation of patriotism!

June 10.—The demonstration over the Rappahannock turned out to be a slaughter of the cavalry. What! Was Hooker again stunned, to make such a deliberate mistake— nay, crime? Such a demonstration never could prevent Stuart from moving, even if our troops had defeated or worried him—even if victorious, our cavalry would have been forced to recross the Rappahannock, and Stuart, having behind him Lee's whole army, which could easily reinforce him, would then move again. Our force of nine thousand men, distant from support, attack a superior force of fifteen thousand, who besides have within supporting distance a whole army! This demonstration prevents nothing, decides nothing, beyond the worst, the most damnable generalship. General Hooker and his chief-of-staff are personally responsible for every soldier lost there.

June 11.—Again visitings to the army. Senators, ladies, magnifico Chase leading on. O, if the guerrillas could sweep them!

June 12.—Crippled men are to be met in all directions, on all the streets. One-third of the amputated limbs undoubtedly could have been saved by the Medical Department, were it in better hands, and above all, if surgeons had been called in from Europe—the domestic surgeons not being sufficient for the demand.

June 13.—The principle of election, the only true one, a principle recognized and asserted as well by antiquity as by the primitive Church, recognized by rationalists, by Fourier, by radical, or any democracy whatever—that principle must undergo an immense improvement before it shall act in all its perfection. The elector must be altogether self-governing, and not governed or influenced by anybody in his choice and vote. The elector himself must stand on an elevated level before by his vote he raises one or several above that level. When the people's vote confers the highest trust to one rather below than in the level, and still less one above the level, then even the most intelligent people in the world, being thus misdirected, misconducted, confused, in a very short time become almost enervated, and, so to speak, loses its self-possession, and its sense of duty and of right becomes shaken, its intellectual light dimmed. *Exempla sunt odiosa.*

June 14.—The cavalry expedition over the Rappahannock was to arrest any further offensive movements of the rebels. But lo! the rebel army, so to speak, spreads in all directions, and takes the offensive. We do not even know positively where Lee is going, where he will appear and strike. We are shaking in, and for, Washington.

"Weh, Messina! wehe, wehe, wehe!"

Mr. Lincoln is unshaken in his confidence in Hooker and Butterfield.

June 15.—By a bold and rapid manœuvre Lee has thrown his troops over the valley, over the Potomac, into Maryland, and God alone knows where Lee will stop. Lee's advance must have been already on the Potomac when the slaughter of our cavalry over the Rappahannock was planned at the various head-quarters. How splendidly Lee's movements have been arrested by that demonstration! Lee is on the Potomac, and it seems that his movements have been ignored. His armies, to be sure, have not been surrounded by a cloud, as the Jews were in their exodus from the land of bondage, but the cloud was hanging over the headquarters in the army and in Washington

June 16.—The North invaded—threatened, shaken to the marrow! The audacity of the rebels is stimulated by our sluggishness. If the accounts in the War Department are true, then from Fortress Monroe to the Potomac, including Baltimore and Maryland, we have about two hundred thousand men, and the rebels dare! O, the rebels! what a desperate conception, what a lightning-like execution! Dutifully re-echoing the words uttered by their masters, the partisans of the Administration console themselves by saying that "this invasion of the North will have the effect of stirring up the North from its lethargy." O, you blasphemers! worse blasphemers than ever have been stoned or burned alive! Is the North not pouring forth its blood and its treasures, and are they not all squandered by counterfeits?

June 16.—The draft is not put in motion, because for weeks and months Mr. Lincoln adjusts the appointments to be made under this law, adjusts them to the exigencies of politicians.　Jeff Davis executes the draft with an iron hand.　Mr. Lincoln thus gives time to the Copperheads, to the disciples of the Seymours, of the Woods, of the *World*, to organize a resistance. Bloodshed may come!

June 16.—This invasion of Pennsylvania ought to be investigated.　Light must be brought into this dark, muddy, stinking labyrinth.　Weeks ago, honest, clear-sighted, patriotic Governor Curtin asked authority to arm the militia of his State, and was snubbed in Washington.　Will this new disgrace serve to strengthen the Administration?　Quite possible.

June 16.—Pennsylvania invaded, the country disgraced, and our helmsmen, our Secretaries of State and of the Treasury, give banquets!　O, what a stoicism! a stoicism *sui generis*.　The homes of the farmers whose sons bleed on fields of battle, are invaded, their hearths threatened with desolation, and the helmsmen sip Champagne, paid for by the people!

June 17.—*Halleckiana*.　Rosecrans telegraphed to head-quarters that he cannot send any troops to Grant, and that if he, Rosecrans, is to attack Bragg, he must have reinforcements.　Answer: "Do what you like, on your own responsibility."

June 17.—Hooker seems to have lost his former *dash*.　He must have known that the rebels extended from Gordonsville to Pennsylvania, and he, moving in almost a parallel direction to that line, ought to have cut it, or at least its tail.

General Ewell at Winchester. Hooker seems to doubt what he can do. The soldiers of his army can do anything ever done by any soldiers in the world—but lead them on, O Generals! Hooker has ninety-four thousand men, and, McClellan-like, waits for more; laments that he is outnumbered. A good general, having such a number, and of such troops, would never hesitate to attack an enemy numbering one hundred and twenty thousand, and the more so, as Hooker's command is massed, while Lee's is not. And I'll risk my head that Lee's whole army, all over the valley, and over Pennsylvania, and over Maryland, is smaller than Hooker's. It is the same old trick of the rebels and of their friends, to throw dust in our eyes by magnifying their numbers. The trick is always successful, because on our side it is wished to extenuate incapacity by the supposed large numbers of the rebel armies.

June 18.—The North rises. New York sends its militia. The people fails not, but how about the helmsmen?

The Democrats—the Copperheads roar for McClellan. Well! the like Democrats glorifying McClellan, show their patriotism, their metal and their judgment. These Copperhead-Democrats may insist upon calling McClellan a captain and a hero, but history will give another verdict, and history will credit to the Democrats the fact that they have adroitly poisoned and perverted the good faith of the honest but credulous Democratic rank and file.

June 18.—The Administration's *simon pure* echoes, politicians, etc., try to persuade everybody that the invasion of Pennsylvania is nothing, a mere tempest in a tea-pot.   Whom do they hope to humbug in this way?   The disgrace is nameless, only they are callous enough not to feel it.   Their cheeks can no more redden.....However, Stanton is not so optimist.   It would look so farcical if it were not so deadly to witness.   Hooker groping his way after Lee; Lincoln and the all-knowing head-quarters in the utmost darkness about Lee, his army, his movements, and his plans. And all this while the country, the people, is kept officially ignorant of its honor, of its fate.   All publicity and communication is suppressed—not to inform thereby the enemy of our movements.   How idiotic, how silly!   As if the march and the movements of an army of one hundred thousand men could be kept secret from a vigilant and desperate enemy, and the enemy wanted to read the papers for it.   Good for us!

I cannot hope against hope, and expect that Hooker, Butterfield, Lincoln, Halleck will out-manœuvre Lee, bold, quick, and desperate as he is.

June 19.—The jobbers, the contractors, the gold, stock, and exchange speculators wish for the prolongation of the war.   For this reason, disasters are rather welcome to them.   Oh! to crush those ignoble and demoniac monsters.

June 20.—I cannot comprehend how Lee could

have dared such a desperate movement, even if relying on the confusion and senselessness prevailing in *our* military movements. Lee must have had some kind of encouragement from the Copperheads before he risked a step, which ought to end in his utter destruction, even with a Halleck, Hooker and Butterfield as our commanders.

June 20.—Hooker has more than ninety thousand men in hand—his rear, his supplies, his *depots* covered by Heintzelman, and by the defences of Washington. This alone is equal to fifty thousand more. And with all this, the treble headquarters, in the White House in G street, and in the army cannot find Lee, and therefore the rebels are not attacked, and lay Pennsylvania waste. O, staffs, O, staffs!

June 20.—More than any other army in the world, the American army requires to have a thoroughly organized staff, with very intelligent staff officers. Such staff officers carry orders to generals and to colonels who, although brave and devoted, may often not altogether comprehend certain sacramental technicalities of an order delivered by mouth, or written briefly in the saddle.

The officer ought to be able to explain the order. Think of it, you wiseacres and organisers of American armies.

June 21.—Small cavalry skirmishes without signification. The curtain is not rended, and the enemy rolls towards the heart of Pennsylvania. How will it end?

June 22.—Nobody of the various upper and lower Chiefs can find Lee. Give twenty thousand men to a bold man even not a general, and in twenty-four hours he will bring you positive news about Lee's army.

June 23.—It seems that Lee waits, if we divide our army, to strike a blow on Washington. Thus he will be baffled; there is a limit even to our military blunders.

June 24.—Incorrigible Seward. France invites our Government to participate in the diplomatic coercion against Russia. Of course, Americans refuse. Mr. Seward, in harmony with the feeling of the people politely snuff off France. But O, Mr. Seward, why pervert history or show your ignorance, even of the national events and of Congressional records. The United States, Adams II., President, sent commissioners to the Congress of Panama, and the United States Congress did it after a discussion of several days. What is the use to deny it now? Then Mr. Seward is insincere to both parties. Speaking of " *a temporary transient revolt here*" he seemingly insinuates, that but for this *transient reuolt* he would perhaps try his hand at the European game. It would look so grand to be in company with the *Decembriseur*. Then the only impediment would be the people's will different from yours, oh, Seward! *The refusal* in the dispatch re-echoes the convictions of the American people ; its shilly-shally conditionality is exclusively Sewardism and only fit to catch a Russian diplomat in Washington.

June 25.—Hooker crosses to Maryland with nearly one hundred thouaud men. Lee is still on both sides of the Potomac. By a blow Hooker could cut Lee's army, break it, and retreive what he lost at Chancellorsville. Oh, how I wish he may do it. But since Hooker has refused to mend his staff, all hope is lost. Stanton sees the condition very clearly, but Butterfield is in good odor in the White House.

June 26.—Lee's movements and invasion puzzle me more and more. The raid into Pennsylvania is the move of a desperate commander, almost of a madman, playing his whole fortune on one card. If Lee comes safe out of it, then doubtless he is the best general of our times, and we the best nincompoops that ever the sun looked upon and blushed for.

June 26.—The reports give to Lee an army of two hundred thousand men. Impossible ! Where could the rebels scrabble together such a number ? The old trick to frighten us. If, however, Lee should have even only from one hundred to one hundred and fifty thousand, then relying on the high capacity of our various headquarters, the rebel chiefs may have gathered what they could take from Charleston and from Bragg, and massed it to try a decided blow on Washington. But this cloud, this dust cannot last long ; whatever be our headquarters, light must come, and the cloud burst with blood and thunder.

One meets in Washington individuals praising sky-high Mr. Lincoln's military capacity, and saying that he alone embraces all the extensive line of military operations, combines, directs them, etc. Pretty well has all this succeeded, and why cannot the younger generation seize the helm in this terrible crisis? How I ardently wish to see there an Andrew, Boutwell, Coffey, and more, more of those new men.

June 27.—From a very reliable, honest, and *not conspiring* secessionist in Washington, I learn that a Northern Copperhead visited Jeff Davis in Richmond, and stimulated the rebel chief to carry into the north a war of retaliation by fire and sword, but that Jeff Davis refused to instruct Lee for devastation. I instantly told Stanton my news; and now I doubt not in the least that the invasion is concerted with Northern Copperheads.

June 28.—The following is this morning the military condition of the city with the forts and defences: Hooker took all he could and all he met on his way. To defend the works around Washington Heintzelman has six thousand infantry, and not two hundred cavalry. The rebels have cavalry all around, within six or eight miles. A dash of twenty thousand infantry, and Washington is done!

June 28.—Admiral Foote dead. Irreparable loss. Foote was of the stamp of Lyon, of the stamp of patriot-heroes. He died of exhaustion, that is, of devotion to the country. Foote was an honor to the navy and to the American people.

June 28. — Yesterday, Friday, the candidate for presidency, splendid Chase, stood up mightily for Hooker. Oh, Mr. Chase! you may be a great or a doubtful financier, but keep rather mute on military matters. You know as much about them as this d— mosquito that is just now biting my nose.

June 28.—At last, Hooker relieved. I pity Meade to receive a command at such a critical moment. But now or never, to show his mettle, his capacity! The army thinks very highly of Meade. Will Halleck soon be sent to California? Then the country's cause will be safe.

June 29.—Yesterday a rebel cavalry raid captured an immense train of provisions, cattle, etc., worth about five hundred thousand dollars, and within eight or twelve miles of Washington! Of course, it is nobody's fault. In other armies and countries, such a large train would have a very strong convoy—here it had scarcely a small squadron of cavalry. The original fault is, first, with Hooker's chief-of-staff, who is responsible for providing the army, and for the security of the provision trains. So at least it is in European armies. Second, with the head-quarters at Washington, who ought to have known that the enemy, ant-like, spreads in the rear of Hooker. The head-quarters ought to have informed the quarter-master thereof, and provided a strong convoy. This train affair is the younger brother of the Fredericksburg pontoons.

Third, the head-quarters of the army and the quarter-masters ought to have inquired at the head-quarters of the defenses of Washington, if the roads are safe. But of course it was not done, as the *big men* here possess all the prescience, and need no valuable information. All of them appear to me as ostriches, who hide their heads and eyes, not to see the danger.

June 29.—General Heintzelman is as thorough a soldier as any to-day in Washington—a soldier superior to head-quarters of the army. Heintzelman commands the military district which south, west and north touches on the theatre of the present campaign. In similar conditions and circumstances, any other government, sovereign, commander-in-chief, etc., would consult with the commander of the defences of the capital and of the military district around the city ; here Heintzelman is not noticed.

June 30.—How will Meade compose his staff ? All depends on that. In the present positions of Meade's and Lee's armies, even a Napoleon could not do much without a very good staff.

Were the staffs of the American armies organized as they are in Europe, no difficulty would exist. In Europe the staffs of the armies are independent from the persons of their commanders. When a commander is changed, the staff and its chief remains, and thus the new commander at a glance and in a few hours can become thoroughly familiar with the position and condition of the army, and with the plans of his predecessor, etc., etc. Often such commanders are changed and sent from one end of the country to the other. In 1831, PASCHKEWITSCH was ordered from the Caucasus to Poland, to supersede DIESBITSCH.

June 30.—Since Calhoun, the creed of the *simon pure* Democratic party intrinsically marked a degradation of man and of humanity. Its logical, unavoidable and final outlets must have been secession, treason, and copperheadism; its apotheosis, South, the rebels; North, the Woods, the Seymours, the Vallandighams and the *World*. The creed of the Republican party is humane. The *simon pure* democratic rank and file, North and South, intellectually and morally constitute the lowest stratum of American society. Progress, civilization, intellectual, healthy activity principally are embodied in the Republican rank and file. True men, as a Marcy, a Guthrie, and some few similar, throw a pure and bright light on the Democratic party; many from among the official and political Republican notabilities throw a dismal and dark shadow on the intrinsically elevated and pure principles of the party.

Eneas — Anchises — General Warren — Aldie — General Pleasanton — Superior mettle—Gettysburgh — Cholera morbus—Vicksburgh — Army of heroes—Apotheosis—" Not name the Generals "—Indian warfare—Politicians —Spittoons—Riots—Council of War—Lords and Lordlings—Williamsport— Shame—Wadsworth—" To meet the Empress Eugenie," etc., etc., etc.

July 1.—It is worth while to ascertain if the Administration is prepared to run. During last year's invasion of Maryland, at the foot of C street a swift vessel was, day and night, kept under steam—(in the greatest secrecy)—to carry away the American gods. *Eneas-Seward* was to carry on his shoulders ANCHISES-LINCOLN. I was told that certain gallant secretaries promised to certain gallant *ladies* to take them into the ark.

July 1.—Meade makes General Warren his chief-of-staff. For the first time in this war, in-doors and out-doors, a man for the place. I never saw Warren, but have heard much in his favor. Then he is young. Then he is not conceited. Then he is no intriguer. Then he is fighting always and everywhere. Then he speaks not of strategy. A brighter promise. Genuine science and intelligence dawn on our muddy, dark, ignorant horizon.

Four weeks ago Meade might have been already in the command of the army. (See after Chancellorsville.) Perhaps Lee would have been to-day shut up in Richmond instead of laying waste Pennsylvania.

July 1.—The people will never know to what extent Mr. Lincoln-Halleck are stumbling-blocks in all military affairs. If Lincoln had even a *Carnot* for Secretary of War, the affairs would not go better than they go now.

July 1.—General Meade is the pure, simple result of military necessity. His choice is not adulterated by any party spirit. Success may be probable, if Meade is in reality what his colleagues suppose or assert him to be.

July 2.—The property of the great patriot THADDEUS STEVENS destroyed by the rebels. I am as sure as of my existence, that the rebel hordes were urged by the Copperheads and by Northern traitors, by the disciples of the *World*, etc.

July 2.—Copperheads and their organs scream to have McClellan at the head of the armies. This enthusiasm for McClellan soon will be a burning shame. For many it is a mental disease, and almost unparallelled in the history of our race. A man of defeats and of incapacity to be thus worshipped as a hero! To what extent sound intellects can become poisoned by lies! O, Democrats! what a kin and kith you are! The stubborn, undaunted bravery of the people keeps the country above water, when McClellan and his medley of believers dragged and drags her down into the abyss. Soon infamy will cover the names of those who wail for McClellan's glory, the names of these deliberate betrayers of the people's good faith.

July 2.—Count Zeppelin was at the cavalry fight at Aldie. In his appreciation, General Pleasanton is almost the ideal of a general of cavalry, in the manner in which he fought his forces. The Count says that our soldiers are by far superior to the rebels, that our regiments, squadrons, showed the utmost bravery, that in single-handed *mélés* our soldiers showed a superior mettle, and that during the whole fight he did not see a single soldier back out or retire.

Count Zeppelin spent three weeks with Hooker. The Count *never* saw Hooker intoxicated, but nevertheless, he does not believe Hooker to be the man for the command of a large army. The Count, an educated officer of staff, deplores the utter absence of that special science in the heads of the staff.

The Count was with the army during its march from Falmouth to Frederick. He admires the endurance, the good spirit, and the cohesion shown by the army marching under great difficulties, such as bad roads, heat, &c.

July 2.—News of fight at Gettysburgh. It seems that this time a plan was boldly conceived, and carried out with rapidity and bravery. It seems that *now a general* commands, and has at his side *a chief-of-staff*.

July 2.—A crystalized section of abolitionists has, it seems, dispatched to England a Rev. Dr. *Conway*, who put on airs, began a silly correspondence with Mason the traitor, and has thrown ridicule on the cause and on the men whom he is supposed to represent.

July 3.—Some details from Gettysburgh. Most sanguinary and stubborn fighting. General Reynolds, the flower of our army, killed. The unblemished patriot, General Wadsworth, fought most splendidly, and is reported to be wounded. His son was beside Reynolds. Mark this, you world's offals in the WORLD. Nothing like you can be found in the purlieus of the most stinking social sewers.

July 3.—Whoever wishes to know how, in Mr. Seward's mind, right and law are equipoised, should read the correspondence between the State Department and the Attoney-General in the case of a criminal runaway from Saxony. *Astraea-Themis*-BATES is always bold and manly when right, justice, when individual or general human rights are questioned. BATES' official, legal opinions will remain as a noble record of his official activity during this bloody tornado.

July 3.—Most contradictory news and rumors. To a great extent, the fortunes of the Union may be decided at Gettysburgh. Copperheads alias Peace-Democrats more dangerous than the rebels in arms. The Copperheads poisoned and paralyzed the spirit of the people ; the Pennsylvanians look on, and rise not as a man in the defence of their invaded state.

July 4.—General Wallbridge the orator of the day. *O tempora Lincolniana !*

It is fortunate for the country and for General Meade that no telegraphic communication exists between Washington and his camp.

July 8.—July 4th, in the evening, I was struck with *cholera morbus.* In two hours I was delirious, and the end of the DIARY and of myself was at hand. Those who may be interested in the DIARY, be thankful to *fatum* and to my friend in whose house I was taken sick. I am up and again on the watch.

July 8.—However, I have lost the run of events. I have lost the *piquant* of observation how the events of Gettysburgh affected the *big men* here. I may have lost the echo of some stories told on the occasion at the White House.

Vicksburgh taken! No words to glorify GRANT, FARRAGUT, PORTER, *and the army of heroes on land and on the waters.*

I wake up and open a paper. Apotheosis! Yesterday evening Mr. Seward made a speech and glorified himself into CHRIST. Why not? At the beginning of this internecine war, Mr. Seward repeatedly played the inspired, the prophet, and even the SPIRIT, having the polyglotic gift. *In illo tempore* Mr. Seward advised the foreign diplomats to bring to him their respective dispatches received from their respective governments, and he, Seward, would explain to each diplomat the meanings of what the dispatches contain. Perhaps the spirit was an after-dinner spirit!

In the above-mentioned speech Mr. Seward exclaimed, "If I fall!" O, you will fall, and you will be covered with ...... I shall not stain the paper. Plenty of lickspittles glorifying Lincoln-Seward.

July 8.—The battles at Gettysburgh will stand almost unparalleled in history for the courage, tenacity, and martial rage shown on both sides, by the soldiers, the officers and the generals. This four-days' struggle may be put above Attila's fight in the plains of Chalons; it stands above the celebrated battle of giants at Marignan between the French and the Swiss. No legions, no troops ever did more, nay, ever did the same. At Waterloo one-third of the French infantry was not engaged in the previous days of Ligny and of Quatres-bras, and three-fourths of the Anglo-allied army were fresh, and not fatigued even by forced marches. I am sure that no other troops in the world could fight with such a stubborn bravery four consecutive days; not the English, not even the *iron-muscled* Russians.

I learn that during the invasion of Pennsylvania, and above all, during the last days, all the country expected something extraordinary from the army at Fortress Monroe, under General Dix's command. But the affair ended in expectations.

A few days ago the President declared in a speech that he dares not introduce the names of the generals. Not to name the victor at Gettysburgh, the undaunted captor of Vicksburgh! The people repeat your names, O heroes! even if the President remains dumb.

Already a back-fire against Meade. I cannot believe that his heart fainted, and that other generals kept him from breaking before the enemy. But Meade is the man of their own kith and kin, and they ought to have known him.

It is now so difficult to disentangle truth from lies, from stories and from intrigue. It will not do, however, to uphold Hooker—it will not do. Hooker is a brilliant fighter, but was and always will be *stunned* when in command of an army. It is a crime to put up Hooker as a captain.

Somebody put in the head of the patriotic but mercurial Senator Wilson that the terrible onslaught of the rebel columns is not the result of their having adopted European, continental tactics, but that the rebels are formidable because they have adopted the Indian mode of warfare. God forgive him who thus confused my friend's understanding! Indian tactics or warfare for masses of forty, fifty, or one hundred thousand men!

I learn that Christ-Seward wishes to force the hoary, but brave, steady, and not at all fogyish Neptune Welles, to recognize to Spain or Cuba, or to somebody else and to all the world, an extension of the maritime league. It is excellent. Such extension is *altogether* advantageous to the maritime neutrals—all of them, Russia excepted, our covert or open ill-wishers.

Mr. Seward, as a good, scriptural Christian, minds not an offense, and is not rancorous. The Imperial *Decembriseur*, and all the imperialist liveried lackeys, look with contempt on the cause of the people, side with secessionists, with copperheads, etc., etc., and Mr. Seward insists on giving a license for the exportation of tobacco bought in Richmond for French accounts. Again Neptune defends the country's honor and interests.

In proportion as the presidential electioneering season approaches, Mr. Seward repeatedly and repeatedly attempts to impress upon the people's mind that he will not accept from the nation any high reward for his services. Well, it is not cunning—as by this time Mr. Seward ought to have found in what estimation he is held by nine-tenths of the people.

This is all that I caught in one day, after several days' interruption.

July 9.—Lee retreats towards the Potomac. If they let him recross there, our shame is nameless. Will Meade be after Lee *l'épée dans les reins.*

Halleckiana, minus. Nobody in Washington, not even the head-quarters, has any notion or idea what means Lee has to re-cross the Potomac.

Halleckiana, plus. I am told that Halleck refused

to telegraph to Meade Mr. Lincoln's strategical conceptions.

July 9.—Chewing and spitting paramount here, require incalculable numbers of spittoons. The lickspittles outnumber the spittoons.

July 10.—The politicians already begin to broadly *play their game.* I use the sacramental expressions. What a disgusting monstrosity is a thorough politician! Not even a eunuch! There is nothing in a politician to be emasculated : no mind, no heart, no manhood. In what a *galere* I got—not by personal contact—but by intellectually observing the worms on the body politic of my—at any rate heartily adopted—country.

July 11.—Repeatedly and repeatedly certain newspaper correspondents announce to the world that Senator Sumner exercises considerable influence on the supreme power. All things considered, I wish it may be so, but I see it is not. Sumner's influence ought to have produced some palpable results. I see none.

The international maritime complications are watched and defeated by Welles.

Drapez vous, messieurs, drapez vous—in the statesman toga, history and truth will take it off from your shoulders.

July 12.—Mr. Seward is very ardently at work—Weed marshaling Seward—to reconstruct slavery and Union, to give a very large if not a general amnesty to the rebels, to shake hands with them, in pursuance of the Mercier-Richmond programme, and to be carried into the White House on the shoulders of the grateful Union-saviours, Copperheads, and blood-stained traitors. The *Herald*, the *World*, the *National Intelligencer* and others of that creed will sing *gloria in excelsis* to Seward.

July 13.—What is *Meade* doing? It is exciting to know why a blow is not yet dealt on the head of retreating rebels. Or is it that though West Point generals—on both sides—tolerably understand how to fight a battle, they subside when the finishing stroke is to be dealt. Oh for a general who understands how to manœuvre against the enemy! ! !

I hear from a very reliable source, that during the excitement brewing before the day of Gettysburgh, the honorable Post Master General by a special biped message insinuated to the honorable governor of New York that the governor may ask the removal of Stanton for the safety of the country and of patriots of the Postmaster's and the governor's species.

July 13.—Besides what *Meade* has in hand, there must be a considerable number of troops in Baltimore, in Fortress Monroe and the volunteer militia. Why not, Lincoln-Halleck! mass them on the south side of the Potomac under such generals as Heintzelman, Sigel, etc., and take the enemy between two fires?

July 14.—Bloody riots in New York. The teaching of the Woods, of their former hireling, the *World*, and of those who pay that offal now. Seymour's democracy; mob, pillage, massacre.

July 14.—Lincoln has nominated so many Major-Generals who are relieved from duty, so many of them, that the Major-Generals ought to be formed into a squadron, and, Halleck at the head, McClellan at the tail, make them charge on Lee's centre. In such a way the major-generals would be some use.

July 14.—I meet many who attempt to exculpate Mr. Seward from *this* or *that* untruth which he is accused having told to the President. Such *Seward's* men often contradict not the fact, but attempt to insinuate that somebody else might have told it. To all this I answer with the Roman Prætor:

Ille fecit cui prodest

July 14.—GRANT has overpowered men, soil —and elements. GRANT, PORTER, FARRAGUT, and their men overpowered land and waters. They overpowered *the Mississippi*, hear: the Mississippi's and its mighty affluents as the Yazoo, the Red River, and others. McClellan caved in before a brook, as the Chickahominy. McClellan had the most gigantic resources in men and material ever put in the hands of a commander, and caved in. O, worshippers of heavy incapacity, take and digest it if you can.

July 16.—Lee re-crossed the Potomac! Thundering storms, rising waters and about one hundred and fifty thousand at his heels! What a general! And our brave soldiers again baffled, almost dishonored by domestic, know-nothing generalship. We have lost the occasion to crush three-fourths of the rebellion. But where is the responsibility ? Foul work somewhere, but, as always, it will be nobody's fault.

July 15.—Stanton in rage and despair. Riots everywhere. All these riots must be the result of a skillfully laid mine. They coincide with the invasion by the rebels. At the best, these riots are generated by Fourth of July Seymourite speeches and by the long uninterrupted series of incendiary articles in New York papers, like World, etc., and in Boston, where emasculated parasites as Hilliard, a Cain Curtis etc., soothingly tried their hands to disgrace their city and to mislead the people. All the Lincoln-Seward-Halleck actions cannot excuse these riots and their matricidal, secret inciters.

July 15.—The Adminstration ought to recall Wool and put Butler in New York. Butler understands how to deal with riotous traitors,

July 15.—Good news from Banks. Now he comes out and will recover the confidence of all good men.

July 15.—If it is true that *Meade* convoked a council of war, and that the generals decided not to attack Lee, then whoever voted and decided so, ought, at the best, to be sent to the hospital of mental invalids, and the army put in the hands of fighting men. Lee's escape will henceforth occupy the cardinal place in the annals of disgraceful generalships of the Potomac army.

July 16.—One of the truest men and citizens in this country, George Forbes, of Milton Hill, returned from England.   Forbes says that aristocracy and the commercial classes (with few exceptions) are generally against us.   But the people at large are on our side.

Oh ! that some method may be found to separate the interests of the good and noble English people, from the interests of the other classes ; then to have intercourse only with the people ; and towards the other English fulfil :

Vos autem o Tyrii prolem gentemgue futuram,

and that not one of those lords, lordlings, of inborn snobs and flunkeys, that not one of that English social sham may ever be allowed to tread the sacred American soil.   And if such an Englishman ever touches these shores, then be he treated as leprous, and as carrying in him the most contagious plague, and let the house of any American that shall be opened to such an Englishman, be torn down and burned, and its ashes scattered to the winds ; and the curse of the people upon any American harboring those snobbish upstarts of liberty.

July 16.—The incendiaries and murderers in New York cheered McClellan and came to his house. Bravo !   Can, now, any honest man who is not an idiot, doubt where are the main springs and the animus of those New York blood-thirsty miscreants, and who are those of whose hearts McClellan got hold ? What a nice Copperhead combination for saving the Union.   Very likely Seymour, Dictator or

President, McClellan Commander-in-chief, or Secretary of War, some of the Woods or Duncans or Barlows in the Treasury, their hireling any Marble for Foreign Affairs, and with them some others from among the favorites of the New York blood-thirsty incendiaries.

I read in one of the New York poison-dealers, *alias* Copperhead newspapers, that McClellan was ruined by politicians. So-called honest, but idiotic conservatives sanctimoniously repeat that lie. It was McClellan, who, inspired by *Barlow*, by the *Herald* and by his aristocratic West Point pro-slavery friends, introduced democratic politics into the army at a time when the army was yet in an embryo state, already in September and October, 1861. O, impudent liars! history will nail your names to the gallows, together with the name of your fetish and of his military tail.

July 16.—In that fated, cursed council of war which allowed Lee to escape, my patriot WADSWORTH was the most decided, the most outspoken in favor of attacking Lee. Wadsworth never fails where honor and patriotism are to be sustained. Warren with Wadsworth. So Humphries, Pleasanton and Howard. Those names ought to coruscate as the purest light of patriotism for future generations. Meade's vote is of no account. He, the commander, ought to have acted up to his vote. If only Meade had imitated *Radetzky*. In 1849 after the denunciation of the Armistice of

Milan, *Radetzky* called a council of war to decide whether the *Po* was to be crossed and Piedmont invaded. All the best Austrian generals—*Hesse* with them, voted against the proposition. Radetzky quietly listened, then rose and give orders to cross immediately.

The result was the battle of Novara and the temporary humiliation of the house of Savoy. That was a model for *Meade*. And this General *French* who advised to entrench! To entrench in pursuit of a retreating enemy! This French honors West Point and engineering. The generals who voted to entrench and not to attack Lee, and Meade with them, they can never, never retrieve. Whatever be their future or eventual success it will not heal the wound given to the country by thus allowing Lee to escape. O, God! O, God!

Such *Frenches* and others asserted that "Lee will attack before he crosses." Oh what *Marses! Lee's position at Williamsport was on heights*, etc., etc., assert those braves.

When a country is hilly and undulating there will always be found one point or hill commanding the others. I shall risk my head on the fact, that around Lee's entrenchments at Williamsport, there exist other elevations which command Wilhamsport, and are within artillery distance. *Natura semper sibi consona.* I am sure that · better positions than that selected by Lee could easily have been occupied by our troops or artillery. The same must have been the case at

Hagerstown.   And if the generals were afraid to fight Lee's whole army they ought to have more vigilantly watched his crossing. There was a time when a part only of the rebel army was facing us, and at least this part ought to have been attacked and crippled, if not destroyed. Sound common sense teaches it. But it seems that no will to fight Lee, or to impede his safe re-crossing, no such will animated the majority of the council of war. It seems that some of the West Point nurslings are still awestruck at the sight of their slavocratic former companions, as they were at the time of their studies at West Point.

I was told by an officer coming from the army that the soldiers are exasperated. The soldiers say that the generals did not wish to destroy Lee's army and finish the rebellion, because their "stars were to set down." Who knows how far the soldiers are right ?

July 17.—In New York the *unterrified* democracy went to arson and murder, hand in hand with the immense majority of Irishry. Meagher, Nugent, Corcoran and thousands like you, are exceptions. The O'Connors, O'Gormans, etc., are the unterrified. For these bloody saturnalia the wedding was consecrated by the Iro-Roman priesthood. As the *unterrified* Democrats pollute the sacred name of genuine Democracy, so the Irishry stain even the Catholic confession. The Iro-Roman Church in this country is not even a Roman-Catholic end. This Iro-Romanism here is a mixture of cunning, ignorance, brutality and extortion.   A European Roman-Catholic at once finds out the difference in the spirit, and even to a certain extent, in the form.   The incendiaries and murderers in the New-York riots are the nurslings and disciples of the Iro-Roman clergy and the Iro-hierarchy.

July 17.—Mr. Lincoln ought to dismiss every general who voted against fighting ; dismiss *Meade* for not understanding his power as commander of an army, and give the places to such Howards, Warrens, Pleasantons, Humphreys, Wadsworths, and all others, generals, colonels, etc. who clamorously asked an order for attack.   If the army shall depend upon such generals who let Lee escape, then lay down arms, and drag not the people's children to a slaughter house.

To excuse the generals, it is asserted that at Chancellorsville Lee has allowed to Hooker to recross the river without annoying us, which Lee could easily do, and damage us considerably.   Well! are our Generals to carry on a mere war of civilities ? If Lee committed a fault, are you, gentlemen, in duty bound to imitate his mistakes ? Imitation for imitation, then rather imitate Lee's several splendid manœuvering and tactics.

July 17.—I learn that the deep-dyed Copperheads and slavery-saviours do not consider Seymour of New York safe enough.   They turn now to a certain Seymour in Connecticut.   It seems that the Connecticut Seymour still more hates human rights, self-government, light and progress, and is a still more ardent lickspittle of slavocracy, of barbarism, and of the slave-driving whip.

July 18.—Splendid Chase urged Wadsworth to go to Florida and organize that country—very likely to prepare votes for Chase's presidency. It is not such high-toned men as Wadsworth who become tools of schemers.

Again rumors say that Stanton joined the scheme of Lincoln's reelection. As far as I can judge, Stanton's cardinal aim is to crush the rebellion.

July 18.—The greatest glory for Wadsworth is that the majority against him in the last November elections is now murdering and *arsoning* New York. All of them are unterrified, hard shell democrats, and cheer McClellan. These murderers are the " friends " of Seymour—they are the pets of that *World*, itself below the offal of hell—they are the " gentlemen" incendiaries of H. E. the Archbishop Hughes. On your head, most eminent Archbishop, is the whole responsibility. These " gentlemen " are brought up, Christianized and moralized under your care and direction, and under that of your tonsured crew. The " gentlemen" murderers are your herd, O most eminent shepherd! You ought to have and you could have stopped the rioters. And now your *stola* is a halter and your *pallium* gored with blood, otherwise innocent as is the blood of the lamb incensed on the altar of Saint Agnes in Rome.

Mr. Seward strongly opposed the appointment of General Butler to New York. Mr. Seward wished no harm to the "gentlemen" of his dear friend the Most Eminent Archbishop, and to the select ones who helped him to defeat Wadsworth.

July 19.—Difficult will be the task of the historian of these episodes of riots, as well as of the whole civil war. If gifted with the sacred spark, the future historian must carefully disentangle the various agencies and forces in this convulsion. Some such agencies are—

a The righteousness of the cause of the North, defending civilization, justice, humanity.

b The devotion, the self-sacrifice of the people.

c The littleness, helplessness, selfishness, cunning, heartlessness, empty-headedness, narrow-mindedness of the various leaders.

d The plague of politicians.

e The untiring efforts of the heathen, that is, of the Northern worshippers of the slavocrat and of his whip, efforts to uphold and save their idol.

f The fatal influence of the press. The republican or patriot press neither sufficiently vigilant, nor clear-sighted, nor intelligent, nor undaunted; not reinvigorated by new, young agencies; the bad press reckless, unprincipled, without honor and conscience, but bold, ferocious in its lies, and sacrificing all that is noble, human and pure to the idol of slavery.

July 19.—The more details about the shame of Ha-

gerstown and of Williamsport, the more it rends
heart and mind. I saw many soldiers and officers,
sick, wounded and healthy. Their accounts agree,
and cut to the quick. Our army was flushed with
victory, craving for fight, and in a state of enthusias-
tic exaltation. But our generals were not therein in
communion with the officers, with the rank and file.
Enthusiasm ! this highest and most powerful element
to secure victory, and on which rely all the true captains; enthusiasm, that made invincible the phalanx
of Alexander; invincible Cæsar's legions and Napoleon's columns; enthusiasm was of no account for the
generals in council. O *Meade !* better were it for
you if your council was held among, or with the soldiers.

The Rebel army was demoralized, as a retreating
army always is ; no doubt exists concerning a partial,
at least, disorganization of the rebels. But Lee and his
generals understood how to make a bold show, and a
bold, menacing front, with what was not yet disorganized, and our generals caved in, in the council.

This July 19th is heavy, dark and gloomy....I wish
it were all over.

July 19.—Thurlow Weed puffs Stanton and patron-
ises him. O, God ! It is a terrible blow to Stanton.
How, now, can one have confidence in Stanton's manhood. Are contracts at the bottom of the puff, or is
it only one of *Weed's* tricks to defile and to ruin
Stanton ?

July 20.—It is almost humiliating to witness how mongrels and pigmies attempt to rob the people of their due glory, how they attempt to absorb to their own credit what the pitiless pressure of events forced upon them. All of them limped after events as lame ducks in mud; not one foresaw any thing, not one understood the *to-day*. Neither emancipation nor the transformation of slave into free states, are of your special, individual work, O, great men; but you strut now.

Mirmidons, race féconde, enfin nous commanndos.

Some say that the generals who let Lee off, intended not to humiliate their former chief and pet McClellan.

July 20.—Cavalry wanted. Stables and corrals filled with horses, but no saddles. No saddles in this most industrious country! No brains in the Quartermasters or in those to whom it belongs. And perhaps no will, and perhaps no honesty. No saddles! Oh! I am sure it is nobody's fault; no workmen are to be found, and no leather, and no men to look after the country's good. That is the rub.

July 20.—Captain Collins, commanding a United States man-of-war, captures an English blockade-runner near an isolated shoal somewhere in the vicinity of Bermuda. England asserts that the shoal is a shore, and that the maritime league is violated. Mr. Seward at once yields, Neptune defends as he always does, the rights of the national *Tritons*, and of the national flag. The supreme power sides with Seward, and an order is given to reprimand Collins or something like it: it is done, and the prize-court decides that Captain Collins has made a lawful capture. I hope Collins will be consoled, and light his segar with the reprimand.

The future historian will duly ponder and establish Mr. Seward's claims to the *salvage* of the country.

July 20.—From all that I learn, *Meade* has a better and larger army than Lee; oh, may only Meade establish that he has the biggest brains of the two.

July 20.—From time to time, I read the various statutes issued by the last Congress, and am strengthened in my opinion that Congress served the people well. The various statutes are the triumph of legislation. They are clear, precise, well-worded results of patriotic, devoted, far-seeing and undaunted minds and brains. All glory to the majority of the Thirty-seventh Congress!

July 21.—A manly and patriotic letter from James T. Brady is published in the papers. Such Democrats, Irishmen and lawyers, like Brady, honor the party, the nationality, and the profession.

July 21.—A mystery surrounds the appointment of *Grant* to the command of the fated Potomac army. *Yes* and *no* say the helmsmen. The truth seems to be, it was offered to Grant, and he respectfully refused to accept it. If so, it is an evidence in favor of Grant.

To give up glory and devoted companions in arms, to give all this up for the sake of running into the unknown, and into the jaws of the still breathing McClellanism, and into the vicinity of the central telegraphic station! Grant believes in volunteers; and for this reason it is to be regretted that he refused to correct the West Point notions.

July 21.—The draft occasions much bad blood, and evokes violent dissatisfaction. The draft is a dire necessity; but it could have been avoided if time, men, and the people's enthusiasm had not been so sacrilegiously wasted. The three hundred dollar clause is not a happy invention, and its omission would have given a better character to that law.

July 21.—If the New York traitors succeed in preventing the draft, then they will riot against taxes; after breaking down the taxes, they will riot against the greenbacks, against the emancipation, and finally force the re-construction of the Union with the murderous rebel chiefs in the senatorial chairs, according to the Seward-Mercier-Richmond programme. Any one can see in the Cain-Copperhead newspapers of New York, of Boston, of Philadelphia, and in the letters and speeches of those matricides, what are their aims, and how their plans are laid out.

July 21.—Again I am most positively assured that some time ago a friendly offensive and defensive alliance was concluded between W. H. Seward and Edwin Stanton. The high powers were represented by

Thurlow Weed and Morgan for Seward, and the virtuous, lachrymose, white-cravated Whiting acted for Stanton. I was told that this alliance drove Watson, (Assistant Secretary,) from the War Department. This would be infernal, if true. I know that no *Weed* whatever could approach such a man as Watson; but Watson assured me that he returns back, and I cannot believe that Stanton could consent to be thus sold.

July 22.—Honorable, virtuous, tear-shedding, jockey-dressing Whiting wanted to make a trip to Europe. Sharp and acute, the great expounder found out at once that Mr. Seward is one of the greatest and noblest patriots of all times. Reward followed. Whiting goes to Europe on a special mission—to dine, if he is invited, with all the great and small men to whom Mr. Adams or Mr. Dayton may introduce him, and to convince everybody in Europe that the Sewards, the Whitings, &c., are the *crème de la crème* of the American people. *Vive la bagatelle.*

July 22.—How putrescent is all around! But it is not the nation, not the people. And as the sun raises above the darkest and heaviest vapors, so in America the spirit of mankind, incarnated in and animating the people, towers above the filth of politicians, of cabinet-makers, of presidential-peddlers, etc. Look to the masses to find consolation. How splendidly acts Massachusetts and New England's sons! And what free State is not New England's son? The youth of Massachusetts are almost all in the field—the rich and the poor, those of the best social standing, and of the genuine good blood and standing ; scholars and mechanics, all of them shouldered the musket.

July 23.—How strangely and how slowly Meade manœuvres ! It looks McClellan-like. O, God of battles, warm and inspire Meade !

July 23.—Only boys in the corps of invalids. It has its good. For scores of years to come, these invalids will be the living legend of this treasonable, matricidal rebellion, and of the atrocious misconduct of our helmsmen. I hope that when returned home, these invalids will be as many extirpators of all kinds of *Weeds* in their respective townships and villages. They will become the lights of the new era.

July 23.—Were it not for the murdered, these New York riots could be considered welcome. The rioting cannibals, and their prompters and defenders showed their hands. No one in his senses can now doubt how heartily and devotedly Jeff Davis was served by his hirelings among the Copperhead leaders and among the New York Copperhead press. The cannibals cheered for McClellan, and the Administration has neither enough courage nor self respect to put that fetish on the retired list.

In the old, flourishing times of Romanism and papacy, such a Most Eminent Hughes would long ago have been suspended by the Holy See. The Most Eminent's standing among the continental European Episcopacy is not eminent at all, whatever be Mr. Seward's opinion. The Most Eminent is a curious observer of the canons, of the papal bulls, and of other clerical and episcopal paraphernalia. The spirit animating the Most Eminent is not the spirit of the Roman Sapienzia. I well recollect what I heard lectured in that Roman papal university.

July 24.—As a dark and ominous cloud, Lee with his army hovers around Washington, keeps the Shenandoah valley, and may again cross over to the Cumberland valley. It seems that the generals whose council-of-war allowed Lee to recross the river unhurt, believed that Lee with all speed would run to Richmond; and now they hang to his brow and eye.

The crime of Williamsport bears fruit. Never, never in this or in the other life, can the perpetrators of the Williamsport crime atone for it.

It may come that the western armies and generals will bring the civil war to an end, the Potomac army all the time marching and countermarching between the Potomac and the Rappahannock. And such a splendid army, such heroic soldiers and officers, to be sacrificed to the ignorant stubbornness of sham military science!

July 25.—I positively learn that Gilmore has scarcely ten thousand men, infantry, and is to storm the various forts and defenses around the Charleston harbor. If Gilmore succeeds, then it is a wonder. But in sound valuation, Gilmore has not men enough to organize columns of attack so that the one shall follow the other within a short, very short supporting distance. And the losses will almost hourly reduce Gilmore's small force. I dread repulse and heavy losses. Some one at the head-quarters deserves to be quartered for such a distribution of troops. With the immense resources and means of transportation, it is so easy to send twenty thousand troops to Gilmore, attack, make short work of it, and then carry the troops back to where they belonged. But to concentrate and act in masses is not the *credo* of the—not yet quartered—head-quarters.

July 26.—Old—but not slow—Welles again gives to Seward a lesson of good-behavior, of sound sense, and of mastery of international laws. The prize courts side with Welles. Because Neptune has a white wig and beard, he is considered slow, when in reality he is active, unflinching, and progressive.

July 26.—O, could I only exclaim, *Exegi monumentum aere perennius*, to the noble, the patriotic, and the good, as well as to the helpless, the selfish, and the counterfeits.

July 27.—*Philadelphia.* Flags in all the streets, volunteers parading and drilling. Prosperity, activity and devotion permeate the country. So at least I am led to believe. All this is so refreshing, after witnessing in Washington such strenuous efforts how not to do it.

Bad news. I learn that Gilmore is repulsed. When the *forlorn hope* entered Fort Wagner, no support promptly came, and the heroes, black and white, were massacred or expelled. Gilmore ought to have been more cautious, and not to have undertaken an operation which was on its outside stamped with impossibility. Perhaps Gilmore obeyed peremptory orders. Who gave them?

Lee's army escapes through Chester Gap, and thus we have not cut the rebels from Richmond, and now they are ahead of us. Again out-manœuvred! and *nobody's fault*, only the campaign prolonged *ad infinitum*. Perhaps it is in the programme!

June 28.—*Philadelphia.* The petty, narrow, school conceit imbibed in the West Point nursery, is the stumbling-block barring everywhere the expansion of a healthy and vigorous activity. I listened to the heaviest absurdities and fogyism on military affairs *oracularly* preached by one of the great West Pointers on duty here.

July 31.—*Long Branch.* Away from personal contact, even from the view of politicians, of plotters, of lickspittles. How refreshing, how invigorating, how soothing!

Mr. Seward, with a due tail, visits Fortress Monroe. What for? Is it to organize some underground road, to re-union on the Mercier-Seward-Richmond programme?

One well-informed writes me that the last programme of Lincoln, Halleck and Meade is, that the army of the Potomac is to keep Lee at bay, but not to attack. If true, how well designed to give time to Lee to do what he likes, to re-organize, to send away his troops where he may please, to call them back—in one word to be fully at his case on our account.   Will this country ever escape the tutorship of sham science?

July 31.—*Long Branch.*   Seward's concession policy towards France bears fruit in Mexico.   Of course the *Decembriseur* outwitted the Weed-Albany-Auburn politician statesman.   But it is not the ignorant foreign policy which strengthened and strengthens the French policy in Mexico.   It is the blunders, the tergiversations, the gropings, and the crimes of our internal domestic policy, which, protracting the war, allows the French conspirator to murder the Mexicans.

July 31. *L. B.*—So the *Decembriseur* amuses himself in creating an Imperial throne in Mexico for some European princely idiot or intriguer.   All right.   I have confidence in the Mexicans.   The future Emperor, even if established for some time on the cushion of treason propped by French bayonets, that manikin before short or long will be *Iturbidised.*   Further : I have confidence in the French people.   The upper crust is pestilental.   Bonapartists, lickspittles, lackeys and incarnations of all imaginary corruptions compose that upper crust.   But I would bet a fortune, had I one, that in the course of the next five years, the *Decembriseur* and his *Prince Imperial* will be visible at Barnum's, and that some shoddy grandee from 5th Avenue, will issue cards inviting *to meet the Empress Eugénie.*

Stanton—Twenty Thousand—Canadians—Peterhoff—Coffey—Initiation—Electioneering—Reports—Grant—McClellan—Belligerent Rights—Menagerie—
Watson—Jury—Democrats—Bristles—" Where is Stanton ?"—" Fight the
monster "—Chasiana—Luminaries—Ballistic—Political Economy, etc., etc.,
etc.

August 2. Long Branch.—The organs of all shades
and of all gradations of ill-wishers to the cause of the
North, and to that of Emancipation, the secret friends of
Jeff Davis, and the open supporters of McClellan are
untiring in their open, slanderous, treacherous accusations of *Stanton ;* others spread sanctimoniously perfidious suggestions against the Secretary of War, and
so does the *National Intelligencer*, this foremost
Whig - Conservative, double or treble-faced organ.
Stanton is called to account for all mishaps, mismanagement, disasters and disgraces which befall our
armies between the Rio Grande and the Potomac.
Such accusations, to a certain degree, could be justified if the Secretary of War were clothed with the
same powers, and therefore with the same responsibilities as is the case in European governments.

But every one knows that here the war machinery is very complicated, because wheels turn within wheels. The Secretary of War is not alone to answer and he is not exclusively responsible for the appointment of good, middling, or wholly bad generals and commanders. Every one knows it. *Stanton* may have all the possible short-comings and faults with which his enemies so richly clothe him; one thing is certain, that *Stanton* advocated and always advocates fighting, and Stanton furnishes the generals and commanders with all means and resources at the country's and the department's disposition. If many respectable men are to be trusted, *Stanton* never interferes with intrinsic military operations, never orders or insinuates, or dictates to the commanders of our armies where and in what way they are to get at the enemy and to fight him. As far as I know Stanton keeps aloof from strategy.

Stanton *is insincere and untruthful,* say his enemies. Granted. I never found a man in power to be otherwise in personal questions or relations. It is almost impossible for the power-holders to be sincere and truthful.

> Trust in thy sword,
> Rather than prince's (president's) word;
> Trust in fortuna's sinister,
> Rather than prince's minister.

But *Stanton* is truthful and sincere to the cause, and that is all that I want from him. Stanton's alleged *malice* against McClellan had the noblest and the most patriotic sources, which, of course, could not be understood or appreciated by Stanton's revilers.

The organs of treason and of infamy refer always to McClellan. *O race, knitted of the devil's excrements mixed with his saliva,* [see Talleyrand about Thiers] your treason is only equal to your impudence and ignorance. If in February, 1862, Stanton had not urged McClellan to move, probably the Potomac Army would have spent all the year in its tents before Washington. McClellan's henchmen and minions thrusted and still thrust the grossest lies down the throat of a certain public, eager to gulp slander as sugar plums. McClellan's stupidity at Yorktown and in the Chickahominy is vindicated by his crew with the following counter accusation : that all disasters have been generated because McDowell with his twenty thousand men did not join McClellan. If McClellan had in him the soldiership of a non-commissioned officer, on his knees he ought to implore his crew not to expose him in this way. When a general has in hand about one hundred and ten thousand men, as McClellan had on entering the peninsula, and accomplishes nothing, then it is a proof that he, the general, is wholly unable and ignorant how to handle large masses. If McClellan could not manage one hundred thousand men, still less would he have been able to manage the twenty thousand more of McDowell's corps.

The stupidity of attempting to invest Richmond is beyond words, and for such an operation several hundred thousand men would have been necessary. [Spoke of it in Vol. I.]   If twenty thousand men arrive not at a certain day or hour when a battle is raging, most surely this failure may occasion a defeat—Grouchy at Waterloo—but in McClellan's Chickahominy operations, twenty thousand men more would have served only still more plainly to expose his incapacity, and to be a prey to fevers and diseases.

The bulk of the rebel army in Richmond was always less numerous than McClellan's; the rebels always understood to have more troops than had McClellan when they attacked him. During that whole cursed and ignominious (for McClellan) Chickahominy campaign, McClellan never fought at once more of his men than about thirty thousand. It was not the absence of twenty thousand men that prevented a commander of one hundred thousand from engaging more of his troops, and for quickly supporting such corps as were attacked by the enemy.

August 3 : *L. B.*—The Colonists, that is, the appendixes of England, as the Canadians, the Nova Scotians, and of any other colonial dignity and name, together with their great statesmen, certain Howes and Johnsons, etc. etc. etc. agitate; they are in trances like little fish out of water. They find it so pleasant to seize an occasion to look like something great.   Poor frogs! trying to blow themselves into leviathans.

Their whelpish snarling at the North reminds one of little curs snarling at a mastiff. How can these colonists imagine that a royal prince of England could reside among something which is as indefinite as are colonists—something neither fish nor flesh.

August 3.—The *Evening Post* contains a letter on the difference between the behavior of Union men in Missouri during the treasonable riots in St. Louis in the Spring of 1861, and the conduct of the Union men in New York during the recent riots. But the Saint Louis patriot is silent—has forgotten the immortal Lyons who saved that city and its patriots, who saved Missouri. (General Scott insisted upon courtmartialling Lyons.)

Also, have you already forgotten the foremost among heroes and patriots, and whose loss is more telling now than it was in 1861. Forgotten one of the purest and noblest victims of Washington blindness, of General Scott's unmilitary policy and conduct. Forgotten the true son of the people? But O Lyons! thy name will be venerated by coming generations.

August 4: *L. B.*—*The Cliques.*

a The worst, and the womb of all evils is the Weed-Seward clique. Around it group contractors, jobbers, shoddy, and all kinds of other social impurities.

b The ambitious, intriguing, selfish, narrow-minded West Point clique.

c The not brave, not patriotic, and freedom-hating, unintelligent McClellan clique.

d Copperheads of various hues and gradations.

Cliques *a*, *b*, and *c*, generated and fostered Copper-heads, and facilitated their expansion.

e Imbeciles, lickspittles, politicians, etc.

f The Lincolnites, closely intertwined with the *genus e;* the Blair men, etc.

g The partisans of Chase. This clique is the most variously and most curiously composed. Honest imbeciles, makers of phrases, rhetors, heavy and narrow-minded, office-hunters, office expectants, politicians, contractors, admirers of pompousness and of would-be radicalism, all who turn round and round, and see not beyond their noses, etc.

Several minor cliques exist, but deserve not to be mentioned. Behind these mud-hills rises the true people, as the Himmalayas rise above the plains of Asia.

August 4.—Why could not Everett, that good and true patriot, preside over our relations with Europe; or why is that thorough American statesman, Governor Marcy, dead! How different, how respected, how truly American would have been the character of our relations with Europe! No prophecies, no lies would have been told, no gross ignorance displayed !

August 4. *L B.*—In the columns of the *Times* a friend of Halleck tries to make a great man of the General-in-chief. Halleck repudiates Burnside and Hooker, but claims the victory at Gettysburgh, because Meade, being a good disciplinarian, executed Halleck's orders.

So from his room in G street Washington, Halleck directed the repulse of the furiously attacking columns. Bravo! more bravo as no telegraph connects Washington with Gettysburgh!

Meade being a good disciplinarian, the crime of Williamsport falls upon Halleck; the commander-in-chief is the more responsible, as the crime was perpetrated under his nose; about four hours' drive could have brought him to our army, and then Halleck in person could have directed the attack upon the enemy.

From all that transpires about Williamsport one must conclude that Lee must have known that he would not be seriously attacked, and that he was not much afraid of the combined disciplinarian generalship.

Further: Halleck claims for himself Grant's success, because Grant obeyed orders, and Rosecrans did the same. How astonishing, therefore, that their campaigns ended in victories and not in such shame as Halleck at Corinth, in 1862. Rosecrans was inspired by telegraph to change defeat into victory; the indomitable Grant received by telegraph the fertility of resources shown by him at Vicksburgh. Oh! Halleck! you cannot succeed in thus belittling the two heroes, and you may tell your little story to the marines.

August 4.—The Proclamation on retaliation is a well-written document; but like all Mr. Lincoln's acts it is done almost too late, only when the poor President was so cornered by events, that shifting and escape became impossible. If I am well informed Stanton long ago demanded such a Proclamation, but Lincoln's familiar demons prevented it. Nevertheless Lincoln will be credited for what intrinsically is not his.

August 5 : *L. B.*—Thomas—not Paul—Lincoln's pet, returns to the Mississippi to organise Africo-American regiments. For six months they organize, organize and have not yet fifteen thousand in field. If Stanton had been left alone, we would have to-day in battle order at least fifty thousand Africo-Americans.

August 5 : *L. B.*—All computed together, among all Western Continental European nations, the Germans, both here and in Germany, behave the best towards the North. I mean the genuine German people. Thinkers and rationalists are seldom, if ever, found on the wrong side. I rejoice to see the Germans behave so nobly.

August 5.—The Peterhoff condemned, notwithstanding all the efforts to the contrary of our brilliant, versatile and highly erudite in international laws Secretary of state. But Mr. Seward will not understand the lesson. How could he?

August 5 : *L. B.*—At least for the fiftieth time, Seward insinuates to the public that we are on the eve of a breach with England—but Seward will prevent it. Oh, Oh! Yes, O Seward! when backed by the iron clads and by twenty-two millions of a brave and stubborn people!

August 5 : *L. B.*—Poor Stanton, I pity him! After Weed comes the "little villain," with his puffs. Happily, the *World* abuses Stanton, and this alone makes up even for the applause of Weed and his consorts.

August 7 : *L. B.*—Coffey, Assistant Attorney-General, published a legal, official opinion on maritime, commercial *copperheadism*; that is, when an American vessel, from an American port, is sent in ballast to a neutral port to load there, afterwards to run the blockade, Coffey proves it to be treason and criminality. The document is clear, logical, precise and not wordy : not in the style of the State Department logomachy. Why, O why cannot such younger men be at the head! Emancipation would have been carried out, slavery destroyed, the Union restored, rebels crushed, and the French murderers and imperial lackeys would cut very respectful capers to please a great people.

August 8 : *L. B.*—I shudder as I pass in review what little is done at such an enormous expenditure of human limbs and of human life, not to speak of squandered time, labor and money.

It seems that the prevailing rule is to reach the smallest results at the greatest possible cost. General Scott, Seward and Lincoln early laid down that rule. McClellan, that quintessence of all unsoldierlike capacities, faithfully continued what was already inaugurated. Halleck almost perfected it ; and so it became a chronic disease of the leading spirits in the Administration, Stanton and Welles excepted. That sacrilegious, murderous method and rule, at times was forcibly violated by Grant, by Rosecrans, by Banks, by the glorious Farragut, by Admiral Porter. The would-be statesmen either see nothing or do not wish to see what ill-disposed minds could consider to be an almost premeditated slaughter.

I know too well that every initiation is with sacrifice or blood. It is a law of progress, absolute, not made by man, but cut out for him by fate or providence. In a stream of his mother's life-blood man enters this world; by the blood of the Redeemer the Christian becomes initiated to another, called a better world. Sacrifice and blood prevail throughout the eons of the initiation of human societies and religions. Through sacrifice and blood the Reformation became a redeemer. Great results are reached at great cost. I am an atom in a generation which, to assert her deep, earnest convictions, never caved in before blood and sacrifice; a generation that has labored and still labors, spreads seed and begins to harvest; a generation which regrets nothing, and cheerfully takes the responsibility of its actions. And with all this, the men of convictions and of undaunted revolutionary courage in Europe, bestowed and bestow more care upon any unnecessary sacrifice of human life than I witness here. By heavens! Marat, Saint Just, Robespierre, could be considered lambs when compared with the *faiseurs* here. And Marat, Saint Just, and Robespierre were fanatics of ideas: here they are *fanaticised* by selfishness, intrigue, helplessness and imbecility.

August 9: *L. B.*—For the last few months men of sound and dispassionate judgment tried to convince me that there is somewhere, in high regions, a settled purpose to prolong the war until the next presidential election. I always disbelieved such assertions; but now, considering all this criminal sluggishness, I begin to believe in the existence of such a criminal purpose.

August 9: *L. B.*—All the open and secret Copperhead organs raise a shrill cry on account of what they pervert into McClellan's general Report of his unmilitary campaigns. When a commander is in the field, he is in duty bound, as soon as possible, that is, in the next few weeks, to send to his superior or to the Government, a Report of each of his military movements and operations. McClellan ought to have immediately made a Report to the Government after his *bloodless victory* at Centreville and Manassas; a victory crowned with maple trophies! Then McClellan ought to have sent another Report after the great success at Yorktown, and so on. Every period of his campaign ought to have been separately reported. It is done in all well organized governments and armies, and it is the duty of the staff of the army to prepare such periodical, successive Reports. Even if the sovereign himself takes the field, the staff of the army sends such Reports to the Secretary of War. Nobody stood in the way of

McClellan's doing what it was his imperative duty to do, and to do immediately.

But it is unheard of that a commander during a year at the head of an army, should take another year to prepare his Report. No self-respecting government would allow such an insubordination, or accept such a tardy Report. If a government should act upon such a Report, it would be rather by dismissing from service, etc., the sluggish—if not worse—commander.

The so-called "McClellan's Report," concocted by a board of choice Copperheads in New York, and of which the *World's* hireling was an amanuensis, that production is certainly an elaborate essay on McClellan's campaigns, is certainly bristling with after-thoughts and *post facta*, as pedestals for the fetish's altar. It must have on its face the mark of combination, but not of truth. Such a Report—not written on the spot, in the atmosphere of activity, not written by officers of the staff, not by the Chief-of-staff—such a Report cannot command or inspire any confidence; it has not, and ought not to have any worth in the Government's archives. McClellan may publish his memoirs, or essays, or anything else, and therein may shine this labor of a *dasippus* assisted by vipers.

August 11 : *L. B.*—In Washington they seem to insist that Grant shall take the command of the Potomac Army. If Grant accepts, he will be a ruined man. Grant ought to have Pope in memory. Grant soon will see stained his glorious and matchless military record. He will not withstand the cliques and the underground intrigues of craving, selfish and unsatisfied ambitions.

If Halleck could only know what in a European army any tyro knows, Halleck would make Mr. Lincoln understand that such an appointment must produce confusion, as no regular staffs exist in our army. (I spoke somewhere about it.)

August 13: *L. B.*—Can it be possible that several from among the Republicans, honest leaders, gravitate towards Lincoln, and already begin to agitate for Lincoln's re-election? If it is so—if the people submit to such an imposition—O, then, genius of history, go in mourning!

August 13: *L. B.*—The Board appointed by Stanton to investigate into the condition of the Africo-Americans, has published its dissertation—very poor—in the shape of a Report. Stanton intended to do a good thing by appointing that Board. It did not turn out so well as Stanton expected. What is the use of expatiating—as do the three wise men in their Report—on certain psychological qualities and *non-qualities* of the Africo-American? The paramount question is how to organize the emancipated in their condition of freedom. When Stanton appointed that Board he wished to have elucidated, if not settled, the way and manner in which to deal with the new citizens or semi-citizens; but Stanton was the last man to look for an old psychological re-hash, without any social or moral signification whatever; a re-hash whose axioms and apothegms are, at least, a quarter of a century *behind* the scientific elucidations on races, on Africans, even on Anglo-Saxons.

August 15 : *L. B.*—Weeks ago Grant sent his Report, embracing the various operations connected with the fall of Vicksburgh.   Grant did not want a year to make a school-boy like composition, as did McClellan with his quill-holders.   Every word of Grant's Report resounds with military spirit and simplicity.   Grant has not to put truth on the rack and throw dust into people's eyes.   Three cheers for McClellan!   Grant has confidence in the volunteers; not so McClellan, who had only confidence in shams.   Grant and his army, at the best, were the second sons of the Administration—not of the people; to the last day McClellan was the pet, the spoiled child, and as such he disgraced his parents, tutors, etc., and ruined his parent's house.

August 15.—A letter published by the Honorable W. Whiting, (who is now traveling,) occasions much noise.   The letter is pointed and keen, but the writer knows mighty little about international laws.   Almost *a priori* he recognizes in the rebels, as he says, "only the rights of belligerents."   Only the rights of belligerents!   Such rights are very ample, and for this reason they belong in their plenitude exclusively to absolutely independent nations.   To recognize *a priori* such rights in the rebels, is equivalent to recognizing them as an independent nation.   In pure and absolute principle of modern (not Roman) *jus gentium*, rebels have not only no belligerent rights, but not any rights at all. Rebels are *ipso facto* outlaws in full. Writers like Abbe Galiano, Vatel, etc., for the sake of humanity and expediency, recommend to the lawful sovereign to use mercy, to treat rebels *in parte* as belligerents, and not as *a priori* condemned criminals.

August 16: *L. B.*—Seward is to promenade the diplomats over the country. He is Barnum, the diplomats are the menagerie. Poor Lord Lyons. Very probably it is Seward's last rocket to draw upon himself the attention of the people.

August 16. *L. B.*—The probabilities of a rupture with France are upon the public mind. I still misbelieve it. I have not the slightest doubt that the *Decembriseur* is full of treachery towards the North, and that his Imperialist lackeys blow brimstone against the Northern principles. But are the French people so debased as to submit? We shall see. Let that crowned conspirator begin a war of treason against the North. Before long the French people will put an end to the war and to the Decembriseur.

August 16. *L. B.*—I learn that Watson has very gravely injured his health by labor, that is, by being the most faithful servant of the country and of its cause. I never, anywhere in my life, met a public officer so undaunted at his duties, so unassuming, so quiet as Watson, in his duties of Assistant Secretary of War, which are as thorny as can be imagined. Watson was, and I hope will be for the future, the terror of lobbyists, of bad contractors, of jobbers—in one word, the terror of all the leeches of the people's pocket. And it honors Stanton to have brought into his Department such a man as Watson. I heard and hear, and read a great many accusations against Stanton ; but I never found any proofs which could virtually diminish my confidence. To use a classical, stupid, rhetorical figure : Stanton is not of antique mould. And who is now? But he is a sincere, devoted and ardent patriot ; he broadly comprehends the task and the duty to save the country, and he sees clearly and distinctly the ways and means to reach the sacred aim. Stanton may have, and very many assert that he has, numerous bristles in his character, in his deportment. Let it be so. It is the worse for him, but not for the cause he serves.

August 16. *L. B.*—Are the people again to receive a President from the hand of intriguers, from politicians, or from honest imbeciles ? If the people will stand it, then they deserve to be kept in leading strings by all that medley.

August 16. *L. B.*—Rosecrans wants mounted infantry. The men of the day, the men who understand and comprehend the exigencies, the necessities of the war, they pierce through the rotten crust of fogyism. That is promise and hope. The great organizers of the army—the McClellans and the Hallecks—could never have found out that mounted infantry is necessary, and will render good servive.   Mounted infantry was not considered a necessity in the West Point halls, and Jomini mentions it not.   How should a Halleck do so?

August 17.   *L. B.*—A defender of slavery, a Copperhead, and a traitor, differ so little from each other, that a microscope magnifying ten thousand times would not disclose the difference.   A proslaveryist, a Copperhead, and a traitor, are the most perfect *tres in unum*.

August 18. *L. B.*—General Meade is absent from the army, and Humphreys, his chief-of-staff, is temporarily in command   I notice this fact as a proof that a more rational, intelligent comprehension prevails in the military service.   A chief-of-staff is the only man to be the *locum-tenens* of the commander. At Williamsport Humphreys voted for fight.   It would be well if Meade should not return to again take the command.

August 18.—A patriotic gentlewoman asked me why I write a diary?   "To give conscientious evidence before the jury appointed by history."

August 20.—On the first day of the draft, I had occasion to visit New York.   All was quiet.   In Broadway and around the City Hall I saw less soldiers than I expected.   The people are quiet; the true conspirators are thunder-struck.   Before long, the names will be known of the genuine instigators of arson and of murder in July last.   The tools are in the hands of justice, but the main spirits are hidden. Smart and keen wretches as are the leading Copperheads, they successfully screen their names; nevertheless before long their names will be nailed to the gallows. The *World*—which, for weeks and weeks, so devotedly, so ardently poisoned the minds, and thus prepared the way for any riot—the *World* was and is a tool in the hands of the hidden traitors. The *World* is a hireling, and does the work by order.

August 21. *L. B.*—The final destiny of the Potomac Army seems to be to keep Lee at bay but not to attack him Oh! the disgraced soldiers and officers! Chickahominy, Antietam, Fredericksburgh, Gettysburgh, are the indestructible evidences of the mettle of the army, and of the poverty or total eclipse of generalship.

August 21. — Impressionable, excitable, wave-like agitated as are my dear American countrymen, they altogether forget *the yesterday*, and shout the last success. Further: the people cannot see clearly through the stultifying or the dirty dust blown in the peoples' eyes; 1st, by the politicians of all hues, from the Woods, Weeds, Forneys, to the Greeleys, by the simon-pures or the lobby-impures; 2d, by the press of all parties and shades of parties. The people may again make a mistake. Is not Lincoln hailed as the new Moses? as the man for the times, as the only one God sent to direct the people, and to grapple with the stern, earnest emergencies and perils? Emancipation is not Lincoln's, is not Sumner's, is not anybody's personal special work. The necessities, the emergencies of the times and of the hour did it. Their current drifted Mr. Lincoln irresistibly along, and to a shore where he must land or perish.

August 23. *L. B.*—From the tone of certain papers, and from private letters, I perceive that Weed-Seward are hard at work to pacify, to reunite, to save slavery and to leave unnoticed humanity and national honor. The unterrified Democrats become Weed's allies, and the alliance is to carry Seward into the White House. *Nous verrons.*

Chase is to overturn Seward-Weed and to secure the prize. Oh, the intriguers.

On the authority of the published "DIARY," I am asked, even by letters, "Where is Stanton?" "I do not know, and I do not care," is my answer. I would however, like to be sure that Stanton is not in that dirty path. I am Stanton's man, as they call it; but only as long as I find him to be *a man.*

August 24. *L. B.*—The Democrats are arrogant in asserting their superior capacity for government, for carrying on the war, and for other great things. However, I am sure that the so-called Northern Democrats would have managed the affairs even worse than do now those sham representatives of the principles of the Republican party. No faith in a fundamental human, broad principle ever actuated the hard shell Democrats. McClellan and the immense major-

ity of generals, have been, or are full-blooded Democrats, and their warlike prowess dragged the people
into deep, deep mire.   Democrats have to thank God
for not being in power; in this way their incapacity
to cope with such gigantic events is not exposed.
The other fortunate occurrence for the Democrats is
that the power-holders for the Republican party are—
what everybody sees.

August 24. *L. B.*—I very strongly and urgently advised Gen. Wadsworth to resign.   No one in the country has fulfilled more nobly his civic and patriotic
duty.   I urged upon his mind that when the war is
finished, the cause of right, of justice, the interests of
a genuine self-government will require true men to
rescue the people from the hands of the politicians.
Vainly I remonstrated.   Wadsworth prefers to remain in the service, and to fight the monster.

August 24. *L. B.*—*Chasiana.* The New York
leaders of the Chase scheme make all possible efforts
and platitudes to *conciliate* Weed and win him over.
What dregs all around !

The immaculate Chase! to look for support to a
Weed!   To Weed-Seward, who for twenty-five years
fanned the anti-slavery flame!   Seward, whom the
anti-slavery wave elevated where he is, and who now
kicks and spits upon the men most ardent in the cause
of emancipation !   O dregs !   O dregs !

August 24: *L. B.*—The question of confiscation
drags itself slowly on, and soon it may resound in the

courts of the whole country. If confiscation is ever stringently executed, it will generate law-suits *ad libitum* and *ad infinitum*. From the first day when the banner of rebellion was unfolded, *each State* became an *outlaw* in its relations with the Union. Such a rebel State has not a legal existence, and any legal act whatever between individual members—or rather, politically, sovereigns in and of the State—such acts are valueless in relation to the lawful sovereign, as is the Union.

The Confiscation Act is based on a wrong principle —the right to confiscate the whole rebel property in America. This right is derived from the public law. A conqueror of a country becomes *ipso facto* the proprietor of all that belonged to the conquered sovereign and what is called public property, as domains, taxes, revenues, public institutions, etc. The rebels claim to be sovereigns—that is each freeman in each respective State is a respective sovereign. The area of such revolted State, with all the lands, cultivated or uncultivated, with the farms, and all industrial, mercantile or mining establishments whatever, is the property of the sovereign, or of the sovereigns. Property of a, or of many sovereigns, is in its whole nature a public property, and as such, *ipso facto*, is liable to be confiscated by the conqueror.

August 24: *L. B.*—The massacre at Lawrence, Kansas, must exclusively be credited to those who appointed for that region a pro-slavery military commander.   But the power-holders are not troubled by more or less blood, by more or less victims of their incapacity and double-dealing!

August 25: *L. B.*—Any future historian must beware not to seek light in the newspapers of this epoch. The so-called good press throws no light on events; that press is not in the hands of statesmen or of thinkers, or of ardent students of human events, or of men having for their aim any pursuits of science or knowledge.   The luminaries of the press are no beacons for the people during this bloody and deadly tempest! For the sake of what is called political capital, the most simple fact often becomes distorted and upturned by this political, short-sighted, and selfishly envious press.

August 26: *L. B.*—All things considered, the inflation of the currency and the rise in gold has proved to be beneficial to the country. The agricultural interest, above all, in the West, was particularly sustained thereby. Wheat and grain would have fallen to prices ruinous for the farmers. When the gold fell, the farmer felt it by the reduction of the price of his produce. The agriculturist, the backbone and marrow of the country, spends less money for manufactured products than he netted clear profits by the rise in gold. If the farmer sold now his wheat for six shillings, without inflation the price might have been four shillings, and then the farmer would have been bankrupt, unable to pay the taxes. The inflation saved the greatest interest in the country. And thus agriculture and in-

dustry flourish, the country is not ruined, is not bankrupt, as the European wiseacres took great pleasure
in foreboding that it would be. So much for *absolute*
laws of political economy.

August 27 : *L. B.*—The New York Republican papers insinuate that a Mr. Evarts, who was sent to Europe by Mr. Seward, has given assurances to European
governments that slavery will be abolished. If such
declaration was needed, why not make it through the
regular representatives of the country, as are Mr. Adams
and Mr. Dayton ? Mr. Seward is incorrigible. I am
curious to know where he learned this original mode
of *diplomatizing*. Such unofficial, confidential, semi-
confidential agents confuse European governments.
They inspire very little, if any respect for our statesmanship, and are offensive to our regularly appointed
ministers. What must the crown lawyers in England
have thought of Mr. Evart's great mastery of international laws ?

August 30.—Our military powers in Washington,
led on and inspired by Halleck, cannot put an end to
guerrillas, or rather to those highwaymen who rob, so
to speak, at the military gates of Washington. Lieber-
Halleck-Hitchcock's treatise frightened not the guerrillas, but most assuredly the gallows will do it. Everywhere else the like banditti would be summarily
treated ; and these would-be guerrillas here are evidences of the uttermost social dissolution. They are
no soldiers, no guerrillas, and deserve no mercy.

August 31 : *L. B.*—According to the *Tribune*, Mr. Lincoln deserves all the credit for General Gilmore's success before Charleston. There we have it! Mr. Lincoln, outdoing Carnot for military sagacity and capacity, Mr. Lincoln approved Gilmore's plans. Mr. Lincoln—Halleck aiding—at once understood the laws of ballistics, and other *et ceteras* which underlay the plan of every siege. And now to doubt that Lincoln, with his Halleck, are military geniuses! O *Tribune !*

August 31 : *L. B.*—I learned that Grant most positively refused to accept the command of the Potomac Army. They cannot ruin Grant—they will neutralize him.

Jeff Davis—Incubuerunt—O, Youth!—Lucubrations—Genuine Europe—It is for gotten—Fremont—Prof. Draper—New Yorkers—Senator Sumner's Gauntlet—Prince Gortschakoff—Governor Andrew—New Englanders - Re-elec tions—Loyalty—Cruizers—Matamoras—Hurrah for Lincoln—Rosecrans— Strategy—Sabine Pass, etc., etc., etc.

September 1 : *L. B.*—Jeff Davis is to emancipate eight hundred thousand slaves—calls them to arms, and promises fifty acres of land to each. Prodigious, marvellous, wonderful—if true. Jeff Davis will become immortal ! With eight hundred thousand Africo-Americans in arms, Secession becomes consolidated —and Emancipation a fixed fact, as the eight hundred thousand armed will emancipate themselves and their kindred. Lincoln emancipates by tenths of an inch, Jeff Davis by the wholesale. But it is impossible, as —after all—such a step of the rebel chiefs is as much or even more, a death-warrant of their political existence, as the eventual and definitive victory of the Union armies would be. If the above news has any foundation in truth, then the sacredness of the principle of right and of liberty is victoriously asserted in such a way as never before was any great principle. The most criminal and ignominious enterprise recorded in history, the attempt to make human bondage the corner-stone of an independent polity, this attempt ending in breaking the corner-stone to atoms, and by the hands of the architects and builders themselves. Satan's revolt was virtuous, when compared with that of the Southern slavers, and Satan's revolt ended not in transforming Hell into an Eden, as will be the South for the slaves when their emancipation is accomplished. Emancipation, *n'importe par qui*, must end in the reconstruction of the Union.

September 2 : *L. B.*—Garibaldi to Lincoln. The letter, if genuine, is well-intentioned trash. I am afraid that this prolific letter-writing will use up Garibaldi. It seems that in letter-writing Garibaldi intends to rival Lincoln or Seward.

September 3 : *L. B.*—More and more manifestations in favor of Lincoln's re-election. All the New York Republican papers begin to be lined with Lincoln. And thus politicians in and out of the press will—

Incubuerunt mare (people) totumque a sedibus imis.

September 3 : *L. B.*—In the great Barnum diplomatic tour, Seward killed under him nearly all the diplomats, and returned to Washington in company with one. Poor Europe, and its representatives, to be used up in such a way! But it is only the official Europe, the crowned privileged stratum patched up with rotten relics of massacre (December 2d,) of official, regal heartlessness and of servile cunning. That crust presses down the genuine Europe, the marrow of mankind. The genuine Europe is ardent, noble, progressive and coruscant; and from Cadiz to the White Sea, that genuine Europe is on the side of freedom, on the side of the North.

September 3 : *L. B.*—Lincoln to Grant, July 13. This letter shows how the President dabbles in military operations. It clearly establishes Mr. Lincoln's right to be considered at least a Carnot, if not a Napoleon, *vide* the Republican newspapers.

September 3 : *L. B.*—State Conventions, and the old party-hacks under arms. Will not the younger generation rise in its might, break the chains of this intellectual subserviency, scatter the hacks to the winds, take the lead, enlighten the masses, find out new, not used-up men, brains and hearts, for the sacred duty of serving the people. To witness so much intelligence, knowledge, ardor, elasticity, clear-sightedness as animate the American youth, to witness all this subdued, curbed by the hacks!—O, youth, awake !

It is the most sacred duty of the younger generation, to rescue the country from the hands of the old politicians of every kind; to call to political paramount activity the better and purer agencies. It is a task as emphatically, nay, even more, urgent and meritorious than emancipation of the Africo-Americans.

September 4 : *L. B.*—In their official or unofficial quality, numerous Americans amorously dabble in International questions and laws. How much the *rights of war*, etc., have been discussed; how many letters, signed, anonymous, official and unofficial, have been published—and very little, if any light thrown on these questions. What a cruel fate of a future historian, who, if conscientious, will be obliged to read all these darkness-spreading lucubrations!

September 5 : *L. B.*—Mr. Lincoln's letter to the Illinois Convention stirs up the whole country. It is a very, *very* good manifesto,—had it not a terrible YES-TERDAY. It is a heavy bid for re-election and may secure it. The Americans forget the *yesterday*, and Mr. Lincoln's *yesterday!* ....is full of shiftings, hesitations, mistakes which draw out the people's life-blood. The people will forget that a man of energy and of firm purpose in the White House, such a man would have at once clearly seen his way, and then a year ago rebellion and slavery would have been crushed.

A man of energy would not have had for his familiar demons, the Scotts, the Sewards the Blairs, the border-state politicians, the Weeds, etc.

September 5 : *L. B.*—The siege of Charleston *tire en longueur;* it has cost thousand of lives and millions upon millions, and will still cost more. And it is already forgotten that when nearly two years ago Sherman and Dupont took Port Royal, Charleston and Savannah were defenceless; it is forgotten that Sherman asked for orders to siege the two cities, *but such were not given* from Washington, because Mr. Lincoln-Seward (literally) was afraid to get possession of the focuses of rebellion, and General McClellan, with one hundred and fifty thousand men in Washington, could not bear the idea that the rebels should be disturbed either in Centerville or in their *chivalric* homes in South Carolina. It is forgotten that civil and military leaders and chiefs then and there refused to deal a death blow to the rebellion.

And as I am *en train* to recall to memory what is already forgotten, and what the Illinois letter intends to wholy erase from the people's memory ; I go on.

In the first days and months after the explosion of the rebellion, Mr. Lincoln was as innocent of any wish to emancipate the slaves, as could be a Seward, or a Yancey, or McClellan, or a Magruder or a Wise or a Halleck. All this is forgotten. It is forgotten that General Butler is the earliest initiator of emancipation, and that to him exclusively belongs the word and the fact of an emancipated *contraband*. It is forgotten that when Butler began to emancipate the contrabands, the *big men* in the Administration, Lincoln, General Scott, and Seward, became almost frantic against Butler for thus introducing the " nigger" into the struggle. The fate of Fremont is forgotten. Fremont was ahead of the times. Fremont emancipated when Lincoln-Seward-Scott-Blair, etc., heartily wished to save and preserve slavery. Down went Fremont.

Early in the summer of 1861 General Fremont wished to do what was now accomplished by the, until yet, *sans pareil* Grant—that is, to clear the Mississippi at a time when neither Island No. 10, nor Vicksburgh, nor Port Hudson nor any other port was fortified. But the plan displeased and frightened the powers in Washington. Fremont was never to be pardoned for having shown farsightedness when *the great men* deliberately blindfolded themselves. Fremont might not be a Napoleon, not a captain ; Fremont committed military mistakes,—other generals commit military crimes.

The angel of justice very easily will white-wash Fremont from military responsibility for the unnecessary waste of human life ; and with all his various faults Fremont's aspirations are patriotic and lofty, and he is by far a better and nobler man than all his revilers put together. But all this seems to be forgotten.

It is, or will be forgotten, what a bloody trail over the North is left, and has been imprinted by the half measures, the indecisions, and the vascillations of the Administration.

The medley composed of politicians, jobbers, contractors, and newspapers, already scream " Hosanna," and attempt to spatter with lies and dust the road to the White House, and thus to prepare the way. And the medley already shakes hands, and enemies kiss each other, because if their *elect* succeeds, there will be peace over, and pickings for all the world. But the justice of history will overtake them all, and the better, younger generation will crush them to atoms.

September 6. *L. B.*—Wilkes' *Spirit of the Times* maintains its paramount, independent position in the American press. I cannot detect any shadow of a politician in its columns. It is all over independent and patriotic. The *Spirit* fights the miscreants.

" *Principles not men*," is an axiom, but the axiom must be well understood and applied, and it has its limitations. Are bad, worthless, insincere, selfish men to be the agencies and the factors of great and lofty principles? Is such a thing possible? Is the example of Judas forgotten? O, you Bible-reading people, can Judases and rotten consciences carry out good principles? The press that teaches and preaches *principles not men*, that never dares to attack bad men in its own ranks, such a press betrays the confidence of the people, and degrades below expression the elevated and noble position which the press ought to occupy in the development of the progress of human society.

September 6.—Computing together and comparing the mental and intellectual characteristics, the manifestations and utterances of passions in the Africo American and in the Irish of the Iro Roman nursery, the anthropologist, the psychologist and the philosopher must give the palm to the Africo-American. And nevertheless Doctors of Divinity and many truly religious men plead in favor of slavery, that is, of brute force. I ask all such to meditate the words of Professor J. W. Dʀᴀᴘᴇʀ, in his great and profound *History of the Intellectual Development of Europe : That brute force must give way to intellect, and that even the meanest human being has rights in the sight of God.*

September 10 : *New York.*—Headquarters of all kinds of politicians, of schemers, of perpetrators of treasonable attempts, of falsifiers, of poisoners of the people's mind. The rendezvous of those who devour the vitals of the country—who, as contractors, jobbers, brokers, stock and gold speculators, *agioteurs*, etc. are the most ardent patriots, and wish that the war may be indefinitely continued. In the columns of the *Herald* the future historian will find the best information concerning all that—not-blessed race. The race deserves to be recorded and *scavenged* in the *Herald.*

And nevertheless New York contains the most pure and the most devoted patriots. New York and New Yorkers have been foremost in coming to the rescue when the matricide rebels dealt their first blow. From New York came the best and the most energetic urgings on the gasping and vascillating Administration.

The New Yorkers originated the Sanitary Commission, for which I can find no words of sufficiently warm praise. New York contains many young, fresh, elevated and noble minds and intellects. Why, O why do some of them disappear in the muddy part of the great city, and others are overawed and overleaped by the hacks and by the politicians, or the so-called wire-pullers.

September 10. *New York.*—It is the place to ascertain the manœuvres of political schemers. Those who know, most emphatically assure me of the existence of the following *Sewardiana.*

1. Seward has given up in despair all dreams of finding people to back him for the next Presidency.

2. Seward hesitated between McClellan and Banks,

3. And finally settled on Lincoln ;

4. And although afraid of being finally shelved by Lincoln, he advocates Lincoln's re-election—

5. As being the paramount means to politically murder Chase.

Oh American people! Oh American people! how those foul political pilferers dice for thy blood and thy destinies!

Years ago, I justified the existence and asserted the necessity of politicians in the political public life of America. I considered them an unavoidable and harmless result of free democratic institutions. [See "America and Europe."] At that time I observed the politician from a distance, and reasoned on him altogether metaphysically, after the so-called German fashion. Since 1861 I have come into personal contact with the genus politician—and oh! what a monstrous breed they are!

September 10. *New York.*—Senator Sumner on our foreign relations. The Senator enumerates all the violations of good comity, of international duties, of the obligations of neutrals, violations so deliberately and so maliciously perpetrated by England and by France.   But why has the Senator forgotten to ascend to one of the paramount causes ? Previous to England or France, the State Department in Washington and Mr. Lincoln recognized in the rebels *the condition of belligerents.* It was done by the Proclamation instituting the blockade.   The *Blue Book* fully proves that already months before Mr. Lincoln's inauguration the English Government had a perfect knowledge of the vascillating policy which was to be inaugurated after March 1, 1861.   At the same time, the English Government knew well that already previous to March 4, the rebel conspirators were fully decided on carrying out their treacherous aim across streams of blood.   A long war was imminent, and a recognition of the rebels as *in parte* belligerents, could not have been avoided. A part of the English nation, a part of the English Cabinet, was and is overflowing with the most malicious ill will, and such ones crave for an occasion to satisfy their hatred.   But our domestic and foreign policy singularly served our English ill-wishers.

I deeply regret that the Senator preferred the halls of the Cooper Institute to the hall of the United States Senate ; that he threw the gauntlet to Europe as a lecturer, when for days and months he could have done it so authoritatively as a Senator of the United States ; could have done it from his senatorial chair, and in the fulfilment of the most sacred public and patriotic duty. How could the Senator thus belittle one of the most elevated political positions in the world, that of a Senator of the United States ?

Not so happy is the part of the lecture concerning *Intervention.* It is rather sentimental than statesman-like. *Intervention* is, and will remain, an act of physical, material force, and history largely teaches that *Intervention,* even for higher moral purposes, was always exercised by the strong against the weak, the strong always invoking " higher motives." Thus did the Romans ; and about a century ago, the Powers which partitioned Poland began by an *Intervention,* justified on " higher moral, etc. grounds."

September 11 : *New York.*—Prince Gortschakoff's answer to the demonstration of lying, hypocritical, official diplomatic sympathies made in favor of the Poles by the cabinets of France of England, and of Austria. The Gortschakoff notes are master-pieces for their clear, quiet, but bold and decided exposition and argument, and in the records of diplomacy those notes will occupy the most prominent place. O, why cannot Mr. Seward learn from Gortschakoff how not to put gas in such weighty documents ? Could Seward learn how to be earnest, precise and clear, without spread-eagle-ism ? The greater and stronger a nation, the less empty phraseology is needed when one speaks in the nation's name.

September 15.—Returned to Washington. From

what I see and hear, Mr. Lincoln is earnestly and hard at work to secure his re-election. I hope that Mr. Lincoln is as earnest in his efforts to destroy Lee's army and to put an end to the guerrillas who rob to the right and to the left, and under the nose of the supreme military authorities.

Governor Andrew, of Massachusetts, always the same—active, intelligent, clear and far-sighted. Andrew is the man to act for, and in the name of the most intelligent community on the globe, which the State of Massachusetts undoubtedly is. As I have observed several times, Andrew is among the leading (*Americanize*, tip-top,) men of the younger generation, is no politician, and never was one. If a civilian is to be elected to the Presidency, Andrew ought to be the choice of the people, if the people will be emancipated from the politicians.

I learn that that monster, the politician, has almost wholly disappeared from New England, above all from Massachusetts. The New England people are too earnest and too intelligent to be the prey of the monster. Sound reason throttled the politician. All hail to this result of the bloody storm! I hope the other States will soon follow the example of Massachusetts.

The State of Massachusetts and the city of Boston noiselessly spend millions for their coast and harbor defences. Governor Andrew has the confidence of the people, and is untiring in procuring the best war material. He sent an agent to England to buy heavy guns.

If the English government take in sail, if it come to its senses and cease to be the rebels' army and navy arsenal, then all this will be due to such quiet and decisive active demonstrations as that above mentioned in Boston, in Massachusetts, and the similar activity of the New Yorkers, and not at all to any persuasive arguments of Mr. Seward's dispatches.

September 16.—Mr. Seward is slightly mending his ways. His last circular for the foreign market is considerably sobered, and almost barren of prophecy. Almost no spread-eagleism, no perversion, although geography and history, of course, are a little maltreated.

And so, Mr. Prophet, you at least recognize the utility of arming the Africo-Americans. And who is it that openly and by secret advice and influence in the cabinet and out of it, who, during more than a year, did his utmost to counteract all the efforts to emancipate and to arm the oppressed?

September 16.—The draft is seriously complained of, and the drafted desert in all directions. To tell the truth, drafting is odious to every nation, whatever be its government. But it is a dire necessity, and it is impossible to avoid or to turn it. The draft became here imperatively necessary by the long uninterrupted chain of helplessness and mismanagement of events, the sacrifice of blood and of time. But for the advice of the Scotts, of the Sewards, of the Blairs, but for the military prowess of McClellan and his *minions*, but for the high military science of a Halleck, Mr. Lincoln would not have been obliged to draft.

In the West, everything is action, operation and victory. Grant, Rosecrans, Banks, their officers and soldiers honor the American name; even good Burnside acts and succeeds;—but here the Army of the Potomac is observing and watching Lee's brow! McClellan's spirit seems still to permeate these blessed generals, and then Halleckiana, and then God knows what. The fear of losing won laurels probably palsies the brains of the commanders; at any rate it is certain that the inactivity of the Potomac army throws unsurpassed splendor on the annals of this war. O, the brave, brave soldiers and officers! how they are maltreated!

September 16.—Matamoras will fall into the hands of the *Decembriseur's* freebooters, and then Texas will be almost lost. Matamoras ought long ago to have been seized by us, or at least very closely blockaded and surrounded; then all the war-contraband to Texas would have had an end.

In 1861, when microscopical specks began to loom over Mexico's destinies, when the *Decembriseur* began to feel the pulse of Spain and of England, I most respectfully suggested to Mr. Seward to blockade Matamoras. No foreign country or government could call us to account for such a step, if the Mexican government would not protest. And it was so easy to satisfy and hush the Mexican liberals. Besides, a paragraph in the treaty of Mexico expressly stipulates that any violation of the respective territory will not be considered as a *casus belli*, but the case will be peacefully investigated, etc., etc. Surely the Mexican government would have preferred to see Matamoras in our hands, than in those of that bloody Forey's bands.

September 17. — "Loyalty," "loyalty," resounds from all sides. Loyalty to principles? Why, no. Loyalty to Mr. Lincoln and to his official crew. If such maxims mark not the downfall of manhood, then I am at loss to find what does. Such a construction of loyalty brings many otherwise honest and intelligent men to foster Mr. Lincoln's re-election.

September 17.—At the beginning of the war, Lord John Russell issued orders for the regulation of the English ports in cases of belligerents. Our great Doctor of International Law in the State Department mistook such municipal, English regulations ; he considers them to be absolute international rules and principles, and concocts instructions for our cruisers, instructions which smell as if written under Lord Lyons' dictation. As always, Neptune stands up for the national interests and for the interests of his tars, because the instructions concocted by the Doctor make it impossible for our cruisers to fulfill their duties. As always, Mr. Lincoln bends rather towards the Doctor, who in his world-embracing *humanitarianism* defends the interests of all the neutrals at the cost of the interests of the country and of our brave navy. The Doctor was right when, some time ago, he compared himself to Christ.

September 17.—The border-State politicians establish that the revolted States are not out of the Union. The States are no abstractions, no metaphysical notions, but geographical and political entities. They are States because they are peopled with individuals, free, intelligent, and who, to give a legality to their rebellion, claim to be sovereigns. It is not the soil constituting a State that represents a sovereignty, but the soil or State acquires political signification through the population dwelling in or on it. When the population revolted, the State revolted. From Jeff Davis to the lowest " clay-eater," each rebel who took up arms claims to have done this in the exercise of his sovereign will and choice. The revolt quashed all privileges conceded by the Union to a State, and the Union reconquers its property in reconquering the former States.

September 18.—Hurrah for Lincoln! He sends an expedition to Texas, say his admirers. He forgets nothing. Well, why has Lincoln forgotten Texas all this time? Notwithstanding all the prayers of the Texans and of the northern patriots, I am not sure that at this moment it is expedient to break up our armies into smaller expeditions instead of concentrating them in Tennessee, Georgia, and here. Strike on the head or at the heart if you wish to kill the monster, but not at its extremities. But perhaps the Government and Halleck have men enough to do the one and the other.

But why not put at the head of the Texan expedition a noble, high-minded, devoted patriot, such as General Hamilton, instead of putting a Franklin, unknown to the Texans, who can inspire no confidence, and of whom the best that can be said is, that he never succeeded in anything, and disorganized everything. See Pope in Virginia, Burnside at Fredericksburgh.

If Hamilton, the Texan, is to participate in this expedition, not Lincoln and his advisers put Hamilton there—the pressure exercised by the combined efforts of the governors of New England States did the work.

Hurrah for Lincoln and for his crew.

September 19.—Governor Andrew's activity and initiative are admirable. More than any body in the country, Andrew has done to clear up, and to firmly establish the condition of Africo-Americans as soldiers, and to push them up to the level with other men.

September 19.—*Hurrah for Lincoln*, who hurries the organization of Africo-American regiments! Oh yes! he hurries them; *festina lente.* And how many regiments have been organized in Norfolk, which ought to have been established as *the* central point to attract and to organize contrabands? Is not Virginia the first in the slave States for the number of slaves? In the hands of a clearsighted man, Norfolk ought to have been used as a glue to which the slaves would have wandered from all parts of Virginia, and even from North Carolina. Norfolk ought to have to-day an army of fifty thousand Africo-Americans born in

Virgina, and not a few regiments of them raised in the North. An Africo-American army in Norfolk doubtless would have more impressed Jeff Davis and Lee, than they are impressed by the marches of the commanders of the Potomac army. And what is done? Oh, hurrah for Lincoln! A General Naglee, or of some other name, appointed by Halleck, sustained by Lincoln, and by, who knows whom—commands in Norfolk. This general so appointed, and so sustained is the most devoted worshipper of slavery. This favored general hob-nobs with the slave-making, slave-breeding and slave-selling aristocracy of Norfolk and of the vicinity, looks down upon the *nigger* with all the haughtiness of a plantation whip, and haughtily snubs off the not slave-breeding Union men in Norfolk, the mechanics, and the small farmers. Mr. Lincoln knows this all and keeps the general. Rhetors roar, Hurrah for Lincoln.

September 19.—Massachusetts and New England men and women! you true apostles! your names are unknown but they are recorded by the genius of humanity. These men and women feel what is the true apostolate. They follow our armies, take care of the contrabands, take care of poor whites, establish schools for the children and for the grown up of both hues, and thus they reorganize society. O sneer at them you fashionables, you flirts, you....; but such men and women, and not you, make one believe in the highest destinies of our race.

September 20.—Grant is the only general who accomplished an object, showed high, soldier-like qualities, organized and commanded an excellent army. But scarcely had *Grant* taken Vicksburgh, when his army was broken up and scattered in all directions, he himself was neutralized and reduced to inactivity. It could be considered a crime against the people's cause—but —hurrah for Lincoln.

After the shame of Corinth, 1862, the Western army disappeared in the same way. But it was nobody's fault, oh no! So it is nobody's fault that Grant is shelved. Will a man start up in the next Congress and call the malefactors to account?

September 20.—This day, General Meade has about eighty thousand men. General Meade himself estimates the enemy's forces in front of him at no more than forty thousand men, and General Meade does nothing beyond feeling his way. O, cunctator!

September 20.—The partisans of Mr. Lincoln admit that he came slowly *to the mark*, but he came to it. Of course, better late than never, but in Mr. Lincoln's case, the people's honor and the people's blood paid for Mr. Lincoln's experimental ways. Mr. Lincoln may now be serious in a great many matters, but if he could have been serious a year ago—how much money would have been economized?

Hurrah for Lincoln!

September 21.—Rosecrans worsted. Burnside joined him not. They say that Burnside disobeyed orders. I doubt it, and would wish to see what orders have been given. Meade or Halleck quietly allow a third of Lee's army to go and help to crush Rosecrans.

September 21.—General Franklin was, in his own way, successful at the Sabine Pass, as every where. But how could the government entrust him with this expedition? He graduated *first* at West Point. Washingtonians and tip-top West Pointers speak highly of Franklin. Enough !—

September 22.—The rebels concentrated every available and fighting man on Chattanooga; we scattered our forces to all winds. The rebels march on concentrating lines, we select radii running out in the infinite, or in opposite directions. That is the head quarters paramount strategy.

Rosecrans is worsted. Hurrah for Lincoln, who believes in Halleck !

And to know, as I know, that our army and country has young men who could carry on the war better in darkness than Lincoln-Halleck do in broad daylight !

September 22.—By depleting the banks by means of loans, by establishing the so-called National Bank, by creating an army of officials, by taking into his hands the traffic in the great staple of the rebel States, by providing the South with the various Northern products, by holding all the money in his hand, Mr. Chase concentrated into his hand a patronage never held by any secretary, nay, scarcely if ever, held by a president.   Mr. Chase has more patronage than even any constitutional king. · It is to be seen how all this will end.

September 22.—On all sides I hear the question put, Who is Gilmore? It seems to me that Gilmore is one of the men generated by new events and not by Washington or West Point estimation.   It seems to me that Gilmore may be one of the representative men of the better generation so luxuriant here, and whose advent to power would save the country ; a generation who alone can give the last solution, and whose advent I expect as the Jews expected the Messiah, and I shall hail it as did Anna, Elizabeth, Simeon, etc. put together.

September 23.—As a result of the Meade-Halleck combined military wisdom, a part of Lee's army fought Rosecrans at Chattanooga, and may in a very short time be again in Virginia, and it is nobody's fault.   O strategy ! thy name is imbecility !

September 23.—Better news from Rosecrans. The stubbornness of the troops, the stubbornness of General Thomas saved the day.   Reinforcements join Rosecrans now.   But why not previous to the battle ? If Rosecrans had had men enough on the 19th and 20th, then Bragg would have been broken, and the rebels almost on their last legs.   But perhaps such glory and victory are not needed !   Hurrah for Lincoln !

September 24.—Many of Mr. Lincoln's partisans admit that at the most favorable calculation, the re-

sults obtained up to to-day by the war and by emancipation, could easily have been obtained by a smaller
expenditure of life, blood, money and time, if any will,
and foresight, and energy presided at the helm. And,
nevertheless, hurrah for Lincoln! And the highest
destinies of the principle of self-government to again
be trusted in such hands!

September 24.—How could Meade let Lee send
troops to Bragg, and why Meade attacked or attacks
not? Those rebel generals show but little consideration for our commanders, and it would be curious to
know what Lee and his companions think of our Marses.
It seems that a conception of a plan of campaign or of
a military operation is altogether beyond the reach of
Meade's *cerebellum.* As commander of a division, of
a corps, Meade had *dash in him*—he lost all when
elevated above the level.

I am sure that Stanton urges or urged Meade to do
something, without telling him how or where. Had
Lincoln, had Halleck meddled? If so, Meade ought
to tell it. The best to do for a commander of the
Army of the Potomac is to keep his secrets to himself
and have in his confidence only his chief-of-staff—not
to tell them to any one in the camp, and still less to
any one in Washington. But it seems that Meade had
no plan whatever in view, and had no secrets to keep
or to tell.

September 25.—It is to-day exactly a week since
Rosecrans was attacked. At the head-quarters they

ought to have known Rosecrans' force, and the imperative, the paramount necessity of reinforcing him in time, as they *ought* to have known that Lee sent to Bragg a part of his army. But probably the precious head of the head-quarters is confused by some translation, or by reading proof-sheets instead of reports. By simply looking on the map, the head-quarters—perhaps headless—ought to have found out that Chattanooga and Atlanta are the keys of the black country, and that the rebels—who neither write silly books nor translate—will concentrate all available forces to stop Rosecrans's advance, and eventually to crush him. Weeks ago the head-quarters ought to have reinforced Rosecrans; it is done to-day, a week after the defeat. Hurrah for Lincoln, who sustains a Halleck!

One of the most cautious men that I met in life, and who is in a position to be well informed, in the most cautious and distant manner suggested to me that Rosecrans is obnoxious to the head-quarters, and that in G street, Washington, they may have wished to see Rosecrans worsted.

Hurrah for Lincoln! Halleck is his true prophet!

Shake an apple tree, and the foul fruit falls down; and so it is with Halleck's western military combinations. All the army of Grant running dispersed on centrifugal radii, Burnside sent in a direction opposite to Rosecrans. Bravo, Halleck! You outdo McClellan!

September 25.—It seems that with a little, a very

little dash, we could go in the rear of Lee, who is weak-ened by sending troops to crush Rosecrans. But we have given Lee time to fortify his position, and of course we will wait until Lee is again strong, either by position or by numbers. Then we march a few miles onwards, more miles backwards, and what not? What splendid combinations coruscate from the head-quarters here, or in the army! Cæsar, Napoleon, Frederick, bow your heads in dust before our great captains!

September 26.—It seems that at Chattanooga the rebels massed their infantry in columns *per* battalion, and Crittenden's and McCook's troops could not with-stand the attack. It was not at West Point that the rebel generals learned the like continental tactics. It seems that the rebels like to learn.

September 27.—In defence of the *Franklinade* at the Sabine Pass, it is alleged that the expedition had bad old vessels, and was poorly fitted out. Then why make it? It is a crime in this country to complain of any want of material and of bad vessels—provided no one steals thereby. In America, not to have an adequate material? What an infamous slander on the most in-dustrious people! Not material, but brains, or some-thing else are not adequate. But, of course, it is no-body's fault, and nobody will be taken to account.

September 29.—Hooker is to have a command, and to supersede Burnside. Probably again a separate command. If generals refuse to serve under each other, under the plea of seniority, at once expel such *recalcitrant* generals from the service; better and younger men will be found. The French Convention beheaded such generals, not on paper, but physiologically. The French Directory was not a master of honesty or energy, but it had sufficient energy to select Napoleon, twenty-six years old, over the heads of older generals, and put him in command of the Army of the Alps, which in his hands became the Army of Italy. And as long as the world shall stand, the consequences of that violation of the rule of seniority will not be forgotten.

September 29.—General Thomas ought to have the command, if Rosecrans failed, but not Hooker or Butterfield.

Halleck's *officina* of military incongruities and to unmilitary combinations ought to be shut up, and the occupants sent about the world. The War Department and the President would get better advice from the young Colonels in the Department, and around Stanton, than it gets from all that concern in G street.

September 29.—The papers say that all over Europe and the rest of the world Seward *ex officio* scatters Sumner's Cooper Institute oration. Well may Seward do it. Sumner suppressed true events, not to hurt Seward.

Now Sumner will find Seward an admirable statesman.

September 30.—The suspension of the *habeas corpus* makes great noise. It was emphatically necessary. But it would not have been emphatically, indeed not in the least necessary, if the domestic and war policy were different. Then the people would not have been disheartened. If the people's holy enthusiasm—so dreaded in Washington—were not so sacrilegiously misused and squandered, volunteers would be forthcoming.

September 30.—If Lincoln-Halleck could create a military department on the moon, they would instantly send thither some troops and a major-general, so strong is their passion to break up the armies into fragmentary bodies.

September 30.—If this war has already devoured or destroyed three hundred thousand men in dead, crippled, and disabled in various ways, then the responsibility is to be divided as follows :

a 100,000 lost by the policy initiated by Lincoln, Seward, Scott.

b 100,000 to be credited to McClellan and Halleck's military combinations ; Halleck by half with Lincoln.

c 100,000 to be credited to the war itself.

September 30.—England mends her ways, and stops the arming of vessels for the rebels. The *Decembriseur* more and more treacherous—as a matter of course.

September 30.—I understand now, what I never could understand in Europe. I understand how an all polluting power can force into alliance men of strong convictions, but of the most deadly opposite social and political extremes. Such extremes meet in the wish to put an end to a power whom they hate and despise.

Aghast—Firing—Supported—Russian Fleet—Opposition — Amor scelerated — Cautious — Mastiffs — *Grande guerre* — Manœuvring — Tambour battant— Warning, etc., etc., etc.

October 1.—Rosecrans, Bragg, Lee, Meade, Gilmore, Dahlgren and the iron-clads keep the nation breathless aghast. A terrible and painful lull. The politicians furiously continue their mole-like work; election, reelection is inscribed on the mole hills.

October 2.—Chase men fire into Blair's men, and Blair's men are supposed to be Lincoln's men. The skirmishing, the scouting before the battle. But the day of battle is yet far off, and the proverb, "many a slip," etc., may yet save the nation from becoming a prey of politicians.

October 3.—News arrives that reinforcements sent from here reached Rosecrans. For the first time the troops have been forwarded with such rapidity. The War Department has brought almost to perfection the system of transportation of large bodies. The head-quarters, who combine, decide and direct the movements, the distribution, and the scattering of troops all over the country could have therefore ordered the troops to Rosecrans, and the War Department would have rapidly forwarded them there. And if Grant's army was not broken, and he himself virtually shelved or neutralized—if he had marched towards Georgia, Secession would have been compressed to two or three States; Bragg crushed, Alabama and Georgia rescued! Hurrah for Lincoln-Halleck.

October 4.—The Russian fleet evokes an unparallelled enthusiasm in New York, and all over the country. *Attrappez* treacherous England and France! The Russian Emperor, the Russian Statesman Gortschakoff, and the whole Russian people held steadfast and nobly to the North, to the cause of right and of freedom. Diplomatic bickerings here could not destroy the genuine sympathy between the two nations.

October 4.—The probable majority in the next Congress is the great object of present calculation and speculation. The Administration seems to be of the opinion, that a small republican majority will do as well, because it will be more compact and more easily to be played upon. God save the country from a majority *twistable* by the Administration! If the majority is small, then it may be unable to drag such dead-weight as was the Administration directed by its master spirit.

The Administration ought to be dusted and pruned. This Administration especially needs to be shaken and kept always on the *qui vive* by an honest and a patrotic opposition. The opposition made by Copperheads is neither honest nor patriotic. Opposition is a vital element of parliamentary government; and as by a curse, the opposition here is made not to acts of the Administration—the Copperheads wish to throttle the principle which inspires the best part of the people. If it was possible to have an opposition strong enough to control the misdeeds of the Administration, to serve for the Administration as a telescope to penetrate space, and as a microscope to find out the vermin: if such an opposition could be built up, it would have forced the Administration to act vigorously and decidedly, it could have preserved the Administration from repeated violations of the rules of common sense, and in certain Administrative brains the opposition could have kindled sagacity and farsightedness:—such counterpoise would have spared thousands and thousands of lives, and thousands of millions of money.

October 6.—Meade will retreat or already retreats. The choice of the army, Meade, has not yet greatly justified itself. And Meade, too, builds up in the army a clique of generals, and therein Meade begins to imitate McClellan. Likewise McClellan seems to have been Meade's model at Williamsport, and, McClellanlike, Meade has wasted precious time.

And thus the month of October sees us on the defensive on the whole line, from the Potomac to the Rio Grande. After two and a half years of military misdirection, of rivers of blood, of mines of money— there we are.

Hurrah for Lincoln and for his apostles!

October 6.—How the world's history is handled, twisted, and *bungled*. Wiseacres put history on the rack to evidence their own ignorance. The one invokes England's example during Wellington's expedition to Spain, as if that war in the Peninsula had been a civil war, and England's integrity, national independence, and political institutions had been endangered. And another compares this war to the civil wars of Rome, and censures the impatience of those who wish for more energy in the Administration. Do the wiseacres wish for an

> Altera jam teritur bellis civilibus ætas.

Others point to Cæsar, and forget that Cæsar fought almost in person everywhere, in Europe, Africa, and Asia.

Great commanders-in-chief point out to their subordinates the example of Napoleon and of Frederick visiting their pickets. Yes, great military scholars! Frederick and Napoleon visited the pickets when their armies faced—nay, when they almost touched the lines of the enemy. But Frederick and Napoleon were with the armies—they were in the tents, and directed not the movements of armies from a well warmed and cosy room or office.

October 6.—Blair, a member of the Cabinet, in a public speech delivered in Maryland, most bitterly attacks the emancipationists and emancipation. Blair is perfectly true to himself. That speech would honor a Yancey. Blair peddles for Mr. Lincoln's re-election. Blair thus semi-officially spoke for the President, and for the Cabinet. Such at least is the construction put in England on an out-door speech made by a member of the Cabinet, or else another member takes another occasion to refute the former. Mr. Splendid Chase is a member of the Cabinet, and claims to represent there the aspirations, the tendencies, and the aims of the radicals and of the emancipationists. Such a conflict between two members of the Cabinet shakes the shaky situation. What will Chase do? Nothing, or very little.

October 7.—Months, weeks and days of the most splendid weather, and Meade, the choice of the West Point clique in the army, Meade did nothing. If Meade had not, or has not troops enough, why is not Foster ordered here with all he has? Keep Fortress Monroe well garrisoned, and for a time abandon the few points in North Carolina. Destroy Lee, and then a squad of invalids will reconquer North Carolina, or that State may then reconquer itself. This, or some other combination ought to be made. I am told that more than seven hundred thousand men are now on the Paymasters' rolls. Where are they? Is it forgery or stealing? Where, oh where are the paid men? On paper or in the grave? If the half, three hundred and fifty thousand men, were well kept in hand, Lee and Bragg ought to be annihilated.

Hurrah for Lincoln and Halleck!

October 8.—From various sides I am assured that Stanton passed into the camp of Lincoln, with horse, foot and artillery. I doubt it, but—all is possible in this good-natured world. Stanton, like others, may be stimulated by the *amor sceleratus* of power.

October 8.—Lee's Report, containing the operations after the battle of Chancellorsville, the invasion of Pennsylvania, and his recrossing of the Potomac at Williamsport, is published now. But Lee, a true soldier, made his report in the last days of July, therefore almost instantly after the campaign was finished. Sympathizers with McClellan's essays on military or on other matters! there is another example for you, how and when such things ought to be done. Meade has not yet made his Report.

October 9.—The cautiousness of Meade and his fidelity to McClellan-like warfare are above admiration. General Buford, brave and daring, weeks ago offered to make with his cavalry a raid in the rear of Lee and destroy the railroads to the south-west—those main arteries for Virginia. The offer was vetoed by the commander of the Potomac army. Had Lee ever vetoed Stewart's raids? Lee rather stimulated and directed them.

October 10.—And the power-holders let loose their mastiffs. And the mastiffs ran at my heels and tried to tear my inexpressibles and all. And they did not, because they could not. Because my friends (J. H. Bradley,) stood by me. And the people's justice stepped in between the mastiffs and me, and I exclaim with the miller of Potsdam, "There are judges in Washington."

October 11.—I most positively learn that even Thurlow Weed urged upon the President the immediate removal of Halleck, and even Thurlow Weed could not prevail. Many and many sins be forgiven to the Prince of the Lobby, to the man who understood how to fish out a fortune in these national troubles.

October 12.—*Cæsar morituri te salutant*, say our brave soldiers to Lincoln.

The Meades and the McClellans, like most of the greatnesses of the West Point clique, have no impulse, no sense for attack, because what is called *la grande guerre*, that is the offensive war, was not among the special objects of the military education in West Point. This is evident by the pre-eminence given to engineering, and to the engineers who represent the defensive war; and therefore the contrast to the *grande guerre*. Some of our generals, as Grant, Rosecrans, Reno, Reynolds, and others, and as I hear likewise of Warren, made and make up in enthusiasm for the deficiency of the West Point education. But the majority of the *educated* Potomac commanders and generals were not, and are not much troubled by enthusiasm.

October 12.—In his answer to the Missouri patriotic deputation, Mr. Lincoln, with one eye at least to the re-election, proves to the observer that he, Lincoln, has not yet found out which party will be the stronger when the election shall be at the door. Mr. Lincoln has not yet made his choice between the radical, immediate emancipationists and those who wish a slow, do-nothing, successive, *pro rata* emancipation. Not having yet found it out, Mr. Lincoln has not yet fully decided which direction finally he has to take; and therefore he shifts a little to the right, a little to the left, and tries to hush up both parties. Our so characteristic military operations are closely connected with the vascillating policy and with the hesitation to cut the knot.

October 13.—Unparalleled in the world's history is the manner in which the war is conducted here, from May, 1861, to this day. The annals of the Asiatic, ancient, and of modern Tartar warfare, the annals of Greece, of Macedon, of Rome, the annals of all wars fought in Europe since the overthrow of the Romans down to the day of Solferino, all have nothing similar to what is done here. This new method henceforth will constitute an epoch in military *un*-science.

October 13.—General Meade in full and quick retreat. The most contradictory rumors and explications of this retreat; some of the explications having even the flavor of official authority. One thing is certain, that when a general who confronted an enemy at once begins to manœuvre backwards, without having fought or lost a battle, such a general is outmanœuvred by his enemy. O for a young man with enthusiasm, and with inspiration! Suggested to Stanton to shun the men of Williamsport, or to look for enthusiasts such as Warren.

Chaos everywhere; chaos in the direction of affairs, and a disgraceful chaos in the military operations. But as always, so this time, it is nobody's fault.

Fetish McClellan finally and distinctly showed his hand, and joined the Copperheads in the Pennsylvania election. McClellan is now ripe for the dictatorship of the Copperheads. Will Mr. Lincoln have courage to dismiss McClellan from the army? A self-respecting Government ought to do it. Let McClellan be taken care of by the *World*. *Par nobile fratrum.*

October 14.—

Nox erat et cœlo fulgebat luna sereno,

and the virtuous city of Washington enjoyed the sleep of innocence: the genius of the country was watchful. Halleck slept not. Orderlies, patrols, generals, officers, cavalry, infantry, all were on their legs. Halleck took the command in person. What a running! First in the rooms, then in the streets and on the roads, and on the bridges whose planks were taken off. And thus about the cock's crow the nightmare vanished, and Halleck, satisfied to have fulfilled his duty towards the country and towards the innocent Washingtonians, Halleck went to bed.

October 15.—Our head-quarters at Fairfax Court House. It is not a retreat. O no! It is only splendid backward manœuvring!

As far as the Virginia campaign is concerned, the situation to-day is below that previous to the first Bull Run. Lee menacing, going we know not where; guerrillas in the rear of our army, at the gates— literally and geographically at the gates of Alexandria and of Washington. Previous to the first Bull Run, the country bled not; to-day the people is minus thousands and thousands of its children, and to see Lee twenty to thirty miles from Washington! What will be the manœuvring to-morrow?

Warren fought well, but if Sykes was within supporting distance, why did they not annihilate the rebel corps? Two corps ought not to have been afraid to be cut off from the rest of the army distant only a few miles. Or perhaps orders exist not to bring about a general engagement? All is now possible and probable. *Our great plans may not yet be ripe.*

When the smoke and dust of the manœuvring will be over, I heartily wish that our losses in the retreat may prove innocent and as insignificant as they are reported to be.

On the outside, Lee's movement appears as brilliant as it is desperate. Has not this time Lee overshot the mark ? Cunctator Meade may have some lucid moment, and punish Lee for his impertinence. And every and any thing can be done with our brave boys, provided they are commanded and generaled.

In military sciences and history, it would be said that Lee has *ramené tambour battant* Meade under the defences of Washington. Such a result obtained without a battle, counts among the most splendid military accomplishments, and reveals true generalship.

October 17.—Meade was decided to retreat, even before Lee began to move, say the knowing ones, say the military authorities. If Meade wanted not to go to Culpepper Court-house, or to march towards the enemy, or to occupy the head waters of those rivers, then why was our army promenaded in that direction ? To amuse the people ? to increase losses in men and in material ? Was it done without any plan ? I supposed, and the country supposed, that Meade marched south to fight Lee where he would have found him ; but it turns out that it was done in order to bring Lee towards Washington and towards the Potomac. What a snare !

October 17.—The electoral victory in Pennsylvania marks a new evolution in the internal *polity* of the country. It is the victory of the younger and better men as represented by Curtin, by Coffey, etc., over the old hacks, old sepulchres, old tricposters and over men who sucked the treasury and the people's pocket ; they did it scientifically, thoroughly, and with a coolness of masters. Oh! could other States therein imitate Pennsylvania, then the salvation of the country is certain.

October 17: *Evening.*—The knowing ones promise a battle for to-morrow. Yes, if Lee will. But if not, will Meade attack Lee? who I am sure will continue his movement and operation whatever these may be. We are at *guessing.*

Repeatedly and repeatedly it is half-officially trumpeted to the country, that this or that general selected his ground and awaits a battle. It reminds one of the wars in Italy during the thirteenth and fourteenth centuries. And if the general who forced backwards his antagonist, if he prefers not to attack, but continues to manœuvre, what becomes of the select, own ground? Who ever read that Alexander, or Cesar, or Frederic, or Napoleon, or even captains of lesser fame, selected their ground? All of them fought the enemy where they found him, or by skillful manœuvring hemmed the enemy or forced him to abandon his select position. Cases where a general can really force the antagonist to attack *such a select, own ground,* such cases are special, and very rare.

And so for the second time in this year, Lee shakes and disturbs our quiet in Wasnington. Oh why is Lee engaged on the bad and damnable side?

October 18.—A new *whereas* calling for three hundred thousand volunteers. The people will volunteer.

Oh this great people is ready for every sacrifice. But you, O you! who so recklessly waste all the people's sacrifices, will you volunteer more brains and less selfishness?

October 18.—And when all the efforts of great men converged to the reelection and election, Lee converged towards Washington. Be the people on their guard and warned!

Note.—The publication of this book has occurred at a culminating period of annoyances and inconveniences which may possibly have left traces in the volume now finished. The Author's residence in Washington—unprecedented delays of the mails—scarcity of compositors—and beyond all, the confusion from unavoidable duplication of proofs, have so annoyed the Author, that it is but just to make this brief explanation and apology.

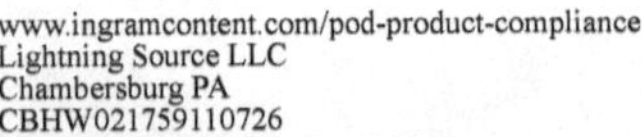